ALLY

ALLY

ANNA BANKS

FEIWEL AND FRIENDS

NEW YORK

A Feiwel and Friends Book
An imprint of Macmillan Publishing Group, LLC
175 Fifth Avenue, New York, NY 10010

Our books may be purchased in bulk for promotional, educational, or business use. Please
contact your local bookseller or the Macmillan Corporate and Premium Sales Department
at (800) 221-7945 ext. 5442 or by e-mail at MacmillanSpecialMarkets@macmillan.com.

Library of Congress Cataloging-in-Publication Data is available.

ISBN 978-1-250-07018-0 (hardcover) / ISBN 978-1-250-14302-0 (ebook)

Feiwel and Friends logo designed by Filomena Tuosto

First edition, 2017

1 3 5 7 9 10 8 6 4 2

fiercereads.com

For G,
my accomplice in all things that probably aren't a good idea.

ALLY

PART ONE

1

SEPORA

THE TIP OF SETHOS'S SWORD ALMOST CATCHES the bridge of my nose. As I sweep back, I use the inside of my foot to kick dirt in his face for daring to come so close to me. These are, after all, only practice sessions, and if he's going to test me this way, I'm most certainly going to return the favor. He glides to his left, an effortless movement, avoiding not only the sand, but the cloud of dust left in its wake.

I'm left infuriated and thrilled all at once.

I can't imagine there could be anyone faster than Sethos, Tarik's younger brother. I haven't seen many of the Master Majai train, as the king's highly skilled army of warriors spend their days at the Lyceum when not on duty, but of these Favored Ones I *have* watched from the balcony overlooking this courtyard, none are faster than Sethos, who only just turned sixteen. Even his shadow cannot keep up with his movements. I wonder whether his father, the Warrior King Knosi, was as nimble on his feet.

Sethos laughs. "Your antics might work—on a lesser warrior. But I'm afraid you'll have to do better than that, Princess, if you're going to overtake me."

We both know I'll never overtake him, no matter how much we practice. And we both know these lessons are not strictly for my instruction. Our sessions together bring us both relief from the delusions we used to call lives. There was a time once when we were both free to make our own decisions, free to marry whom we chose—or, at least, the illusion of that choice—and free to leave the palace walls.

Freedom now is like the hinge of a door rusted in place from lack of use.

Sethos and Tarik's relationship has become strained. Where there used to be easy banter between them, it comes with sharper barbs and insincerity. Where there used to be shared opinions, Sethos takes the opposite side of Tarik, no matter the subject. It is difficult to watch sometimes, the deterioration of the affection these brothers once had for each other.

I shake my head, lowering my sword. Catching one's breath in the stifling Theorian heat seems almost as impossible as merely shaving Sethos with my sword. I want to graze him so badly, to at least nick him, anything to get that smug look wiped from his face. But other Majai cannot, and so when I get close, I know he is just toying with me. "Trust me when I say I'm doing my best," I tell him.

He makes a *tsk*ing sound with his tongue. I've come to abhor that sound, so mocking and condescending. "You know you're not. You know you could—"

"Do not say it," I hiss, lifting my sword again. I'm growing tired of this, the same conversation we have each session. He's bent on seeing me Forge, bent on teaching me to use my ability to protect myself. He insists that if I could produce spectorium fast enough, I could use it to scald my opponent. I suppose he's right. But even if I wanted to Forge, I couldn't. Not here in the open. I know it. Sethos knows it.

Our two impervious kings, Tarik and my father, have decided that my Forging should be kept a secret from the kingdoms. That my power, as the only Forger of spectorium, puts me in danger. And that my well-being is of the utmost importance.

Indeed. Tarik's sense of duty makes my well-being his concern. But Father? His intentions strike the opposite direction entirely. Every day, he grows impatient of my "well-being," threatening to chain me in the dungeon (the palace in Anyar, the heart of Theoria, has no such dungeon) until I Forge spectorium for him. He has thrown outrageous fits in our moments of privacy, demanding that I Forge, and when we are in the company of the Falcon King, he finds many diplomatic ways to suggest the same to Tarik. But for some reason, Tarik is not willing—not yet, at least—to force my hand. The Falcon King must think I will acquiesce, that I will give in and eventually supply him with the spectorium needed for the plague.

He is wrong.

I will no longer supply any of the five kingdoms with spectorium. Not Theoria for its plague nor Tarik's leverage, not Serubel for its economy nor Father's ambitions. The ice kingdom of Hemut will have to make do without the element, as will Wachuk and Pelusia, which I'm thankful have shown no interest in it in the past. The age of spectorium has ended.

I will no longer be used as a pawn in a game of power. And I will no longer trust anyone to decide what is and is not for my well-being.

Which, sadly, must include Sethos. How am I to know whether Sethos is secretly siding with Tarik, planning to bring him the fresh spectorium I Forge during our training sessions? Sethos, though one of my favorite people at the moment, is conniving and cunning enough to pull off such an act of betrayal. Perhaps that is why he constantly pesters me to Forge—Tarik has put him up to it. Though, the thought is truly unlikely. Sethos barely speaks to Tarik anymore, and while I'm not a Lingot as Tarik is, having the ability to discern the truth from a lie, I'm not a fool, either. It is plain that Sethos considers his older brother a tyrant—and the fact that Tarik has ordered him to wed the Princess Tulle of Hemut is irrefutable proof of that accusation. It came down as a royal order, one that the entire kingdom of Theoria knows about and one that Sethos cannot forgive his brother. No, Sethos is not trying to betray me. Not for Tarik.

Truth told, our practices together are the only time Sethos resembles himself anymore. Something happens to him after we finish—after we are sapped of energy and of sweat, after we've returned to our lot in life. When he arrives for the evening meal in the palace—another one of Tarik's requirements—he is sullen and quiet and bereft of charm.

He is no longer Sethos.

I know that it is his imminent marriage to Tulle that has him so depleted of his usual charm and so filled to the brim with ill temper. I cannot fault him there, for a marriage without love is what we are both facing, and the prospect of it makes most of my food lose its taste. But Sethos's circumstances are unique in that he actually despises his betrothed, whereas I have resolved to simply remain aloof. Any love Tarik and I once felt for each other has been twisted into something that resembles manners and diplomacy.

With Sethos, manners and diplomacy have never come easily.

"Why do you loathe Princess Tulle?" I immediately regret the question, which was blurted as an afterthought. I watch the moment he closes himself off to me. Our lesson is all but over now; I can see it in his eyes. Disappointment makes my sword even heavier.

He gives me an odd smirk when he says, "Don't worry, Princess. Tulle harbors no love for me, either. You're fortunate to be able to marry for love."

All at once, my face is full of warmth, a flush I know cannot be concealed. I should not have this reaction to Tarik, not after everything he's done. There was a time when I would have married him for love. But our time for loving each other has passed. And so has my willingness to marry him.

Yet Sethos grins wickedly. "You and my brother assume I'm blind, then? Did you know that you do not steal glances of each other no fewer than a dozen times at the evening meal alone?"

I lift my chin. I'd been working on that, not looking at Tarik. Not giving attention to his presence at all. And I've been failing, apparently. "I'm merely striving to be attentive. Perhaps you could set aside a portion of your busy day to reflect upon good manners." It is a blow, suggesting that Sethos is busy. He has been assigned to the security of the palace, and according to him, the place runs by itself. The only distraction he finds is when he feels of the mood to round up a group of guards, portraying himself as an intruder and tasking them with finding him, how he got in, and what he was after. This only serves to irritate him in the end; his ego does not allow him to be captured, and so the guards must resign themselves to another session resulting in failure with a Master Majai berating them incessantly. It is not good for anyone involved.

"Attentive?" Sethos is saying. "Your execution of 'attentiveness' is flawless, Princess. Coincidentally, so is my brother's."

I slide my sword into its sheath strapped across my back, as is the Theorian way. "If you are so proficient about judging everyone's apparent feelings, how is it that you could not secure the affection of Tulle?"

Sethos spits on the ground beside him. "Why are you so bent on seeing me tethered to someone as vile as Tulle? What have I ever done to you?"

"Aside from purchasing me for your brother's harem? Nothing. Why are you so bent on avoiding this discussion?" If I cannot beat him with a sword, I shall best him with words.

Or, perhaps not.

He closes the distance between us quickly, grabbing my arms before I can squirm—before I can even think of squirming. "Run away with me, Sepora. Run away with me tonight."

I try to step away, try to wriggle out of his grasp, but to no avail. His hands are large and my arms are small, and he has his shins and groin protected with platelets of copper. So much for learning to defend myself.

"We could settle ourselves in Wachuk. Make a life together there," he practically yells. "Say yes, and I'll see to it that you can bring Nuna, your glorious Defender Serpen. I'll never make you Forge. Not a drop."

I feel my eyes grow wide, darting frantically about the courtyard partly for help and partly to make sure no one is hearing this madness. "Sethos, has the heat gotten to you?" I hiss. "Let me go!"

"We'll make beautiful babies," he bellows, pulling me closer. I swear his shouting would wake the dead entombed in the pyramids on the other side of Anyar. "I want a girl with eyes just like yours."

Babies! If I kicked hard enough, surely the copper couldn't protect—

"If you ever wish to sire children at all, you'll unhand her directly," a familiar voice calls from behind. We both face Tarik, whose fury cannot be hidden by the golden body paint forced upon him by royal obligation.

Sethos releases me and laughs heartily. It's no wonder he was yelling. From his vantage point, he knew the moment Tarik arrived. Scoundrel.

"I'm going to kill you," I decide as I say it, reaching for the sword at my back.

But Sethos is already walking away and is, decidedly, not concerned. "You really must sport with my brother more often, Princess. As you can see, it's great fun," he says over his shoulder. When he passes Tarik, he doesn't deign to acknowledge him. But Tarik wouldn't have noticed anyway. He's staring at me now, as if I'm the one who'd planned to raise heathen children with his heathen brother in a heathen kingdom.

I cross my arms. "What are you doing here?" I nod to the bronze sundial situated in front of the courtyard wall, though I can't readily tell what it reads. "My lesson is not over."

Tarik raises a brow, making it a point to eye my sheathed sword. "Your tutor seems to think it is."

"You're early," I insist, nearly stomping my foot. The one liberty I do have is that I may practice self-defense with Sethos daily in the courtyard, though Tarik is not elated about extending this courtesy. Still, he does, and so I take full advantage of escaping the goings-on of the palace and my new place in it. When my lessons are cut short, I make it a point to be difficult.

"Your mother is early as well," he drawls. He is good at keeping his emotions to himself of late. His expressions, his body language. The Master Lingot Saen taught me how to learn like a Lingot to watch for these things, that there is more to what a person says than their words. But Tarik shows me nothing. If he is excited to meet my mother, or if he dreads it, I couldn't know. "Queen Hanlyn arrived moments ago by Serpen in the far courtyard. I thought you'd like to visit with her before the evening meal."

Queen Hanlyn. My mother. She wasn't scheduled to arrive until tomorrow; she'll be joining my father to attend the royal engagement procession, as is the custom in Theoria. In the procession, Tarik and I will lead by chariot what I'm told is a rather ostentatious exhibition of the throne's wealth and integrity, bestowing gifts on all of the citizens and, in effect, sealing my fate with Tarik. The thought of it brings shivers to me despite the heat. Or perhaps it is the look Tarik gives me now, one filled with curiosity—and something else I can't quite name.

Against my will, I hold his gaze. To back down now would be too telling.

To calm the sensations swirling in my gut, I try to focus not on his face, but on his words. It will be the first time I've seen my mother since she sent me on the journey to Theoria months ago. Her short visit to Theoria will reveal whether I have failed, and I'm more than curious to see whether she holds praise or wrath for me, with the outcome such as it is. Surely sacrificing myself in marriage will count for something. And it will be a relief to burden Mother with the task of keeping Father at bay where my Forging is concerned. She alone can handle him best, even at his worst, and if she cannot, she can at least manage to distract him long enough from his endeavors until she *can* handle him. But before we discuss the matter of my father, we must discuss the matter of Tarik.

That the great Falcon King is a Lingot, able to discern the truth from a lie.

And that as such, he *cannot* be handled.

2

T A R I K

TARIK ROLLS AND UNROLLS THE SCROLL SET BEFORE
him, wrapping the small message around his finger tightly and
unwinding it rapidly so that it spins. He is more than a little preoc-
cupied with the thought that at this very moment, Sepora is visiting
with her mother, the queen of Serubel. What must Sepora be saying to
her? What impression is Sepora giving to the queen before Tarik has
a chance to prove he is worthy of her daughter? And why does he care
so much what Queen Hanlyn thinks of him?

Rashidi, who has been sitting patiently across from Tarik's day-
chamber desk, clears his throat gently. As his father's most loyal adviser,
and now Tarik's closest friend, he has every right to show some impatience at his king's apparent detachment. Yet he is long-suffering, as
though he understands to where Tarik's thoughts have strayed.

"Perhaps we could discuss this another time, Highness," Rashidi
says. "We have a few days yet to sort out the details of the engagement
procession." He lifts the kohl chalk from the map of Anyar. Obviously,
he'd been tracing a pathway for the procession. Tarik can see that
from the Half Bridge, the course is set to return to the palace. Normally
this would go without question.

But nothing in his life is normal anymore.

Tarik shakes his head, tensing for the disagreement he knows will come with his next words. "We must include the Baseborn Quarters in our procession, Rashidi."

The old adviser groans but does not appear surprised. "I had a notion you might say that."

Tarik smirks. "You knew that I would. The Baseborn Quarters are made up of the descendants of the freed Serubelan slaves. I must include my future queen's own people."

"That is not the point of the procession, Highness. Nor the custom."

"Do enlighten me, then, Rashidi." Though he's well acquainted with the tradition of the procession and the custom. Rashidi had tutored him on both months ago, the moment he'd decided that Tarik should wed Princess Tulle. And if he had married Princess Tulle, this would not be a discussion.

Ah, but so many things become a discussion where Sepora is concerned.

His friend leans back in his seat, resting his silver walking staff against his chest. Tarik can tell Rashidi is deciding how to choose his words. With words, Rashidi has conjured up peace when there was no peace, arranged marriage when there was no affection, and assuaged pride when pride was the only thing that was left. Rashidi and his words are powerful. But Tarik will not bend on this point, no matter the sway of Rashidi's diplomacy. "The point of any royal engagement procession is to display the wealth and power of Theoria," the adviser begins, "to impress upon the one marrying into our kingdom that they are by far on the receiving end of the most advantage. If they do not believe that to be the case, they are free to incorporate their own customs to display their superior wealth, Highness." To Tarik's knowledge, this has not happened before in the history of Theoria, for a kingdom to try to outshine Theoria. And Tarik doubts Serubel has the ability to do so. Yet, Rashidi's eyes light up. "Perhaps King Eron and Queen Hanlyn could host a Serubelan feast for all the kingdom and include their own people. Surely that would appease the Baseborn Quarters and, of course, your queen."

"That would do nothing to make the Baseborn citizens loyal to *me*. And to Sepora. It is not simply a matter of pleasing Sepora. I want to be able to count those people among those willing to fight for Theoria, if the time comes."

Rashidi scowls. Tarik knows his thoughts are drawn to the kingdom of Hemut, where the possibility of war may already loom. "A wise thought, of course." The adviser grimaces, a sign that Tarik will not like what he has to say. "Forgive me, Highness, but it would be difficult for any in our kingdom to remain loyal to Princess Sepora after what she has done. I think even the Baseborn class would take exception, since it was the work of *those* citizens she destroyed."

So. Rashidi is not so concerned with tradition as Tarik had thought. No, he wishes to punish Sepora for what she has done. Or rather, for what she *hasn't* done. Tarik works to keep his expression neutral. Rashidi is still resentful of the fact that all this time Sepora could have Forged fresh spectorium for Cy the Healer to use against the Quiet Plague, but instead chose to remain quiet about it. If Tarik is being honest, he himself is still bitter. Bitter, and betrayed. But for some inexplicable reason, he feels the need to defend Sepora—something he resents as well. Still, among these complicated emotions agitating him to no end, he knows that allowing any servant—even Rashidi—to speak ill of his future wife could potentially start an avalanche of this sort of behavior that may be difficult to control. He and Sepora must stand united, even if she does not yet realize that.

"She has a dangerous gift, Rashidi. She sought only to protect it." Which is true enough. He still remembers the look on her face when she saw the explosion of cratorium for the first time in the courtyard. It was a look of familiarity and of terror. She was afraid the weapon would fall into the wrong hands. And who could blame her for that?

Yet a small bit of blame does ease its way into his mind and settles there, where it will stay until he has the opportunity to confront her about her . . . *decisions*.

"At the expense of your own father's pyramid?" Rashidi spits. "When the kingdom learns of that—"

Tarik jumps to his feet, leaning across the desk. He did not mean to startle his friend—but perhaps his friend needed a change of pace. He is speaking dangerously just now. If the people knew she could have prevented the dismantling of their dear King Knosi's burial place, they would most certainly riot. "And how will the kingdom learn of that? I believe I made it quite clear that no one must know of Sepora's Forging abilities. Tell me now, Rashidi. Do you intend to tell the people what has taken place?" He is, after all, an ambassador of the people. Tarik well knows that what he asks of his friend goes against his loyalty to the citizens.

His adviser inhales deeply and exhales his wrath in a slow, steady breath. Rashidi is prone to tantrums, especially when they keep private company. Tarik respects that he takes care to rein in his temper. Still, it does take a moment for his gaze to reach Tarik's. When it does, Tarik can see that his friend has calmed down. "No, Highness. I would never defy you."

The truth. Pride of the pyramids, but he needed to hear that. If he lost Rashidi's loyalty in the face of all that he knows is to come . . . He cannot even think of the desperation in which he would be left. Tarik takes his seat again, leaning his arms on the rests of the chair. "You think that I have forgiven Sepora for forcing my hand in taking down my father's pyramid." It is not a question. His father, the Warrior King Knosi, had meant a great deal to Rashidi. It is natural for the family's oldest friend to be bitter. Natural, and loyal, Tarik reminds himself. Rashidi's reaction is as it should be.

"She has secured your heart, Highness. I was hoping that despite this, she has not secured your reason."

"She has not." Even he can sense the turmoil in those words. Is reason not always inconveniently intermingled with the desires of the heart?

"If I were but a Lingot, so that I may know how you truly feel."

Tarik taps his fingers on the armrest. "I understand. You need reassurance from me, friend. And I have no idea how to give it to you."

"By not bringing honor to someone who has dishonored you on so many occasions. Highness, including the Baseborn Quarters in the procession tells your future queen that she can dance upon your pride and you'll do nothing about it."

Tarik sighs. "I cannot punish her for a crime she doesn't know she committed."

Rashidi stares at him for a long time. "Do you mean to say that you have not told her of your father's pyramid?"

"No, I have not."

"Why in the Five Kingdoms not?"

Tarik longs to wipe a hand down his face, but it would ruin the art painted so carefully there, and he doesn't have time to reapply it before the evening meal. "I've not had the chance to. We've barely spent time alone, and those times did not lend themselves to bringing up something so . . . precious to me. I must have time to think on it more, Rashidi. Right now she is bent on defying me in any way she can."

"You're afraid she will not have the proper respect the situation deserves."

"I am." And he is afraid of how it will make him feel if that happens. If Sepora were to brush off the discussion or to treat it with the defiance she has grown so fond of and without due care, he shudders to think how a lifetime with her would be possible.

It simply would not.

"And what if she never composes herself? What if she intends to act this way for her entire rulership and marriage to you?"

"Oh, I'm quite sure that is her intention."

"What will you do?"

"Sepora and I will not live our lives as strangers to each other— I won't allow that. If I have to woo my own wife all over again, that is what I will do. When she is mine, in every sense of the word, that is when we will speak of this matter. But not a moment before. You see, I cannot risk a fight between us. That would give her an excuse to run away or to try to end our union. We need the Serubelans, as much as I hate to admit it, now that we have likely offended Hemut."

Though, truth told, he is more concerned about losing Sepora than of having to face the Hemutians without the likes of King Eron on his side. But this he cannot confess to his best adviser. For this alone proves that Sepora truly has stolen his reason along with his heart.

Rashidi actually smiles then. "Your father would be proud of you, Highness. He did not name you the Falcon Prince in error. You truly do see matters from a loftier view than most people."

If only Rashidi were a Lingot. Then he would see through me and I could be relieved of the burden of this farce. Tarik picks up the kohl utensil Rashidi had been using to mark the path of the engagement procession and circles the part of the map denoting the Baseborn Quarters. "So then, we will include the Baseborn Quarters in our royal procession. And we will shower them with more gifts than the people have ever seen."

3

SEPORA

I FIND MOTHER WAITING FOR ME ALONE, INDULGING herself in a quiet tour of my bedchamber. Nothing about her has changed; she still wears her golden-brown hair, sliced through with gray, in the same long, thick braid that trails down her back. She still moves silently and with purpose—never without purpose—and she still wears the same old-fashioned Serubelan gown, which she has in at least a dozen different, and drab, colors. Mother is not one for extravagance or garnering attention; she's always taught me that men listen better to a woman when they are not distracted by her appearance. I wonder what she will think of my Theorian attire now: a pair of flowing, nearly sheer white pants gathered at the ankle and a matching linen top that doesn't cover the shoulders and leaves my midriff exposed. My hair is piled high atop my head in many braids and silver clasps of dragonflies with delicate wings that flutter with my movements; it took nearly an hour this morning for Anku, my head attendant, to scrawl the silver and black swirling designs around my eyes. For now, as I am not yet queen, I have chosen not to adorn myself with the full-body silver paint that comes with the duty. Silver for the queen and gold for the king. Tarik is not happy about this, but somehow wearing the paint feels as though I'm admitting defeat and sealing my fate prematurely. As it is, Mother will notice that I have been exposed to the sun in inappropriate places for Serubelan royalty, but that, of course, could not be helped.

I watch her for what seems like an eternity, gliding elegantly about the room as though she has wheels instead of feet hidden under her long gown. I cannot help but feel pride at the expression on her face, which is that of being thoroughly impressed. It is how I felt when I was first introduced to my new accommodations as queen of Theoria, and that first night in the grand bed made of silver and curtained with sheer blue silk was a sleepless one, despite the extreme comfort of the linens and the soothing scent of fresh lavender awash among my pillows and bedding.

I still have not become accustomed to the luxury and splendor Tarik's mother fashioned for herself—and of course, for future queens of Theoria—in what is modestly called a bedchamber. Everything is accented with the most gleaming silver, from the sconces on the walls, which I'm sure would normally be filled with spectorium for lighting but which will be lit with fire as soon as the sun reaches the western horizon, to the silver carvings on the bed, to the legs of chairs and tables and even vases of desert flowers brought in fresh daily. Only the finest silver is appropriate for a queen of Theoria.

Flamboyant for a princess of Serubel.

Mother stops at a design embedded into the wall made entirely of blue Seer Serpen scales, iridescent and pearly and embellished with silver vines, as if the scales were the petals of a rare desert flower. I bite my lip as she frowns. I'd thought about having it removed; Seer Serpens are gentle creatures used by my people only for their gift of sight, and walking past this design day in and day out reminds me that Theorians treasure only their giant cats as pets and will kill any Serpen merely for its beautiful scales. It is as wasteful as killing a camel for just one of its hooves. But asking for the design to be removed is a sensitive matter, because Tarik's mother arranged it herself and the servants assigned to me in these quarters have boasted so admiringly of it. It is apparent they served—and loved—their previous queen. If they are to be of any use to me at all, I must gain their trust and loyalty; destroying something so dear to them is not the way to go about it.

"I must endure it," I tell my mother. "The servants adore it, and extracting it would put their loyalty to me in peril."

Mother visibly startles. When she turns around, her smile fades as her gaze drips from the top of my head to my bare feet; I'd discarded my shoes the instant I'd hit palace floors. I rarely wear them anymore, and when I do, they are not slippers as is the Serubelan custom but are leather sandals, usually encrusted with jewels. I choose to go without, in most cases on account of modesty but on others because of the comfort that jeweled sandals cannot provide.

My mother recovers almost instantly, straightening her shoulders and approaching me for an embrace. When she folds me into her arms, her grip is fierce, yet her words are gently spoken. "You are right not to have it removed," she says in my ear. "Loyalty from those closest to you is indeed necessary. But we will discuss that later." If she is appalled at my attire, she does not say so. She would know that if I am to be queen of Theoria, I must dress the part.

She releases me then and leads me to a sitting area close to the balcony. I feel silly, following Mother around my own bedchamber when it is I who should be hosting her. But I follow just the same, as if things are how they always used to be. And in a way, they are. I am anticipating her telling me how to fix this mess. I am anticipating being the pupil and she the instructor once again.

The easy breeze from the arched entryways makes the light drapery dance in the setting sunlight, and Mother drinks it in for a moment before looking at me. Her gray-blue eyes are steady, even steely, when she says, "We cannot trust your father, Magar Sepora. He would never exchange the annihilation of Theoria for a union with it. He could have had an alliance with Theoria for decades, had he chosen to meet King Knosi even halfway."

Magar Sepora is my full name, and Mother never uses it unless she's trying to impress something upon me. Before, when I was a child, that something could have been the importance of not overeating at dinner or rising early enough to Forge for Father. Now, it seems surreal to have such a conversation with her. A conversation that involves impeding my father. And she makes a good point. I had not thought of it in that way, that Father could have formed an alliance as easily as he could have started a war all this time. I assumed he wanted peace when he learned of Tarik's power and assets, and that the kingdom of Theoria was prepared for his attack. Obviously, Mother does not think that is the case.

That is why I need her here now. I cannot juggle two kings with different interests. My Serubelan tutor, Aldon, never prepared me for such unlucky circumstances. Certainly he never envisioned me betrothed to the king of Theoria nor Father approving of the arrangement.

Tarik has already said that he mistrusts my father. That Father dances around the truth with murky words like "peace" and "for now." The only thing that rings clearly true is that Father intends for me to marry the Falcon King. There is no deception when he speaks of the impending wedding.

"What could he be planning?" I ask Mother, suddenly aware that she is scrutinizing me.

"I have not spoken with him yet. His correspondences to me since he's arrived here have painted a picture of happiness and contentment. Your father does not have contentment in his nature. Ambition has always driven him, in everything he does. You must not Forge, Magar. You must not give him that power."

"I haven't. I won't. But . . . there is something you must know. There's a plague, the Quiet Plague, in the midst of Theoria. Master Cy, a Healer at the Lyceum, has created a cure for it. And the cure requires spectorium." I breathe out, relieved of the burden of this conundrum at last. Mother will have the answer. She always does.

Mother crosses her legs beneath her gown. "Tell me of this plague."

"It killed King Knosi; he was, in fact, the first victim. Since then it has swept through Theoria. It killed many before Cy found the cure. He mixes spectorium—old spectorium, because I will not Forge—with an element called nefarite that we harvest from the River Nefari. Together, they restore the patient to perfect health. The success rate has been absolute."

"Interesting." She taps a finger to her temple. "Nefarite, you say? An element long desired by all the kingdoms. How do they avoid the Parani?"

So Mother knows of nefarite and how it is found only in the River Nefari. I shouldn't be surprised, of course. Mother is from Pelusia, where the River Nefari empties into the great ocean. Parani at the mouth of the river can grow twice the size as the Parani in Theoria. Aldon said that creatures of the oceans are always much bigger than creatures of the river.

I wonder if Mother knows that Parani are not creatures at all. Well, not exactly.

"And where are they getting this old spectorium?"

"Some of the citizens donate it when their family members become ill. But mostly it comes from dismantling structures made from it. They will run out of it, sooner than later."

"Have it out, child. I can hear in your words that something ails you."

Of course she can. "If . . . When Theoria runs out of spectorium, what am I to do? I will be the queen. How can I stand by and watch the citizens die, when I have their remedy at my fingertips?" The question is telling, I know. It reveals that I care for the people of Theoria, while all my life, I was raised to think them my enemies. But I hope that it also reveals that I am dedicated to becoming a good queen if I must—and that I still defer to Mother's judgment.

She thinks on this a long time. I am both relieved and irked that she considers it so carefully. On the one hand, it means that she cares about the fate of the people of Theoria and that she wants me to succeed at being their queen. On the other hand, it means that she fully *intends* for me to be queen. That she will not be helping me find a way to escape this marriage. I'm quite sure now that Mother has no interest in the emotional trespasses Tarik has caused. That he was going to marry another, until it was convenient to marry me. She would say, in her current state of mood, that he did what any good ruler would do.

Yet I had hoped she would be my ally in this. And the disappointment is almost unbearable.

Finally, she says, "This Cy, the Healer at the Lyceum. How trustworthy is he?"

Cy and I are friends, that I know. He wished Tarik and me well when he learned we were to marry, and when he's with us, he is no longer formal and stiff. But I well know where Cy's loyalty lies. "Cy's allegiance belongs to Tarik. If he had to choose between the two of us, he would choose the Falcon King."

Mother nods. "It's as it should be. And the boy king? How trustworthy is he?"

I fidget my hands in my lap, an action that does not go unnoticed by Mother. I would like to say that Tarik is trustworthy. As a king, he is dutiful beyond measure. But in being so dutiful, he has betrayed me so terribly. He would have wed Princess Tulle, even though we shared such intimate feelings for each other. He had apparently expected me to stand aside while he took her to his bed to produce an heir—something he himself would never stand for if our roles had been reversed. And then he chose to use the weapon cratorium, a mix of spectorium and Scaldling venom, against my father in what he thought was an impending war. He had chosen to inflict harm on my people. I clench my teeth and lift my chin, leveling my gaze at Mother. "He would use spectorium in any manner he sees fit."

"Hmmm" is all Mother has to say about that. Then, "Let me think on this, Magar. Spectorium cannot fall into the wrong hands. But I'm not so sure that the Falcon King could bear blood guilt the way your father could. My spies tell me he is fair and decisive."

Spies? I had no idea Mother had spies. And I had no idea they reached as far as Theoria. I have much to learn from her about being a queen.

"Still," she continues, "power is power, and it tends to go to a man's head, to where even his heart can be fooled by it. Yes, I must think on it, child. Until then, however, you mustn't Forge. How have you hidden it so far?"

"There is running water in the lavatory. It eventually dumps into the Nefari. I Forge only small bits at a time, late in the evening after everyone has gone." It is an understatement, to say the amount of spectorium is small. Before, I didn't worry about purging in the lavatory, Forging into the hole leading to the Nefari to regain my strength. Few people would be venturing toward that part of the stream, where the refuse ultimately settles. Besides, if the spectorium had been found, all that could have been assumed was that it had come from the palace—not directly from my chamber. Now, though, Father knows I must Forge every day. He'll know where to look. But even his scrutinizing eyes will not see what I do. The spectorium I Forge now is mere droplets, as small as beads of sweat; if they make it to the Nefari, their glow could be mistaken for the reflection of the sun or a mirroring of the stars upon the river's surface. They are even too small to meld together, too tiny for any ill intentions he may have. In fact, it takes me all night, Forging this way, to regain my energy only to have it stolen away again by lack of sleep. Even now, I long for my bed. But we have the evening meal to attend and begging off is not an option. I want to see how Mother will entertain Tarik, how she will manage his ability.

Just then, Anku quietly opens the great door to the bedchamber and allows herself in. She carries with her a lighting torch. The only acknowledgment she gives us is a slight nod as she proceeds to light the sconces around the immense set of rooms. Darkness creeps in from the balcony and settles over us as if a haze of kohl dust has wafted in. Mother yawns, covering her mouth with the back of her hand.

Standing, she says, "My darling, it is wonderful to see you again. I must go and ready myself for the evening meal now. And it looks as though your face paint could use some touching up." With this, she embraces me once more, the way a person might embrace a muddy child, all angled and without affection. A show of decorum although Anku is not watching.

Perhaps our meals will be less awkward with Mother here. She knows how to entertain Father, and she is an exceptional hostess. For a reason I cannot explain, I want her to impress Tarik, to show him that Serubel is not a kingdom of crude barbarians with primitive customs. If there is anyone who can prove this, it would be my mother.

Oh, but there is one thing I've forgotten. Perhaps the most important thing. I grab Mother's arm before she gets to the door left open by Anku. "Mother, do you know what a Lingot is?"

4

TARIK

TARIK ISN'T SURE WHAT HE EXPECTED OF QUEEN Hanlyn, but this is not it. Perhaps he expected her to be ornery and unpleasant with forced manners, as King Eron is. Or perhaps he expected her to be quiet and submissive, merely an ornament at her husband's side. More important, he expected her to leak puzzling untruths and deceit with every word, as the king of Serubel does—or, at the very least, emanate insincerity through body language alone. He had hoped to garner more clues as to what the two of them truly have planned for his union with Sepora.

But the queen's body language is straightforward and confident, and her words strike true to his ears. The only thing she seems to be hiding is how tired she is from her journey to Theoria. She is so bent on hiding it, in fact, that she has taken over the dinner as though she were the hostess and he were the guest.

And he finds that he doesn't mind at all. Entertaining Eron for so many nights has been exhausting in its own right. The king of Serubel speaks only of war, of the need for cratorium, or of the importance of forcing Sepora to Forge. In so doing, he has admitted to beating her when she resisted back in Serubel. "Sometimes she needs more punishment than encouragement, you see," the king had said. "Nothing a good rod couldn't fix." If it had not been for Rashidi placing a gentle hand on his shoulder, Tarik would have had his own hands around Eron's neck before he could take his next breath. Even now, it is an easy thing, for his mind to wander with thoughts of doing the Serubelan king harm.

It is a wonder Sepora did not desert her father sooner.

Yet, Tarik enjoys a sense of relief that Queen Hanlyn seems to be of a completely different nature altogether. She speaks highly of Sepora, assuring him that she will one day make a great queen. She slides glances of encouragement to her daughter when she thinks no one is looking. She compliments Tarik on the food, the décor, and the well-appointed fleet of servants attending them. She has even tried to coax Sethos into conversation more than once, which is twice as many times as Tarik. Yet Sethos seems impervious to the enchantment of Hanlyn, setting upon moving food around his plate instead of inhaling it for once.

In more ways than one, she reminds him of a girl who once escaped his harem and led his palace guards on a merry chase. A girl with effortless courage and a penchant for solving problems.

Of course, it should not surprise him that Sepora should resemble one of her parents. And for all the physical traits Queen Hanlyn passed on to her daughter, such as her full figure and lips, it is the quieter traits he admires the most about them both, such as their shared unapologetic confidence and their strategic wit. Already this evening, Queen Hanlyn has put Rashidi in his place and handled Sethos's intolerable mood with an ease and a smile that suggests hospitality is an art to her. Too, it is not lost on Tarik that Sepora studies every move her mother makes, hangs on her every word, eyes filled with pride.

Tarik is thankful Sepora has one even-minded parent, since the other seems to be quite mad.

"When Sepora first learned to ride Nuna, she would sneak out at night to practice," Queen Hanlyn is saying. "When it was time for her studies the next morning, she would fall asleep at the table." She shakes her head in mock exasperation. "Even *I* would not dare fall asleep in the midst of a lesson from Aldon. It was not long before he made her stand for her lessons, and she learned very quickly that sneaking out at night would have to stop."

"You *knew* she was sneaking out and did nothing?" Eron says around a scowl.

Hanlyn smiles at her husband—her first disingenuous action this evening. "Of course I did. A mother always knows what her daughter is up to. Oh, don't be angry with me, dearest. It was not important enough to bother you with. Besides, I had faith that Aldon would straighten her out, and he did." She takes a dainty bite of her honey cake, effectively ending any further commentary on the matter.

So. The queen is not fond of her king. The word "dearest" rang solidly in Tarik's ears as false. As did the bit about not wanting to bother him. Curious, though, that she apparently *does* know everything her daughter is up to, or so she believes. Tarik is left feeling envious of this revelation, of how it must feel to have experienced firsthand all there is to know of Sepora.

It also makes him wonder what Sepora has told her—and in how much detail—so much so that he very nearly squirms in his seat. Some things are better kept private, surely Sepora knows. A number of their kisses come to mind, but Tarik forces the memories away as soon as they appear. Blushing in front of his guests will simply not do.

"Queen Hanlyn," Rashidi says, his face full of diplomacy. His adviser is ever diligent, it would seem. "Princess Sepora tells us you are from Pelusia."

The queen takes a sip from her chalice, and Tarik wonders if this is a stall. Curious, that she would need to suspend before answering such a simple question. After a moment, she says, "Indeed, I am. My father was Serubelan, my mother Pelusian, but I was raised in Pelusia. Until, of course, I married Eron."

"And do you still keep up correspondence with your home kingdom?"

Another moment passes before she nods. "Yes, I do. Quite often, in fact."

The truth. But Rashidi is digging for more than just that, Tarik can tell. The older man says, "Do you suppose it possible that if we were to war with Hemut over this marriage alliance, that Pelusia would offer their support?"

Tarik pinches the bridge of his nose. The queen has only just gotten here hours before and now she will be interrogated at dinner? It will be an unpleasant thing, to chide his oldest friend later in private.

"Of course they would," Eron cuts in. "Pelusia has been our ally since the splitting of the kingdoms. We would have their full backing."

To Tarik's relief, the king trusts in his words. It is good to know that Pelusia, a neutral kingdom by decree, would support their efforts, were Hemut to pursue war with them. Thus far they have heard nothing from that kingdom, which could mean a swift retaliation is underfoot. Hemut will not catch Theoria by surprise, but they may well catch them insufficiently prepared. The Majai are ready at all times, of course, but Anyar's other means of protection are not quite in place. Orders have been given and projects set in motion, but will they have enough time to complete all that has been set forward? Tarik doesn't know. His highest commander does well to pledge with words his loyalty to his king, but his body language suggests he agrees with Eron—they need cratorium, and as much of it as they can get.

Tarik glances at Sepora, wondering if he should not share more of that pressure with her. She is to be queen one day. She must be able to view unpleasant situations more objectively, he thinks. But at the moment, his most pressing issue is to ensure that she is queen at all. For all the ways they interact, she seems more likely to run away again than to wed him.

"Pelusia could provide ships, in fact," Eron is saying. "With ships, we could attack Hemut's border from the north, where they go whaling. They would never see us coming."

This could be true. Like Pelusia, Hemut is situated on the northernmost part of the Five Kingdoms, bordering the ocean. Because of Pelusia's notorious neutrality, Hemut would not likely suspect an attack from them at their own northern border.

Tarik remembers one visit to Hemut when he was very young, when Sethos was too small to travel. His father and King Ankor had taken Tarik whaling one day, and though they came back to shore empty-handed, Tarik had found the experience exhilarating. He had never been upon a ship before; the only boats he was familiar with were the small, slender fishing vessels used to navigate the Nefari. The whaling ship had ropes and sails that creaked and groaned with each hearty wave of the ocean. He'd been unsteady on his feet at first, but by the end of the trip he was climbing the ladder to join the lookout far above deck. He wonders how a Pelusian trading ship compares with a massive Hemutian whaling vessel.

"Yes, well," Rashidi is saying, "of course, our hopes are that we will not need to bother your Pelusian friends with the burden of war. I'm confident King Ankor can be reasoned with. After all, our kingdoms have been strong allies for centuries as well."

"Yes, well," Eron says, mocking Rashidi. "You're quite the optimist. I do hope you're not so idealistic that you aren't actually preparing for the worst—and as far as I can tell, you are not. That, friend, is a folly."

Tarik sighs. Another of Eron's attempts at steering the conversation toward preparing for war—and one likely to turn into a plea to pressure Sepora into Forging. He's curious to know how Queen Hanlyn will handle this delicate situation and if she is of the same opinion as her husband.

Still, Tarik knows how *he* will handle it. Sepora already views her marriage to him as an obligation, and he'll not ask her for more than that at the moment. Perhaps he is the optimist, but he wants Sepora to trust him enough to Forge of her own volition, not because he demands it of her. And he's willing to wait a little while longer for that to happen. As it is, fresh spectorium is not needed so badly for the plague now that the nefarite works so well combined with the dying supply they have of the other element. And pride of the pyramids, he'll dismantle every Forged piece of spectorium in Theoria if he has to, in order to give Sepora the time she needs to trust him again. And then he will show her how much he has entrusted her with already; he will tell her of his own father's pyramid.

Yes. Like pyramids, trust takes time to build. Time and patience.

Which is why he'll not allow King Eron to bully Sepora further. "There are many ways other than creating cratorium to prepare for war, King Eron," Tarik says. "And we are doing those things in abundance." Indeed, they are. In fact, just today, he signed a ruling for his engineers to construct ten more Slingers. Normally, the mechanism that rapidly dispatches dozens of arrows per second runs on the power of spectorium, but his chief engineer showed him a design where the thing could be set in motion by springs, though it would now require two men instead of one to operate it. Still, using more manpower is a small price to pay for not depending upon an element that he may never see again.

That the Five Kingdoms may never see again.

Eron waves his hand in dismissal. "Yes, yes. You're doing exactly what Hemut expects. But we need the element of surprise. And they will never suspect—"

"You speak as though we will be attacking them first, which is not the case," Tarik says.

"I can assure you Hemut will meet with surprise if it intends to go up against our Master Majai," Sethos interjects, no doubt on Sepora's behalf. If Sepora does not want to Forge, Sethos will defend her right not to, probably to the death. With Sethos, everything is to the death. "The Majai are not going to tickle them with pitchforks, you see."

Tarik winces. Sethos means to insult Serubel—a kingdom whose army Sethos often jests is made up of volunteer farmers. If he were sitting closer to his brother, he would kick him under the table. Putting Eron in his place is one thing; insulting Sepora's home kingdom is quite another.

"Speaking of the Majai, how goes your *palace* duty?" Eron returns with a sneer.

"It goes well," Sethos says, lifting his chalice. "Though, I had wanted to tell you, sending secret messengers to your advisers in the middle of the night is not necessary. This is a palace, not a prison. I'm sure my brother would hope that you felt comfortable in corresponding with your own men."

Eron slams his fist on the table. "If this is not a prison, then why am I being watched?"

Hanlyn brings his fist to her mouth and kisses it gently. Tarik is forced to note that despite his like for the queen, she is an exceptional liar with her body language. He's quite sure only he—and perhaps Sepora—can discern that she detests the man she shows such adoration for now.

"Dearest, I'm sure at this sensitive time, everyone is being watched, is that not so, King Tarik? It's a precaution we should all strive to observe. The line drawn between peace and war is fragile at the moment."

Tarik nods. "I couldn't agree more. And I assure you Sethos has not been assigned to watch you."

"No," Sethos drawls. "I do it strictly for entertainment."

Sepora, for all her show of silent disinterest, actually giggles, earning her a severe look of disapproval from her mother. In an effort to please, Sepora tucks her lips together in a straight line. Tarik hides his own smile behind his dinner cloth as he dabs at the corner of his mouth.

"So then," Rashidi says, pressing his fingertips together over his plate. Tarik dreads what he could possibly bring up next. But to his surprise, his adviser merely seeks to lighten the mood. "Now that we've discussed alliances and battle plans, perhaps we could steer the conversation toward a more happy occasion: the royal engagement procession tomorrow, of course."

At this, Sepora stands. "I'm not feeling well." A lie. And one she doesn't even bother to try to hide from Tarik's knowing ears. She has a way of evading that he's never seen before. Her bluntness simply shows her disregard for his feelings in the matter. He chooses not to take offense.

Sepora holds up her palm to her mother, who had begun to stand as well. "I must excuse myself. But please, finish your meal, all of you. I'm just going to rest in my chamber." Not the entire truth.

Will she be sneaking out with Nuna again tonight, then? It would seem Sepora had taken up old habits of late; it has been reported to him that she flies Nuna out of her stall almost every evening. Since she has always returned, Tarik has not intervened. He hopes he does not regret that decision tonight. Standing him up at his own royal engagement procession could be a slight Sepora may well not be able to resist.

"I'll have a servant bring you the rest of your dinner, in case you feel well enough to eat it later," Tarik says, standing as well. If she is going to beg off, he will let her. If discussing the royal engagement procession makes her uncomfortable, he'll not force her to listen. But if she intends to evade the procession itself tomorrow morning, or the marriage altogether after that, he will have to take action. "It is good that you rest up. I'll not have you swooning during the procession, unless of course, it's over me."

He earns chuckles from around the table, but from Sepora, he receives a dire look. "Trust me when I say, Highness, that I do not swoon." She turns and leaves the great dining hall then, her long sheer cloak trailing behind her with the lie.

5

SEPORA

NUNA FOLLOWS MY COMMANDS, LANDING US gently in the majestic main garden of the palace, sliding us smoothly along the grass so as not to make too much of a trail. Coming to the garden is bittersweet for me. It is here, in this spot, that I first saw Dody, the Seer Serpen I trained for Tarik. The beast's motionless body had lain in the grass by the grand marble fountain, having been shot from the sky by Tarik's wall guard. Though Dody was the Serubelan general Halyon's Serpen, I had come to accept him as my own. And how could I not? I saw him every day. Had been the one to feed him and exercise him and coo words of endearment into his ears before putting him away at night. Having Nuna back helps soothe some of the sting of his loss. But the memory of Dody still pierces my heart now and again.

With Nuna, I will be more careful. I will protect her, the way I couldn't protect Dody when we fell from the sky together. In fact, as a precaution, I've already taken steps to ensure that Nuna and I would not be shot down when we sneak out at night. I am not supposed to leave the palace walls by order of the Falcon King. Yet, Sethos was more than happy to help me maneuver around that rule. He has somehow persuaded the guards to let me and Nuna fly away unbothered, and though he couldn't promise that the king would not be notified of our nightly escapes, so far Tarik has not acted upon this information.

Until now.

After the way I acted at dinner, I shouldn't be surprised to find Tarik sitting on the ledge of a fountain just outside the shadow of a citrus tree as we land. I wish I had seen him from above before, but I have the suspicion he had taken care that I wouldn't.

He'll ask questions about my behavior at dinner. Out of an irresistible urge to defy him, I'll decline to answer. He has forced my hand in almost every way. I'll not relinquish control over our informal conversations. After realizing I'll not bend, he'll leave my company, brooding, and I'll let him go, hoping I've bested him.

It is the way of things now.

"I see you're feeling better," he says. There it is again, his impassive expression. Either he doesn't believe I felt ill, or he doesn't care. Most likely it's both. He pats the marble next to him on the ledge in an invitation to sit.

"Surely you jest." I train my eyes upon Nuna, aware that doing so turns my nose up ever so slightly.

Out of the corner of my eye, I see his chest fall in a burdensome sigh as he rises and makes the short walk to where I rub Nuna behind her ear. She deserves a good rubbing down after the flight I took her through this evening, but that will have to wait until Tarik has left us. Rubbing down Nuna takes the better part of an hour, and since she was particularly obedient tonight, I'll run along her spine to help ease the tension in her muscles there.

"You were quiet at the evening meal," Tarik says.

"If only *you* were so quiet."

"What? Surely you're not angry that I expressed my wish for you to swoon over me." There is a playfulness in his tone that I can't quite ignore. Blast.

"Such wishes should be kept private."

"We are in private now." He leans upon Nuna, cocking his head at me. It feels like even more of an intrusion, because Nuna seems at ease with this Falcon King. And why wouldn't she be? He comes to us often enough in her stable, feeding her apples and slivers of meat while attempting polite conversation with me. He even pets her absentmindedly while asking me how my day has been. Indeed, he has lowered the defenses of my Defender.

Since the evening meal, Tarik has washed his body of the royal paint, and his hair is a bit straggled, as though he's just awakened. I used to prefer him this way, as Tarik and not the Falcon King. What's more, he knows it. The thought of him coming to me as himself instead of as my ruler forces me to tread warily with my emotions. Perhaps I would not be so nervous if I had not left him with such an intimate lie earlier at dinner—a lie that only he could detect.

"Were you sleeping in the garden, Highness?" I say, hoping desperately for a change of pace. I do not like how his eyes stay trained upon mine.

He gives me a passive shrug and an equally lazy grin that still does not soften the intensity of his gaze. "I might have dozed off waiting for you." He slides closer, his shoulder nearly touching my jaw. "I'd hoped you might stop by the garden before putting her to rest for the night. The guards tell me you visit often." His voice is almost a whisper, and yet it resonates with me down to my bones.

"If you needed to see me, you could have just asked. Though I can't imagine a moment of the day when we're not thrown together over kingdom matters as it is." Which is true enough.

"Nothing I have to say tonight could be counted as kingdom matters."

I feel the burn of a flush at my cheeks as he moves ever closer. His breath is a delicate breeze on my hair when he says, "In fact, at this moment, I am not a king at all, but a servant. *Your* servant, Sepora."

Saints of Serubel. Now he's as serpentine as Sethos can be. "My servant? Well then, Tarik My Servant, go throw yourself from the Half Bridge."

He pushes a tendril of my hair from my face. I try to turn away, but he grabs my arm and pulls me to him. I could easily pull away, just as easily as I could have missed his reach altogether. Nuna stirs uncomfortably behind him. Tarik's eyes are intent upon mine. "Perhaps I'm not being clear. By saying I'm your servant, I meant that I'm here to offer my services."

My eyes go wide and I hate myself for it. He sees everything, even the smallest of flinches. He knows his words do not fall on deaf ears—at least not completely.

"Services?" We are not yet married. What *services* an unmarried Tarik could offer an unmarried Sepora, I do not know. Or perhaps I do. And that is why my voice cracked in the first place.

"You said that you do not swoon. I thought that to be a shame, since swooning over someone can be quite enjoyable. So, here I am, ready and willing to help you swoon."

"I do not need help swooning." *Well played, idiot.*

"No? So you *do* swoon?" His teasing is relentless, his gaze even more so.

"Stop that. Immediately."

"I'm afraid I can't. You challenged me at dinner."

"I did no such thing." It doesn't take a Lingot to hear the desperation in my voice. "You really should see a Healer for these delusions. Surely Master Cy can help."

"And unfortunately—for you—I accept."

For all of my bluster and everything that has come between us, I still do not move away when he entwines his fingers in my hair and pulls my lips to his. When he opens my mouth with his tongue and demands an answer from me, I give it to him. When he presses his body into mine, I allow it. I more than allow it. I press until there is no space left between us.

And when he groans into my mouth, I return one in kind.

With one hand in my bun of tresses, he uses the other to lace our fingers together. But he is not satisfied with that for long. He moves his hand from my hair, his fingertips blazing a trail down to the small of my back where his palm lies flat against my bare skin.

With his touch, he has halted the world and left me here melting under his attentive supervision. And I'll not have it. Yes, he can make me swoon. Of course he can. I'm angry with him, but not impervious. Never impervious to Tarik.

But blast it all, I can make him swoon, too.

I unlock our hands and move mine behind his neck, then wrap my legs around his waist. He groans, leaning me against Nuna, his hands grasping my thighs, pulling me more tightly around him. I revel in the feel of being at eye level with him, but my concentration is quickly stolen when he slips his fingers along my waist, intermittently tucking them between my skin and the fabric of my nearly sheer pants. Not to be outdone, I arch against him, surprising myself with my boldness and with the immediate need the action created within me. Despite my intentions to make *him* swoon, heat fills me everywhere, and I suddenly regret my adventurous decision to seduce him.

Because kissing Tarik is not possible to do without involving my heart. Not in my dreams. Not in my wakefulness. Not ever.

Tarik senses the moment I consciously withdraw from the kiss, because he pulls his lips from mine. Has he won? I'm not sure. Still, I'm pleased to see that he is as breathless as I am. He lets my legs and arms drop slowly so that I'm standing before him. A cloud passes over the moon, blocking out the light, but not before I catch a glimpse of his expression.

He is as affected as I am.

He runs a hand through his hair. We look at each other's shadow for a long time. I see him swallow once. I fidget with my hands, thankful for the darkness. When the moon peeks out again, revealing Tarik's face, I take a step back, pressing myself into Nuna.

His face is awash in frustration. "I was wrong to approach this as a game," he says gruffly. "I can see I'm well matched." He steps toward me, tilting my chin up with the crook of his finger, and none too gently. "But the next time you kiss me like that, I'll take it as an invitation to bring relief to the both of us."

He turns abruptly then and I watch as he takes the garden steps two at a time toward the palace.

6

TARIK

WHY MUST SEPORA ALWAYS KEEP ME WAITING? But then, couldn't one argue that waiting for Sepora has now become the essence of life? And did last night's kiss not prove that in every way? He'd initiated the kiss and he'd ended it—that was the pitiful extent of control he'd possessed when his mouth had melded to hers. But Sepora? She'd accepted his farce of a challenge and made it into a real one, seizing him, all of him, with her lips. It had not taken long for him to realize that while he is the one issuing orders and commands all day, Sepora is the one in supreme control of his world.

And that kissing her could never be just a game. Not to him, at least.

Uncomfortable with that thought, Tarik shifts his weight from one foot to the other in his ceremonial chariot—the same chariot that had made King Knosi appear as though he were the sovereign of all the five kingdoms. Despite Tarik's ornate, tall headdress, his gold body paint, and the fact that his broad shoulders nearly span the width of the thing, he still feels woefully unworthy to man the chariot. How could he ever appear as majestic as his father did in it? The people—or worse, Sepora—may well laugh him out of the royal engagement procession today, finding him unfit to ride in such a creation. Made of gleaming mahogany, the finest of specimens to be found in the Wachuk forests, the chariot's labyrinthine carvings tell the history of the Theorian kingdom—a proud tale outlined with the voyage across the Dismals, the victory of battles, and the building of pyramids. Behind him, banners of blue and gold fly in the dry wind, and flowers, dyed blue for the occasion, adorn the front of the chariot.

Rashidi had missed no opportunity to be as extravagant as possible when commissioning the chariot for King Knosi, and none today when having it bedecked with splendor for Tarik.

But none of this matters. What matters is that Tarik stands here in this, the beginning of his royal engagement procession, without the benefit of an actual future queen by his side. Of course, he is not so obtuse to deny that he could be the one to blame. Yes, she'd been in full control last night, but the way he'd ended their kiss had been callous and not how he'd intended. Yet . . . Yet. No matter what that kiss proved, nor the consequences it brings today, he'll not regret it. Moments like those may be all he has to look forward to in their marriage, what with her mistrust of him now. And if so, he'll grasp each one and cherish them as sacred. Though, truth told, he'd rather she come around and forgive him sooner than later. However stupid enough he is to want even a floundering marriage with Sepora, he's also hopeful enough he'll have one filled with love and respect and eventually, even trust.

Just as Tarik decides Sepora is actually keeping the entire party, including her own family, waiting on purpose, Queen Hanlyn speaks up from the chariot directly behind his.

"It would be my pleasure to retrieve my daughter for you," she says, a bit of agitation coloring her tone. Still, she tells the truth. While

Tarik is sure that King Eron finds Sepora's tardiness a potential insult, and therefore vastly amusing, it is evident that his wife does not.

He refuses to find it humiliating that Sepora's own mother recognizes her daughter's brazen disregard for his pride. Today is their engagement procession, an important moment in the beginning of their lifetime together. And Tarik will not allow bitter thoughts to ruin it. He turns to Queen Hanlyn and smiles, hoping it does not appear as sour as he feels. "I would not think of sending you to fetch her," he says amiably. "If she is too much longer, I'll have one of the guards inquire after her." *After all, Sepora is used to guards chasing her throughout the palace.*

Queen Hanlyn nods. "Of course, Highness." But her frown suggests she really had personally wanted to retrieve Sepora—perhaps for the benefit of a well-placed motherly scolding. Tarik is glad his own mother isn't here to see this indignity, not because she'd be angry with Sepora, but because she'd enjoy watching her own son squirm under the pressure. She would say what she always said: "Conundrums sharpen the wit and dull the boredom."

Just as Tarik reaches his own sharp wit's end, Sepora materializes by the chariot. And promptly steals his breath.

"My apologies, Highness," she says quietly. "I've been held captive by my servants all morning. I hope my appearance is well worth it, as it will take hours to get out of this ensemble alive."

The truth. With relief he offers her his hand to step up into the chariot, trying not to let his mouth fall open. His future queen is nothing short of stunning. "Believe me when I say, it was time well spent."

She wears a silver, cylindrical headdress encrusted with diamonds and sapphires, a silver falcon adorning the front of it; a heavy-looking silver collar bib made of more diamonds and sapphires, intricately woven into swirling designs; silver cuffs around her upper arms with the same falcon on them, only they clutch at sheer blue fabric that spreads wide behind her in a flowing cape. The cuffs around her wrists also hold the sheer material like wings, giving her the appearance of a falcon herself. Set against the silver body paint—Tarik could not be more pleased that she did not fight the body paint on this day, as is the custom—her kohl and blue makeup appear as beautiful swirls upon her face. The gown itself is a light blue silk that extends to her feet.

He knows he pales in comparison to her. Though his ensemble is similar, only with gold, she looks like an exquisite silver figurine, yet achingly human. He'll feel a bit like a fool standing next to her, and not just because she has kept him waiting. As it is, he cannot shake the feeling of being a boy masquerading as a king.

As she steps into the chariot, Tarik smiles to himself as he sees that she opted to wear no shoes at all.

She smiles, too, if only for a moment. "The sandals were made of solid silver," she says, as if scolding him for designing them that way. As if he could have dreamed up this kind of elaborate creation for her himself. "If I'm to be on my feet all day, I must at least be a little comfortable, wouldn't you agree?"

"Ah, but I would agree to anything at all right now."

He can tell that were it not for her silver paint she would be blushing, though she turns away to hide it, pretending to inspect the palace as they pull off for their journey. But she only lets her gaze linger there until the palace disappears from sight. Once they are well on their way, she keeps her focus straight ahead, though the Superior Quarters are still far off. She is tense, her stance rigid as she clutches the handle in front of her so tightly her knuckles whiten with the strain.

"Are you well, Princess?" he whispers sideways, not wishing to alert her parents of anything amiss.

"I'm nervous," she blurts, leaning closer to him. The revelation is somewhat of a shock. In all the time he has known her, she has never admitted to being anything less than excessively confident. Perhaps he had rattled her more than he'd thought with his kiss last night. He could not be more pleased. "What if the citizens do not approve of me as their queen?"

Ah, but he cannot take credit for her anxiety. Swallowing a small bit of disappointment, he says, "The citizens have not had a queen for a very long time. They will most certainly approve."

She sighs. "So it is not *me* they approve of, just the fact that there is a queen at all. In that case, would Tulle not suffice?"

"I was hoping that Princess Tulle would not make her way into our conversation today."

"How can she not?"

At this, he places his hand over hers where she grips the front of the chariot, feeling the instant she stiffens under his touch. Still, he does not miss her slight shiver, either. "I do not even think of her. You, and you alone, consume my thoughts."

She glances back, offering her mother a small, counterfeit smile. So, she is bent upon keeping this particular conversation private, just as he is. Relief steals through him.

"That is not enough," she whispers back.

"Tell me what I can do, Sepora," he says, but they are drawing near to the Superior Quarters and will have little chance to speak to each other after this moment. "There is nothing I would withhold from you."

Still, she has no answer. Or, perhaps, she has too many answers to discuss at the moment.

Inhaling deeply, she begins to smile as they approach the first line of Superior citizens, who are dressed in their finest. He follows her lead, despite Rashidi's strict instructions to show no emotion whatsoever in greeting his people. If Sepora wants to win over the throngs, he will help her. He nods and smiles with approval, watching as the people gently toss rubies and emeralds at the line of chariots and Majai forces, even as the convoy tramples the pathway of desert flowers and jewels beneath them. From behind, he can hear Queen Hanlyn gasp, and he can't help but smile wider.

Leaning in to Sepora, he says, "This is the only part of the tour that will involve the citizens showering *us* with gifts. It is the custom for the Superiors to display their wealth in a show of economic strength of our kingdom. Anything less precious than jewels would be an insult to the throne."

Sepora raises a brow at him, unimpressed and very obviously disgusted. He laughs, gaining him a staunch look of disapproval from Rashidi, who rides on a lavishly appointed horse directly in front of them, beside Sethos. When Rashidi turns around, Sethos spares Sepora the briefest of winks.

"Must Rashidi always look like a provoked cobra?" Sepora whispers through a smile.

"Of course," Tarik whispers back. "It is the only way children would ever leave him alone."

Against her will, Sepora snickers, and again, Rashidi whips around in his saddle. "You would laugh at the offerings of your citizens?" he hisses.

Sepora returns his glare, and just as soon as she opens her mouth for what looks like an articulate insult, Tarik grabs her hand again and points ahead to the crowds waiting for them. "Do you hear that? They are shouting your name. I would say they definitely approve of you."

He didn't mean to lean in so closely, he really didn't. He had just wanted to make sure she heard him. But the look she gives him, the way her gaze lingers over his mouth then trails up to his eyes, the manner in which her gaze holds his in surprise and what he recognizes as desire . . . His heart races in a staccato of beats, matching the trumpets that continually sound their arrival. All at once, the memory of last night's kiss cradles him in a daze.

Sepora is the first to recover, clearing her throat and pulling away from him—and to his disappointment, retrieving her hand from his—as she smiles and waves at the people lining the road before them. He's thankful that she has the mind to show courtesy to their citizens, as he had lost his own sanity in that space of a moment.

Tarik uses her newly formal countenance to compose himself. He tries to concentrate on his citizens, as he should, and on the occasion at hand. The last time he made a procession like this had been for his father's funeral. At that time, taking a wife had been the furthest thought from his mind. And now here he is, only a few months later, more than ready to call this feisty enticement standing next to him his queen.

It is enough to knock the air from him. Still, he waves and smiles, smiles and waves, as slowly, the Superior Quarters disappear from their sight. He glances at Sepora just as she exhales loudly. "It wasn't that bad, was it?" he asks.

She shows him her hand, which is shaking considerably. "Being on such display is a bit unnerving. I've never done anything like this."

"That's not true," he teases. "You've been hauled before audiences plenty of times, if I recall correctly. Once, when you escaped the harem, then when you jumped from the Half Bridge. Also, when you—"

She nudges him in the ribs none too gently. "But I've never willingly put myself upon display," she insists.

He shrugs, doubtful. "I'm told the Superiors put on the biggest exhibition. The rest of the tour should be much less intimidating. When we made the funeral procession for my father . . ." But he cannot continue. Because the funeral procession ended at a pyramid that is no longer there—a loss that even his people have mourned. To them, dismantling that pyramid made Tarik wise and calculating, showing that he would stop at nothing to give the people what they needed at the time they needed it. To Tarik it made him a fool.

Sepora's fool.

Tarik forces himself to swallow down the bitterness rising in his throat.

"Yes?" Sepora asks.

"It was nothing. I can see the Middling Quarters ahead. Or at least, the citrus fields." His teasing tone is gone, he knows. But he cannot resurrect it for her at this moment any more than he can resurrect the pyramid that once stood so proudly guarding his father's remains.

"I didn't mean to press about your father," she says solemnly. "I hope . . . I hope our engagement procession does not remind you too much of your loss."

It didn't, at first. But it does now. And she still does not know the true extent of it.

7

SEPORA

THE RESIDENTS OF THE MIDDLING QUARTERS, thankfully, do not toss their resources of vegetables and nefarite at us when we arrive, but rather leave their offers of wealth in baskets in front of them on either side of us, creating a makeshift road of its own. I'm glad for it—it is one thing to be struck in the face with the occasional stray ruby, but it would be quite another to be pelted with an ear of corn. Too, I can't express my gratitude enough, or at all really, that the Middlings hold large palm fronds over us as we pass, creating an archway of greenery and of glorious shade. Out of all the riches of Theoria, I have come to value shade the most. Shade, and water, which Tarik occasionally hands me from his camel-skin flask he keeps at his feet. I take care not to gulp, if only for Mother's sake behind me, though it's a difficult feat because Anku had ensured my silver body paint would be invulnerable to sweat. My sweat has nowhere to go, and my body screams for a release from the heat.

Ahead of us, six Majai on horseback disperse baskets of shimmering gold and silver. The crowd is respectful, taking their gifts and moving back to formation with their fronds. I'm in awe of how different a royal wedding is treated here in Theoria than it is in Serubel.

In Serubel, we would not parade about the kingdom for all to gawk at, but we would quietly accept gifts from our lords and ladies wishing us well—Father would never think of dispersing treasures among the people—and only a select group of the most important and loyal citizens would be invited to the actual wedding, which would be held in the ballroom of our castle. Rashidi tells me that the wedding for Tarik and me will be held on a pedestal—which is still being constructed of the finest Wachuk wood—for all of Theoria to witness. He says it's so that no one may ever question the vows of loyalty the royals make to each other, nor the vows of loyalty the new queen makes to the citizens.

I suspect it's because Theoria strives to be lavish in even the most mundane of things, that when given the rare occurrence of a special occasion, such as the wedding of the king, Theoria's ambition exceeds "lavish" and aims for "spectacular."

The atmosphere is different here among the Middlings than it was in the Superior Quarters. Despite their bigger workload, these citizens emanate a certain vitality that I did not feel from the upper class of citizens. They should be exhausted from their workload of farming and harvesting, yet their excitement for our arrival is beyond measure. Sun-darkened children squeal as we pass and call out "Princess Magar!" in hopes that I'll look their way. And of course I try, I do. But the procession moves at a steady pace, as we have much more ground to cover, and swiveling left and right to acknowledge every person who shouts for my attention would leave me dizzy at the very least.

Beside me, Tarik nearly glows with pride. Even his golden paint cannot hide his affection for his people, and deep within me, I want to feel that same connection with them. As much as I want to deny that I'll soon be their queen, and as much as I'd hoped Mother would be the one to save me from a marriage born out of obligation, I still feel the need to please these people.

Perhaps it's the feeling of inevitability that has settled over me the moment our chariot left the palace, or perhaps the eagerness with which the citizens greet me, that makes me yearn to become their queen. It could be the internal need I feel to make Mother proud in becoming a capable ruler that makes me want to become the queen of Theoria. But if I'm honest, if I'm truly honest with myself, my need to become queen of anything at all is trumped by my need to wed Tarik.

Even now, I feel the heat of last night's kiss on my lips, and for the first time today, I thank Anku for caking so much body paint on me that the possibility of blushing simply does not exist. It would be a mess of a blush, in any case. One filled with heat from our kiss, and one filled with loathing at my weakness to still want to wed him even after all that he's done and despite the fact that he only wants me for an alliance, and for my abilities. I wish desperately that I was a Lingot, so that I could discern whether his kisses were real, whether his words are empty flattery to encourage me to cooperate or if they spring from sincere feelings for me. Will I ever know how he truly feels?

Get ahold of yourself, dolt. Now would be a most inconvenient time to recollect all that Tarik makes me feel. And he was right, of course; this is not a game. We will truly be married very soon. And very soon I will need to decide what kind of wife I will be. I'd set my hopes on dutiful, but Tarik has the ability to melt dutiful into loving. Doting, even. And I'm not willing to dote on Tarik. Not when his actions have already delivered a message contradicting his words.

"We'll be heading to the Lyceum next," Tarik is saying. "Cy assures me they'll not be throwing anything at us there." I give the king a rueful smile. I had been so consumed by my thoughts I had not noticed that we were already departing from the Middlings, and what's worse, Tarik has mistaken my silence for displeasure at the procession. A procession that thus far, he has been very proud of.

"Apologies, Highness," I say with some regret, knowing he'll discern my words as the truth. "I've become distracted by thoughts of ruling such loyal subjects." Only a half-truth and something Tarik will also detect. Despite the curiosity that registers on his face, he says only, "They are honored to have you as their queen."

As we make our way to the Lyceum, I'm haunted by thoughts of not living up to Theoria's blind loyalty. And what they would think of me were they to learn of my Forging—and the fact that I refuse to supply them with spectorium.

8

TARIK

AFTER VISITING THE MIDDLINGS AND THE LYCEUM, AND spreading baskets full of gold and silver to each venue, Tarik is disgusted with himself for feeling a sense of pride in impressing King Eron and Queen Hanlyn, and most of all, the stunning creature standing beside him, whose outward composure would have impressed even his father. At the Middling Quarters, when his soldiers had begun dispersing the fine coin, Hanlyn had gasped, and Eron had snorted—his only way of showing that an impression had been made, by Tarik's estimate. Sepora had watched wide-eyed. "I trust this will not bankrupt the throne, Highness?" she'd whispered to him in between waves to the crowd at the Lyceum.

Not by far. But instead of being boastful, which he didn't feel would go well with Sepora, he simply laughed. He also tried not to let it bother him that in past engagement processions, they'd also dispersed chunks of spectorium. "What do you think, Princess?" he'd said. "Shall we tax them mercilessly to regain it all?"

Sepora had smiled—until her father spoke up. "That's precisely what you should do," King Eron had said, ruining the jest altogether. "Every last bit of it." Tarik thought he heard the sound of a grunt, probably in response to a well-placed elbow by Hanlyn, but he did not grace the king with a reply, nor Hanlyn with the reward of a grateful smile.

To her credit, Sepora had appeared mortified at her father's suggestion.

As the caravan turns west, Sepora peers up at Tarik in confusion. "But are we not going to the Bazaar?"

He shakes his head. "In honor of us, the Bazaar will be closed today."

"But how will the people procure their daily bread? Make their living?"

"Have I been deficient in generosity today, love? Do you doubt they will be repaid tenfold for their act of loyalty to us?"

She chews at her bottom lip. "Of course not. I just . . . I've never seen the Bazaar closed. It would be . . . Well, it would be odd." She gives him a curious look. "The city of Anyar still seems so alive in the evenings."

Of course she refers to her evenings gallivanting through the sky with Nuna, but Tarik is reminded of their night spent on the great pyramid so long ago. She had first refused his kiss then. He's sure she would refuse it again now, especially after last night. Still, it's worth finding out. *But it may not well be worth the feeling of rejection when she declines.* "Perhaps Nuna would not mind a second rider this evening?"

"I'm sure I'll be quite exhausted at the end of our journey today. Perhaps another time?" It is the truth, rather than an excuse. She has put much effort into performing her part today. She is already showing signs of fatigue, stealing yawns when they leave a venue and allowing her shoulders to slump in between visits. She has not bothered to rearrange the tendrils of hair falling loose from her headdress, and he has noticed that she shifts her weight from one foot to the other often.

Yes, Sepora is tired indeed.

He leans in, his nose brushing her cheek lightly. "I will hold you to that, Princess."

She doesn't look at him, but her words are not laced with resistance as they have been these past days. "I know." Of course she does. What she doesn't know is how surprised he is with himself for suggesting it, especially after the confusing evening they'd shared just hours ago. Not to mention his earlier realization that she is indeed in control of him, though he is the one constantly throwing them together. He pulls them closer; she pulls them asunder.

Will it always be this way?

As the procession draws away from the Half Bridge after unloading untold riches to the merchants and their families, it changes course to due south. Again, Sepora peers up at him. "But this is not the way to the palace."

"We've one more stop to make, Princess."

"Anku said the merchants were the last stop. To where do we travel now?" So, she had known, at least a little, what would happen today. Perhaps Tarik had bored her with the earfuls of information on custom and tradition. If he had, she did not let on, always asking questions and prodding him for more. He'd found her curiosity to be genuine.

"I have resolved to include the Baseborn Quarters in our procession."

The setting sun catches the glistening in her eyes. "Why?"

"How could I not? They're your people, Sepora."

She turns away from him then; her stature suggests she would like to withdraw into herself, to be left alone. He will allow her that, a private moment to sort through her feelings about this; but he wants to make sure those feelings steer in the general direction of what he intended by including the Baseborn Quarters. "We will make changes,

Sepora. Spread the wealth more evenly among the quarters. Provide better public education for the Serubelans. Give more of them the chance to attend the Lyceum. They may become a part of our society in every sense, if they wish it."

"They do not need to become part of your society," Eron says from behind them. There is a bluster behind his words that Tarik does not trust. He has struck a nerve with his esteemed guest. "They belong in Serubel, their homeland."

Tarik turns. "Then why do they stay?"

"Because you keep them too poor to travel home," the king says quickly. "They can barely afford to live day to day, isn't that so, Sepora?"

Sepora is frowning up at Tarik. She must believe at least some of what her father says. Tarik handles it the only way he knows how. "After today, King Eron, the Serubelans will not be poor. They will have the means to travel back to their 'homeland.' If they wish to leave, I'll make no move to stop them."

But he is distracted then, by Sepora placing her hand on his forearm. "Look," she says quietly, nodding ahead of them. "They're waiting for us."

And indeed they are. Tarik sucks in a breath at the sight of the masses of blond heads forming lines on either side of the procession, shouting words of welcome and excitement. The setting sun behind the Baseborn Quarters brings with it a hypnotic feel, casting rich gold and purple fingers of light across the widely spread tents, as if this were its very own flourishing city instead of a poverty-stricken corner of Anyar. It is peculiar that a people who wear no fine jewelry or linen or paint still manage to exude happiness and well-being and, from what he can see of the smiling faces, contentment.

"Do you think they approve of us? Of me, becoming the queen of Theoria?" Sepora whispers as they pass the first handful of Serubelans.

"I think we're about to find out," Tarik says. At the front of the procession, the Majai guard calls for a halt in line, just as Tarik had ordered him.

"What is the meaning of this?" Eron grunts, but almost instantly is hushed by Queen Hanlyn.

"Dearest," she says, "do you wish to ruin this romantic gesture for the Falcon King?"

Eron grumbles something under his breath, but the way his murmurs are delivered tells Tarik he will comply with his wife.

Tarik steps down from the chariot and holds his hand out to Sepora. She does not take it.

"What are you doing?" she says, wide-eyed. "You said we must stay in the chariot at all times. For safety."

He shrugs. "I may have been too severe. Come, Sepora, and let us show the Baseborn Quarters how we feel about them." He nods toward the back of the caravan, where the strong men bring baskets upon baskets of bread. Gold and silver are also offerings, but not in the form of coins. To celebrate the Serubelans, he had commissioned the gold and silver to be melded into small figurines of each kind of Serpen. As one of the men strides by him with a basket, Tarik snatches one of the silver creations from the top and offers it to Sepora. "This one," he says. "With the thicker underbelly. This is a Defender Serpen, yes?"

She stares at the figurine for a long time. Finally, her gaze meets his. "It is, Highness."

He offers his hand to her again. "Sepora, join me," he pleads. "Join me in honoring your people."

She takes his hand but pulls back a bit. "What if they do not accept me?" But that is not the real question hidden in her words. Curious.

He glances around in all directions, bringing her attention to the applause and enthusiasm surrounding them. "I think the chances of that, Princess, are nonexistent."

Without further warning, he lifts her down from the chariot by her waist, and she lets out a small squeal, giving him a look that clearly says he'll pay for that later. "As much as I hate to say this," he says, "I think we should separate. You take one side, and I'll take the other. The men will follow you with baskets of gifts. Make sure to pass them out personally as often as you can. Sethos will accompany you for protection."

And, as if he'd spoken him into their presence, Sethos places a hand on the small of Sepora's back. "Shall we, Princess?" He grins. Together they leave to accompany citizens on the right side. For all his annoying attentiveness, Sepora will not be in danger under Sethos's watch, Tarik knows.

It is something Sepora should know, too. But as Sethos guides her away, she looks back at Tarik, biting her lip. Something is troubling the princess. Something more than what she says. Perhaps it had been a mistake to come here. Does she not feel safe among her people?

But he pushes the thought aside. The citizens here adore her, he can tell. If she fears for her safety, she will be pleasantly surprised.

It is with this thought in mind that Tarik takes the opportunity to tend to the Serubelans on the left.

Over the general drone of the crowd, Tarik can hear words shouted out. Praises such as "Hail Princess Magar, our future queen!" and "A happy marriage for the Falcon King and the Princess Magar!" and "The perfect girl for the boy king!" The latter could be taken as an insult, but Tarik chooses to overlook it this day. After all, when he is with Sepora, he does feel like a lovesick boy.

Speaking of boys, a crowd of the braver ones approaches Tarik, hands out—hands more bony than Tarik would like to see—each bowing before him. "My Falcon King," one boy says, "if you could spare bread for us, we've six to feed."

Tarik smiles. "Then you shall require at least a dozen loaves." He nods to the guard holding the basket of bread, who loads the boy so full with it that he can barely see over the stack of loaves. He giggles in delight, peering up at Tarik. A loaf drops to the ground and the young one swoops to pick it up again. And when he does, Tarik's smile halts in place.

Toward the back of the crowd, clutching the thin skin of his mother, is a boy too shy to approach him. Too shy, or too wary. For the boy at his mother's side has silver eyes. Silver, not gray or blue, as is the normal Serubelan trait. And not a mirage playing tricks on Tarik in the heat. Those eyes shine like coins at the bottom of a fountain, glistening in the sun.

The boy is dirty, but through the grime, he has all the obvious Serubelan features. The pale skin, the white hair, the straight nose. Barely within earshot, Tarik can tell he carries the stubborn accent, though they've lived here for centuries, of a Serubelan speaking Theorian. But this boy is different from the rest. This boy has one distinguishing feature—the one feature no one should have, save Sepora.

And his mother has just caught on to the fact that Tarik is staring. She turns then, whisking him away and disappearing into the crowd behind her. Tarik wants to follow, to assure himself of what he saw. But doing so would make a scene. A scene that he cannot afford to make in the company of King Eron and Queen Hanlyn.

Could it truly be possible? Serubelans usually possess blue eyes, but Tarik has seen some today with brown, green, even lavender or hazel eyes.

But not silver.

Never silver.

King Eron had once told Tarik about the history of Forgers. That they always pass over a generation at a time. That Sepora's grandfather, Eron's own father, had been a Forger, and that the ability had been passed down from him to her. *Did not King Eron also say that only Forgers have those glinty silver eyes? Yes. Yes, he did.*

Tarik glances behind him to seek out Sepora and Sethos. They are quite a bit ahead of him on the other side and not paying the least bit of attention to him. But King Eron and Queen Hanlyn both watch Tarik closely from their chariot just horse lengths away. Instinctively, he moves his body away from the procession, crouching down to speak to the boy in front of him with all the loaves of bread.

"The boy with the silver eyes. Who is he?" he says, trying to keep his tone friendly.

But the young one bites his lip, his cheer turning swiftly into trepidation.

"You've nothing to fear from me," Tarik assures him. "I'm merely curious. What's your name?"

"Trykan." He says it proudly, as if Tarik should already be familiar.

Tarik grins. "Well, Trykan, if you must protect the boy with the silver eyes, I understand. But know this: I'll find out who he is eventually, and the person who tells me will be rewarded. It would be a shame if that person were not you."

Tarik hates himself for bribing a child and for the lightness in his tone. It's unfair to the boy, this position that Tarik is putting him in. He may get in trouble if he tells. He may be punished. But a boy serving extra chores as penance is nothing when compared with the need to know if there is another Forger in Tarik's midst.

Trykan considers for a long time. Then his shoulders slump. "His name is Bardo, Highness."

Tarik smiles widely, even as he commits the name to his eternal memory. "Thank you, Trykan. Tell me, are you having a good time today?"

The abrupt change in subject has the boy smiling again, his transgression all but forgotten. "Oh yes, Highness. When they told us you'd be visiting our quarters today, our teachers canceled our lessons for the whole day!"

Tarik smiles. This boy has no inkling of the importance of the parade or the fact that it came to the Baseborn Quarters in honor of Sepora. He merely cares that his lessons were canceled for the day. Still, Tarik can't help but wonder how the boy Bardo spends his time away from lessons.

Does he Forge?

Certainly he must. Eron had said that Sepora must Forge, else she'll feel ill and weak. Does this boy suffer the same effects if he does not release the energy? How has his gift been hidden for so long? And why?

The questions tug Tarik's mouth into a frown.

"Take these to your family as well," Tarik says quietly, handing him as many gold and silver Serpens as the boy can manage. "And tell them the King and his future queen wish them well. Especially them."

"Yes, Highness!" the boy says with glee, then turns and disappears into the masses. He may not understand the importance of the message he carries with him. But his parents will understand perfectly. They will know that the Falcon King has uncovered Bardo's secret. Either they will flee, they will tell Bardo's family of what has taken place, or they will await his next communication with them. He will not force them to come to him. He will give them the choice, just as he has given Sepora.

Sepora. *Does she know?*

The crowd presses in on him, but Tarik is now too distracted for the task at hand. He instructs the guards to continue in their distribution.

Quietly, he turns in the direction of the chariot.

9

S E P O R A

I WATCH AS THE REST OF THE ROYAL ENGAGEMENT procession pulls away from us and into the night. We stand by our own chariot in the crisp moonlight just outside the Baseborn Quarters, where the festivities of the evening seem to be just beginning. Tarik had requested a private ride home with his future queen, and since everyone—even Rashidi—had been too exhausted to put up an argument, it had happened as the king requested.

I had a thought that I should be nervous, that whatever the king wanted, whether it was a more thorough seduction of me or perhaps even a confrontation over our last kiss, I should at least try to mentally prepare to parry with him. Still, my mind is so weary of having survived this day that I don't think I could utter anything coherent in the way of argument.

When the sounds of the caravans cannot be heard and only vaguely seen, Tarik offers his hand to me to climb into the chariot. I take it, not even caring that I use his shoulder to steady myself as I step up. He takes his place beside me and picks up the reins, gently urging the horses forward and even the smallest movement jars me out of my state of near collapse.

For a time we ride in silence, and I take in the view of the inky sky with its pinpoints of white stars that sparkle like tiny morsels of daylight. While I hadn't thought I'd have the energy to think of anything at all, I do remember now that Serubel rarely offers a view such as this; though the mountains are high, they are mostly covered with clouds in the evenings. At home, a starry night is something one must be constantly on the lookout for.

At home. How odd to think of Serubel as my home again. In the beginning, when I had fled Serubel, I had accepted the fact that I would live out the rest of my days in Theoria, had come to acknowledge Theoria as my new home. Perhaps it was when I left this place on the back of Dody that I began to view Theoria as a foreign kingdom again. Or perhaps the arrival of my mother made me long for Serubel—after all, Mother represents everything that is Serubel, in my eyes. Even after the engagement procession today, after the citizens of Theoria were so vocal in accepting *me* as their new queen, it did not feel as though *they* were my people. I suppose only after I'm settled into marriage with Tarik will I begin to feel at ease here again. I wonder how many years it will take for the tension between us to dissolve. How much time must pass before my feelings for him wane and I can hold conversation with him without emotion lurking behind my words.

"Sepora, we must talk, you and I," Tarik says softly, and it reminds me that I have much further to go until time dilutes my reactions to him.

Still, I know this is what he had wanted when he'd requested a private ride home and am again reminded that perhaps I should have prepared in some way to anticipate what this could be about. Perhaps he'll simply want an explanation for our kiss, and I have none to give him. It simply won't do to confess that his kiss drives me beyond sense—he might be so incorrigible as to kiss me again. Nor will it be fitting to tell him that I accepted his challenge and made the decision to reciprocate—he might find another challenge hidden somewhere in my admission.

I think of all the direct questions he could ask me and all the indirect ways I could answer without lying. There are woefully few paths I can take to evade his gift of discernment. And his gentle tone does not hide the tension hidden just beneath his voice. "Must we talk?" I ask, trying not to sound as desperate as I feel. "It would ruin the perfect evening, I think." I sweep a heavy hand upward to the sky, as if he possibly could have missed its brilliance before.

"We must. The desert is the only place I know that does not have ears."

I cannot help but stare at him in the moonlight as he stops the chariot to remove his headdress and run a hand through his hair, which is matted against his head and set in place by a day of sweat. He combs his fingers through the mess, scratching in places where the headdress must have been tightest. He looks at me for a long time.

"Tarik?"

He leans forward then, resting his forearms on the front of the chariot and staring ahead of us as if he can see something in the stretching desert that somehow the darkness does not swallow. "Soon, I will not be the only person making decisions for the kingdom," he begins. "My hope is that you'll take an interest in being Theoria's queen, despite all that has happened between us."

Take an interest in being queen? Perhaps I don't think of Theoria as my home, but I certainly cannot be accused of neglecting my new duties. "You'll have to elaborate, Highness. Have I not already taken an interest in the affairs of the queen? Do I not stand with you at court, and hear the people—"

"You perform the burdens of a queen well enough, Princess. But I must know your motivations. A queen puts her needs—her innermost feelings and longings—aside to become what her people need her to be. Is it in your heart to do this, Sepora? Have you grown fond enough of Theorians to place more import on their needs than on your own?"

Can he discern my thoughts as well? But never mind that. What he's suggesting is absurd. Duty and obligation are not enough to please him anymore? Now I must rule with my heart—the same heart he sliced through with word and deed alike? Nonsense. "A queen does not rule with her heart, but with her mind. The heart is fickle. The mind is strong." It's almost word for word what my mother once told me. I know when I say it that Tarik cannot find fault in Mother's wisdom.

Yet, he regards me with a neutral expression. I despise the fact that he can read me like one of his many scrolls, but I, however, cannot tell in this moment whether he heard me at all.

"I agree that the heart should not be used to rule, but it should be used to determine what motivates you to do so."

"I'm afraid you'll have to be more direct, Highness. What more do you require of me than to perform my duties?"

He sighs. "I need to know that my people are safe in your hands. That *our* people are safe in your keeping."

"Are you asking if I mean to hurt the citizens of Theoria?" The question makes me breathless—because his answer is more important to me than I expect it to be. Does he truly think me capable of hurting his people—of hurting *anyone*? What's more, I still can't comprehend why we're having this roundabout conversation in the first place. What does he hope to gain by speaking riddles at me?

It occurs to me then that he *wants* to ask me a direct question—but he's not sure if he wants to hear the answer. That Tarik is unsure, and perhaps even afraid, of what I will have to say causes a feeling of unease to settle over me.

This conversation will be about my Forging.

"I don't think you would purposely *hurt* them. But I'm not sure if you would choose to *help* them, either."

"Help them in what way? Must I beg you for candor?" Though with each word, I know his meaning. How could I not? Still, I feel the need to taunt him, because I'm in no mood to make anything easy for him. Perhaps this morning I was. Perhaps this morning I could easily have seen myself loyal and doting on the Falcon King. But somehow I've recovered some of my sense.

One simply does not dote on the person who has broken one's heart.

He stands straight and crosses his arms. I see the moment when Tarik disappears and the Falcon King materializes before me. And the Falcon King can be difficult to sway. It means I must step aside as Sepora and reason as a queen. Reason as my mother would reason.

"I speak of the past, Sepora. When you had spectorium at your fingertips, quite literally, and not once did you Forge to save Theoria from the Quiet Plague. I speak of this very moment, when you still refuse to Forge, knowing we have an impending war."

So then. I've prepared for this very conversation. Truthfully I'd thought it would come much sooner than this, with all the pressures he faces from his commander and my father. Yet, I cannot deny that it stings, the very real disappointment in his voice when he accuses me of withholding spectorium now. He has never betrayed any emotion about it until now. *No. Emotion does not belong in this conversation.*

"That is hardly fair. You know my reasons for all of it. And you yourself tell my father daily that spectorium is not needed." All along, he has made it clear to my father that it is my decision whether to Forge. And all along, he has hidden his own bitterness about the fact that I choose not to. A tinge of guilt overcomes me as I acknowledge that, although spectorium has proven to be the cure, we have not yet tried fresh spectorium. Because Tarik is right. On principle,

I've refused to Forge it. In refusing to be an obedient pawn between two kings, I've been very stubborn. And I do not like the way it makes me feel. I wonder if Mother would feel so culpable or if she would allow a bit of remorse to soften her, as I am now.

But for what? Tarik has voiced his belief, his confidence that Master Cy will conquer the illness soon. Why, then, must we talk of spectorium? And so once again, I get the sense that he dances around the true question. It feels odd, for me to be the one insisting on directness and for Tarik to be the one evading me with his words.

He waves at me in dismissal, his irritation showing through his face paint. "Yes, yes, I know your reasons. Truth told, it's not the spectorium at all. It's the fact that you've kept secrets from me. It takes skill to deceive me, Sepora, and I know you're more than capable of the feat."

I would argue that simply being around Tarik takes skill and is exhausting at times. His abilities make it so, and yet, I can't resist the challenge. "Ask me a direct question before I go mad!"

"Are you keeping secrets from me?" he bellows just as quickly. He pinches the bridge of his nose, and exhales sharply. "Apologies, Princess. I did not mean to yell. It's just that I *know* that you're keeping something from me. I even know *what* you're keeping from me. Perhaps I even know why. But the point is, you're keeping something from me in the first place, and I won't have it."

"Saints of Serubel, if you know so much about my secret, why are we even speaking of it, then?" I turn and jump down from the chariot, aware that part of my ensemble stays behind, caught between some cracks in the wood. Not a graceful exit, to be sure, and Anku will be angry that I've torn her creation, but having such a ridiculous conversation in such a state of exhaustion in such close proximity to the instigator is beyond what I can bear this night. Forcing my tired bare feet to make tracks in the still-warm sand, I head in the general direction of the caravan and, hopefully, the palace. Aware that I'm in the throes of a tantrum—of which Mother would never approve—I call over my shoulder, "To think you've kept me from my bed just to say you know my secrets! Of all the childish—"

But a hand catches my arm and whirls me around. I didn't even hear him disengage from the chariot. Yet here he is, towering over me, blocking out the moon behind him so that darkness covers his face and his expression is once again unreadable. "Unhand me at once!"

To my surprise, he does. "As you wish. But move from that spot, Princess, and I'll secure you to the chariot with your own attire."

I believe him. There's a desperate anger in his voice that paints a clear picture of him throwing me over his shoulder and carrying me back to the chariot. My hands settle on my hips. I won't be hauled back to the chariot but feel obligated to be difficult all the same because of the threat. "Be quick with this, Highness. Ask me a question or forever wonder the answer."

He shakes his head. "That is not how trust works. You are keeping a secret from me. I'm placing the burden upon you to tell me."

"Has the desert heat drained you of sense? Of course I have secrets. Everyone is entitled to their secrets, Tarik. I'll not lay bare all mine just to sort out the one you want most to hear."

At this, he stiffens. "You have more than one secret?"

"Everyone does!" It takes all my restraint not to stomp in the sand.

"I do not."

"No? You're the only person, then."

"Rashidi does not. I would know."

"Has Rashidi ever been in love?"

"What? How could I know that?"

"Have you ever asked him?"

"Of course not."

"Then that is a secret Rashidi keeps from you. He doesn't openly offer the information, and you don't directly ask about it. So, it's a secret."

"Why must you be the most unaccommodating person in all the five kingdoms?"

"Is that truly the question you want to ask me? If not, you're wasting my time and squandering my patience."

He is quiet for several moments. My gaze swivels from my left to my right, anyplace other than his shadowed face. I don't want to hear the question; I know it as surely as I know my name. For what could it be? What if he asks how I truly feel about him? What if he asks how I enjoyed our kiss last night? What if he asks, now that we've visited the entire kingdom, if I'm excited to rule as their queen? He could ask any number of questions that I would not be comfortable with answering. And if he asks them directly enough, I will not manage to hide my sentiments.

Still, of all the possibilities, I do not expect the one he actually inquires after.

"How long have you known about the boy Forger, Bardo?"

My mouth falls slightly open as everything clicks into place. We visited the Baseborn Quarters. We were intimately involved with the residents there. He must have seen Bardo. But how could he know that I knew of his existence? Perhaps he doesn't know. Perhaps this is his way of asking if I did.

And Saints of Serubel, why did Bardo's parents allow him to greet the king? Perhaps they didn't. Perhaps Bardo is a rebellious child and couldn't pass on the opportunity to meet his pharaoh. But none of this matters. What matters is that there is no evading the Falcon King now.

He crosses his arms. "You wanted a direct inquiry. You now have one, Princess."

"Did . . . did my father see him?" And what about the others? But to ask such a revealing question is not in my best interest. I feel so vulnerable. I'm not sure what I should admit to and what I should hold close to my heart.

My answer—my question—gives him pause. "Your father doesn't know, then?"

"No."

In the moonlight, I see his shoulders relax. With not a little relief, he says, "I made sure not to bring attention to him and spent the rest of my time distracting your parents from the crowd."

I know this to be the truth. He had been waiting for me at the chariot when I had finished dispersing the treasures of Theoria to my side of the Baseborn Quarters. No wonder he'd wanted a private audience with me. And no wonder it would be as soon as possible. Another Forger—many Forgers, according to my servant Cara—within my father's reach is not a thing to take lightly.

Tarik knows it. I know it.

But what about another Forger within *Tarik's* reach? Should I be afraid for the boy?

"Does your mother know of the boy?"

I shake my head. "I haven't told her yet."

"But you intend to."

I nod. There is no use in denying it. I'd intended to take Mother's counsel on the other Forgers. I'd intended to take Mother's counsel on everything. But what does he expect? That I will suddenly grow a fondness for Rashidi and invite him over for confections and honey milk and chatter on about how to rule a kingdom? Rashidi would have better luck procuring rain for all of Theoria. And no one else qualifies to advise me on kingdom matters, especially on the matters about which I disagree with Tarik. It must be Mother.

Tarik folds his hands atop his head. "You have kept many secrets from me. I ask that just this once, you keep a secret *with* me."

Little tinges of betrayal sting in my belly. "We can trust my mother. She would never tell my father."

He mulls over this, and I know he's looking for the truth. "That is what you believe," he says finally. "I must spend more time with her before I will believe it. Surely you understand that."

I understand it, but I don't like it. I have ways of evading Tarik's questions. Mother has ways of asking inescapable questions. And she has spies. What will she think of me when—not *if*—she learns I have been keeping this secret from her? Will she decline to help me further? Too, while Tarik and I both agree that we cannot tell my father of Bardo, I'm still not sure what it means for the boy now that Tarik knows of him. "What will you do to Bardo?"

"What will I *do* to him?"

"Will you force him to Forge?"

Again, he stiffens, squaring his shoulders and shaking his head. I'm thankful the darkness hides his expression at this moment. I know it would be one of scorn. "Will I lock him away in the palace, steal his childhood from him, punish him for having the misfortune of having such a rare gift?" He scoffs. "If you have to ask that, then you do not know me at all."

He stalks toward the chariot, leaving me in the sand to either follow or be left behind altogether—and for a few moments, I'm not sure which I'd prefer.

10

TARIK

THE SETTING SUN STREAKS FINGERS OF DYING light into Tarik's day chambers as he unravels another scroll sent to him by his Lingot council. There has been a pattern to these reports of late, and he suspects this parchment holds nothing good in the way of news. Crime has always been present in the city of Anyar, even when his father ruled, and it would be unreasonable for Tarik to think he could abolish it in his own reign. Thievery, brawling, and price gouging—those are the things he had witnessed sitting alongside his father at court whilst being groomed to one day take the throne. Those are the issues he knows how to deal with. Those are the things his Lingot council knows how to deal with.

But the stack of scrolls in front of him are those cases to which the Lingot council had no answer, the cases where they deferred to his judgment. The cases where judgment was simply that, where no true answer simply presented itself to him, and so he is forced to have an opinion not backed by a specific written law. And he wants none of it.

As he scans this new scroll, he rubs at his temples, as though that is where the brunt of his frustration gathers, as though his growing concern will ebb away with the tips of his fingers. He reads through the court case again, blinking at the sordid details and wondering what sort of madness has taken over his citizens. A man from the Middling Quarters, a servant to one of the Superiors, stole his master's fine silk robe and wore it to the Bazaar—an easily punishable offense at court as it is outright thievery, but something that would normally be dealt with inside the household with a proper dismissal and docking of wages. But the theft is not the actual complaint. Oh, if only it were. The actual complaint did not even come from the Superior master himself, but originated with a merchant at the Bazaar who accuses the Middling servant of wearing nothing *but* the robe in front of his young daughters—apparently he'd forgotten to steal the sash to tie around himself—and insisting on paying for the goods he wished to purchase with plain river pebbles that he called "the finest nuggets of spectorium he'd ever seen." The servant subsequently offered to lick the merchant's face in exchange for a good deal on his wares. When asked at court if the merchant was correct in his accusations, the servant had insisted that he had been dressed like the Falcon King himself and that the spectorium he'd offered to pay with was the freshest there was to be had in all the kingdom. Tarik's Lingot council reports both the merchant's accusations *and* the rebuttal of the Middling to be true—or at least, something each *believes* to be true.

Tarik shakes his head. Clearly this Middling has committed an offense—but a crime? Even his secondhand reading of the events shows that the Middling had no ill intent toward the merchant nor his Superior master. He is simply and clearly out of his mind. Tarik is at a loss at where to even begin. Treating this man as a criminal would be like treating a wounded kitten like a vicious beast if it lashed out against help. This servant needs to be taken care of, tended to, not sentenced to work in the salt mines south of Kyra or worse, thrown from the Half Bridge. There is no place in Anyar for a man such as this; in the rare event where a citizen becomes mad, their family is expected to care for them properly and keep them out of trouble. Yet, this Middling has no living family and his Superior master will surely not obligate himself or his resources to the man's care, no matter how long he has served him.

Again, Tarik shakes his head. If it were only the one instance in his court scrolls, Tarik would appoint the man a caretaker himself and be done with it. But the scrolls contain more incidents like this, as many as Tarik has fingers. Something more must be done. He must speak with Rashidi. His old friend will not like what Tarik will suggest—that the throne should take on the expense of creating a sanctuary for mad citizens—but after a bit of bluster and diplomatic arguing, Rashidi will concede. The question is, how quickly can such a place be built—and who can he trust to care for these people?

And more important, what is stealing the minds of his citizens in the first place?

Sighing, he stands and makes his way to the balcony, where he hears the angry clinks of swords down below, a small tinge of jealousy knotting in his stomach. He is careful not to be seen as he peers just outside the archway of the window leading to the balcony, keeping most of his body shielded by a potted shrub stationed at the entrance. Below him, Sethos and Sepora battle out their own frustrations with each other.

Or rather, Sepora grunts and growls, taking every opportunity to strike at his brother, as Sethos parries, deflects, and occasionally laughs. Tarik is surprised at how skilled Sepora has become with a sword; Sethos is breathing heavily, which means that while Sepora's attacks are amusing, they are still worthy of at least some effort on his brother's part.

"You hold your sword like a child," Sethos is saying.

"You babble on like an old woman," Sepora informs him, sweeping her leg wide as her opponent easily jumps over it. "The least you could do is say something interesting."

"Very well," Sethos says, easily deflecting an otherwise deadly blow to his neck. "Rumor has it that the citizens of Theoria are overjoyed that the Falcon King has chosen to marry for love, instead of for duty. What say you to that?"

She rolls her eyes, and out of clear annoyance, stabs directly at Sethos's heart. He leans right, pushing her sword away with his bare hand and clicking his tongue with not a little condescension.

"Rumor *also* has it," she purrs, repeating the move to catch him off guard, "that the citizens of Theoria are slowly going mad. I'd not take the word of lunatics so seriously, my esteemed Majai."

Tarik grimaces as both rumors ring true to his ears. Apparently he had done his part to show himself a lovesick whelp during the engagement procession a few days ago. And apparently this new lunacy that has overtaken a handful of citizens in the city is a concern for all.

How delighted Rashidi will be.

Tarik eases away from the balcony, unsure if he can handle more alarming truths for the day. There are some who long to have the Lingot abilities, to know a truth or a lie as soon as it falls upon one's ears, but those ones never consider how inescapable words can be, how utterly useless it can be to know the truth, or how utterly infuriating it can be to hear a lie but not have the power to act upon it.

As Falcon King, he has the power to act upon most lies, but every once in a while there comes along a lie that should not be acted upon, one that should be acknowledged and tucked away for a later time. The morning after had been one of those times.

He, Sepora, and Queen Hanlyn were breaking their fast in the great dining hall—Eron had begged off, sending a messenger who enacted a dramatic rendition of the king's grave headache (which had been ultimately true, Tarik had surmised). Hanlyn had easily taken her husband's absence in stride, jumping at the opportunity to confess to what an exhilarating time she had during the royal engagement procession, asking him how he had enjoyed the outing and complimenting him on his kitchens for turning out such exceptional meals. While he found her charming, he had not quite been awake for more than an hour as of yet and had met her with somewhat abbreviated graciousness, giving her no more than one or two words in return for her many. Though he still longed for his bed—even Patra had slept beneath his feet at the grand table, unable to keep her eyes open enough to mind the meat she'd been served—he still found the queen of Serubel refreshing. He wondered what his own mother would have been like, sitting in a foreign dining hall entertaining a foreign king, and only hoped she would have been half as charming as Hanlyn. It was a gift, he knew, for her to be so jovial all the time. A gift that her daughter did not inherit—Sepora's eyelids had fluttered shut several times during the course of conversation and Tarik had the inflated hope that perhaps she'd been kept up last night, that perhaps she'd thought of nothing else but the kiss they'd shared, as he had. Most likely, though, she'd spent the evening thinking of their argument in the desert after the procession. She tends to cling to their disagreements more than their accords of late.

Just as he was about to suggest he and Sepora join the Lingot council to hear out some court cases, Queen Hanlyn told the most striking lie he'd ever heard. It had jolted him immediately, and he wondered if he'd been paying close enough attention to the queen after all. Sometimes a person can be so honest and forthcoming that his Lingot abilities will relax in their presence. Is that what had happened with Hanlyn this morning? He couldn't be sure.

Hanlyn had paused from her merriment in retelling the engagement procession from her point of view in the chariots behind them and had said, "My husband will see to it that we have decades upon decades of peace between our kingdoms."

The lie had resounded between them as if it had been a staccato of trumpet blasts echoing off all of the walls. Sepora nearly missed her mouth with her forkful of fruit. She'd blinked up at her mother, casting Tarik a suspicious glance when the queen had refused to acknowledge her daughter.

Sepora and Tarik had the same question, he could tell.

What was amiss?

"And how will he see to it, Queen Hanlyn?" Tarik said cautiously. Tarik did not doubt that Hanlyn was well aware that he was a Lingot. So then, she knew he would have discerned the ridiculous idea of everlasting peace presented in her words.

She'd folded her hands in her lap. "I'm not sure yet, Highness. He doesn't speak to me often about his plans, but I know he has some."

The truth. A game indeed, but with what purpose? Did the queen have knowledge of Eron's spies in the dining room, as Tarik had already learned? That his own servants had taken a bribe from the leader of Serubel and had sworn to report back to him all that they'd heard? If she knew these things, what else did she know? What else could she tell him?

It had not taken much pressing to find out.

"To be honest, I did not trust Eron when first he came to Theoria," Tarik had said with a smile. "My suspicions were that he wanted me to marry your daughter so that he could get close enough to me to use my own resources against me to overtake my kingdom. Silly, isn't it?"

She'd laughed. It was insincere, even though it tinkled around the room innocently enough. "I assure you, Highness, my husband would think of no such thing! Indeed, Eron has no ill will toward you at all. He is very anxious to see our kingdoms united in harmony."

The lie was as transparent as the breath Sepora had sucked in through her teeth. Queen Hanlyn had wished to warn him that Eron was up to something. Yet, this was not news to Tarik—surely she knew that. He had been discerning deceit from King Eron since the moment the king opened his mouth to greet him. Was this a play on Hanlyn's part? An attempt to show him that he could trust her? He hoped not. At this point, he didn't feel he could trust any Serubelan, even, sadly, Sepora. She had kept many secrets from him. Too many to trust her at the moment.

"I am glad to hear it" was all he'd said. Sepora had given him a bewildered look, which had made the impression that, whatever game Hanlyn had played at this morning, Sepora had not been a party to it. He was not sure if he should have been relieved or disappointed that she and her mother had not been allies in this showing of support for Tarik. Only time would tell, he supposed. It had been at that particular moment when he'd been forced to acknowledge what his Lingot abilities had shown him, and had been obligated to tuck the information away for a later time.

And so, the Falcon King had been powerful and powerless all at the same time, in spite of his abilities. Being a Lingot was not easy. Knowing the truth could be difficult, and knowing a lie could be worse.

But ignoring them both would make for bad kingsmanship.

"Uria," Tarik calls to the door now, summoning one of his messengers. The thin, loose-jointed man came to him at once, sliding through the open door like parchment through a crack, and presented himself, head bowed.

"Deliver a message to the Princess Sepora this evening, Uria. Tell her to meet me at the servants' entrance at dawn. Tell her we are to have an outing tomorrow."

Sepora will know what that means—that they will walk the kingdom as Tarik and Sepora, leaving their royalty behind in the palace, as they had done several times before. Only this time, Tarik had an agenda. He would consult with his friends at the Bazaar, with Cy at the Lyceum, with the Middlings and the Superiors. He would get their take on the rumors abounding so broadly in Anyar but never appearing so directly in his court. He would take note of the true needs of his people, and together, he and Sepora would act on their behalf.

At least, that is what he hopes for, as he settles back at his table of scrolls. It is yet another bid for Sepora to show interest in the kingdom that will one day be hers. And if he is truthful with himself, he is not sure how many more of these invitations he can afford to extend.

Uria, clearly confused by the message but willing to please nonetheless, bows farther. "It will be as you wish, Great Falcon King." With the quiet ease of Patra, the servant exits the room with bare feet padding silently on the stone floor. Just as the door closes, however, it opens again, wide.

Before him stands Ptolem. "Apologies for interrupting your evening, Highness," he says gravely. The tone of Ptolem's voice quells the small feeling of excitement Tarik had when he'd thought of visiting the Bazaar with Sepora. This will not be a good report, he can tell.

Ptolem has been newly appointed as a trusted informant to Tarik. But Ptolem, at this hour? Curious. He'd sent Ptolem to officially inquire after Bardo and his family and arrange a meeting with them.

Ptolem enters his chamber carrying the chest of gold with which he'd been sent to Bardo's family. This could only mean they have refused his offer of riches in exchange for the boy's Forging. It was something he'd anticipated, but disappointment still ravages his insides. He'd promised Sepora that he would not force the boy to Forge. He had not promised her that he would not bribe him.

"Ptolem, friend, I see that my offers have been declined," Tarik says, trying to keep the bitterness from his voice.

Ptolem bows ceremoniously, and before he can rise from the

gesture, Tarik waves for him to be seated at the table with him. Ptolem places the chest of gold in the middle of it and looks at it for a long time before speaking again. "I inquired after the family of the boy Bardo as you requested," he says. "I was then sent on a merry chase to find someone who knew of them. It seemed as though no one knew the boy. For most of my time there, I was convinced you'd seen a spirit with silver eyes."

"They are hiding him," Tarik surmises. He folds his hands behind his head. Bardo is no spirit. Sepora had already confirmed that for him. "That is not unexpected."

Ptolem nods. "They are hiding him, yes. Protecting him, as it were. But my visit to the Baseborn Quarters was not in vain, Highness."

"How so? You've brought back my gold and returned without the boy or even a message from his family." Or perhaps he does have a message and I've all but cut him off. Tarik does not mean to sound so bitter. But he'd had high hopes when sending Ptolem to the Baseborn Quarters. More than that, he'd been desperate for spectorium. More desperate than he could possibly let on in front of Sepora.

"You see, Highness, I did not find the boy Bardo with the silver eyes. I found many citizens with silver eyes. Dozens, at the very least."

Dozens? Impossible. His friend had been on a long journey, having stayed two days in that part of the kingdom. Surely the exhaustion has gotten the better of him. "Perhaps they had gray eyes, Ptolem, but not silver. Serubelans are known for their blue eyes to turn gray at times with old age."

Ptolem straightens his shoulder. "I'm not mistaken, Highness. Their eyes were silver—and these citizens could not be older than you or I. Eyes the very same silver as Sepora—er, that is, Princess Magar—has in her own eyes."

"You're sure, Ptolem? Much depends on your being right about this."

"I'm sure. What's more, the Great Council has invited your servant Tarik to speak to them on your behalf."

"Great Council?"

Ptolem swallows. "It would seem, Highness, that the Great Council is a body of elderly Baseborn citizens who rule as a separate entity within your laws. And they are willing to speak with only Tarik, the high servant of the Falcon King, regarding any questions you may have for them."

"How do you know this?"

Again, Ptolem swallows. "Because they took me to the Great Council far off in the desert when I began inquiring after the boy, Bardo."

"They accompanied you to the Great Council without your having to ask?"

Ptolem shakes his head. "They took me, Highness. Blindfolded and my hands bound. I could not tell you where their lair is located even now. The travel there and back was very far."

The Baseborn Quarters have now, in effect, kidnapped a servant of the Falcon King. He cannot let this go unpunished. Or can he? What do they have to say for themselves? Obviously something important, if they request the presence of the highest servant, Tarik.

"Prepare my chariot, Ptolem. I will go to them tonight." *And I will have answers.*

"Tonight? Are you sure that's the best course of action, Highness? What if they mean you harm?"

"If they mean me harm, they will have the entire kingdom of Theoria to contend with. I'll make sure my whereabouts are known with Rashidi." And it will be an unpleasant affair to do so, he's sure. He waves to his servant. "All will be well, Ptolem. I thank you for this information. You may take your evening meal now and rest peacefully tonight. You've been useful to me already, friend."

Ptolem nods and stands, dismissing himself before Tarik can call for the door to be opened for him.

Rashidi will not like this. He will be set against Tarik going alone, which is not unwise, he knows. Yet, he must speak with the Great Council.

Dozens with silver eyes, Tarik thinks. Ptolem is onto something even bigger than the boy, Bardo.

TARIK'S CHARIOT PULLS PAST THE FIRST FEW TENTS of the Baseborn Quarters unnoticed. He doubts he will remain so very much longer, as the night is quiet and his horses are loud. And sure enough, he is right. A line of blond-haired men dressed only in shendyts begins to form in front of him, halting his way ahead.

Certain that he must show humility and goodwill, he steps from the chariot and pushes his hands in the air in a show of peace. "I am Tarik, high servant of the Falcon King. I've come at the request of the Great Council."

The smallest and perhaps youngest man of the group steps forward, his stature and composure signaling that he is clearly their leader. "We've been expecting you, Tarik. Before we take you to see to your affairs, we must take certain precautions, you see." He nods his chin to the man beside him, who steps forward in the moonlight, clearly holding a rope in one hand and a thick sackcloth in the other.

"I understand completely," Tarik says, turning his back to them and crossing his arms so that they may be tied. Tarik smiles into the darkness as he envisions what Rashidi would do were he to witness such an act of submission from the Falcon King to the lowest class of the kingdom. He makes a note to tell him of it when he returns to the palace.

The men waste no time in binding him and placing the cloth over his head. Suddenly, he is lifted by several of them and carried as though he were a plank of wood over their heads. They travel for a long time in this fashion, and Tarik's muscles ache where his captor's hands push into his flesh. He is certain that they take him in circles to confuse him before setting on their true course to meet with the Great Council. He takes note of all the turns and finally decides that they head south, below the boundaries of Anyar.

Then, too, they seem to walk in more circles. It is paramount to them that the Falcon King does not know the location of the Great Council. This does not sit well with Tarik. What sorts of business does the Great Council conduct? Do they coincide with his own laws for Theoria, or do they intentionally hide their undertakings because they do not comply with the law of the land? No matter that tonight, however. He is not there to undermine a council that has apparently been set in place for centuries. He is there to secure spectorium.

And plenty of it.

At long last, he is set upon his own two feet and the sackcloth removed from his head. He faces a round one-story structure clearly made from very old spectorium—no doubt a building they designed and Forged the materials for themselves. There is a single, dark entrance, and he follows the young leader into it, his hands still bound behind his back. He might have been concerned about this, had he sensed any type of deception in Ptolem's account of his meeting with them or in the body language of the men surrounding him. But there is no malicious intent in their gaits, no tension of any sort emanating through their mannerisms. They are simply there to transport him safely—and possibly to ensure the safety of the council.

Tarik is not surprised to find that the inner chamber of the structure is round and well lit with white, fresh spectorium. The Great Council is a collection of elderly men and women seated on the ground in a half circle before him. He turns to the young leader for guidance.

The man says, "You may sit, High Servant Tarik. The Great Council does not bite, for many do not have the luxury of teeth."

This earns a chuckle from a few of the council members, and Tarik finds himself relieved at the rather informal atmosphere, despite the trouble taken to secret him here. Tarik does as he's told, sitting in the sand and crossing his legs in the same fashion as the council members. There are nine of them, and Tarik wonders if the odd number is to decide matters in case of a tie. That is why he had chosen three Lingots for his own council; in case two were at odds, he'd have a third's opinion to sway the outcome of the case.

Out of respect, he waits in silence. Finally, one of the two women speaks. "I am Olna, eldest of the Great Council. Please accept our welcome, High Servant Tarik."

"Please accept my gratitude for your meeting with me on behalf of the Falcon King."

She nods. "We do not believe in standing upon ceremony here. Please tell us why the king is interested in our Forgers."

Tarik appreciates the directness of her words. He decides to return the favor, in view of the lateness of the hour. "You've no doubt heard of the Quiet Plague, Olna."

Again, she nods. "We have."

"The plague has ravaged the kingdom. The king's Master Healers have found that only spectorium helps ward off death and bring back vitality."

She considers this. "When you visited our quarters during the royal engagement procession, it became clear to us that Princess Magar is a Forger herself. Are you aware of this fact?"

"I am."

"And why has she not Forged for His Highness, knowing that it is the only cure?"

Tarik is not sure how much to tell the Great Council. How loyal are they to King Eron? But there is no ulterior motive behind Olna's questioning. She is simply curious. "She is afraid her father will weaponize the spectorium."

"Weaponize it how?"

"It would seem that when mixed with Scaldling venom, it creates a rather powerful explosive. Princess Magar is afraid her father will use it to cause war between all the kingdoms."

Olna glances to a man at her left, who nods. It is then that Tarik notices the man has blond hair, but the dark skin of a Theorian. Could he be a Lingot, then?

Olna returns her gaze to Tarik. "We have been watching King Eron. We've heard reports about how he rules his kingdom. He is a selfish king. Princess Magar, however, appears not to have inherited that trait." She taps her finger against her lip. "You still have not answered why the princess will not Forge for the Falcon King. Does she not trust his ability to keep the spectorium from King Eron?"

"She and the Falcon King have had their differences, I'm afraid. But it is my belief she trusts him in this regard."

Again Olna looks to the man at her left. Again, he nods.

"It would seem that Princess Magar puts a great deal of trust in the Falcon King, to have even spoken of it to him. Too, she did not see a reason to withhold the fact that there are other Forgers in the Baseborn Quarters."

So, the Great Council thinks Sepora openly shared this information with him. If only that were so. If only he were here because he could trust his future queen. But that is not the case any longer. Bitterness steals through him as he thinks back to the royal engagement procession. How they'd stayed behind in the desert night, and how she'd lied to his face about keeping other secrets from him. And what of his Lingot abilities? Is he slipping? The Great Council all but said she knew of the other Forgers. He will ask her directly sometime tomorrow, while they steal away to the Bazaar. He will ask her, and if she lies again, he must make a decision.

A decision his heart does not want to consider.

Instead of answering and giving himself away to the Lingot closely watching him now, he says nothing. After all, Olna did not ask him a question, she merely stated an observation.

"In light of that fact, we will consider the king's need for spectorium." She nods to her left and to her right. "We must confer on the matter at length, however. We will return an answer to him soon, in view of the dire circumstances of the other classes."

This catches Tarik's attention. "Do you mean to say that the Baseborn Quarters have suffered no casualties of the Quiet Plague?"

"We find it interesting as well, High Servant Tarik. We have suffered few casualties, and those who did contract the disease were of mixed blood. Not a single Serubelan has perished from it." Tarik was not aware that mixed blood existed in the Baseborn Quarters. He'd thought they always kept to themselves, not intermingling with the rest of the classes.

He has been under many wrong assumptions, it would seem.

He wonders what Cy will do with this new bit of information. It cannot be a coincidence. It simply cannot. "When may I tell the king you will give him an answer?"

Olna purses her lips. "Can the king assure us the source of the spectorium will be kept from Eron?"

"I can say with the utmost confidence that the king will do everything in his power to make it so."

Seeming satisfied, she says, "As I said, we will return an answer soon."

"Shall he send me again to collect your response?"

"We will send word to him. We thank you for your time, High Servant Tarik. And for your honesty."

"The king sends his highest regards and gratitude for this meeting. He looks forward to your reply."

The guards come to collect him then.

He has much to think about on his journey back to the palace. Even if he does secure more spectorium for Cy—will that cure the insanity running rampant in his kingdom? Battling the Quiet Plague is one thing, but what if the cure itself is causing the madness? He must speak with Cy. He must have more solid answers before he infects his entire kingdom with lunacy.

11

SEPORA

IT OCCURS TO ME THAT I'M ALWAYS IN A BLASTED good mood when Tarik takes me into the city. We get to visit some of Tarik's merchant friends, hear outrageous rumors, and perhaps, if only for a moment, steal a sliver of the life of a normal citizen of Theoria. Each trip, as soon as we leave the palace walls dressed in servants' attire and armed with only bread and cheese for our journey, I feel as though my body somehow floats over the sand on the way to the Bazaar. In fact, I'm already smiling as I head toward the palace kitchens now to meet Tarik. I will even be outside of Mother's reach today, and I couldn't be happier. Her knowing eyes tax my mood at times.

As I turn the corner of the servant kitchens where the entrance leads out into the morning sun and eventually outside of this blasted palace, I'm forced to halt at one of the long wooden bread-making tables a few feet from my destination. I take in the scene, assessing whether it is a display of male idiocy or a true emergency. The one guard posted at this entrance has his arm locked about Tarik's neck, holding him so tightly that Tarik's face is a bit red and his eyes a bit bulging. Tarik is in some pain, and not a small amount of it.

I purse my lips in indecision.

On the one hand, this is Ptolem. Ptolem has become more relaxed with Tarik, as he always comes to the kitchens as himself and not the Falcon King when he seeks to exit the palace. Tarik has a sort of rapport with Ptolem, an ease of friendship that almost always comes along with the knowing of Tarik himself. I wouldn't want to interrupt their banter. But the longer Ptolem holds him in place, I wonder if I can really call this banter.

Because, on the other hand, citizens in this city are going mad. What if Ptolem is one of those touched with delirium? He certainly appears to be enjoying the way Tarik's face changes from red to blue, his grin getting wider as his king angles a failed sweep at his tree-trunk legs. I steal a glance at Patra, who rests at the entrance door, her tail flitting to and fro, as if she, too, cannot decide whether to put an end to this, or if she's simply dejected about being left out of it.

Testing whether I should intervene, I clear my throat at the two. "Ahem."

As that goes unnoticed by the both of them and even by Patra, who keeps a close watch on Tarik, I'm forced to consider my options. The quickest way to undo . . . whatever this is . . . is to approach Ptolem myself and disarm him. But since he's a good foot-length taller than Tarik and wider, even given my training with Sethos, I get the feeling I'd be nothing more than a snack to this young man. Still, he is distracted at the moment by one very foolish Falcon King. Perhaps it could work.

Or, I could do it the uninteresting way and simply call for help. I try to remember the last time I did anything the uninteresting way, and deciding that surprising them both would be great fun no matter the circumstances, I spring forward feeling only a little of the disappointment Mother would be wearing on her face right now.

I've gained a good sprint by the time I reach the end of the long bread table; avoiding Sethos's blade has made me quite fast. I pass a bread knife that could have been worth the taking—and imagine Sethos shaking his head at me—but just in case this is truly gameplay, I leave it next to its crumbs.

I jump then, and that is when the pair finally notice me. Time slows to a crawl while I'm in the air. Their struggling ends abruptly as they stiffen in unison, Ptolem releasing his king so quickly he all but shoves him away. Tarik does not appear so concerned about that as he does about the fact that I'm now flying through the air, scheduled to land on Ptolem's person within the next two breaths. Ptolem turns quickly, showing me his muscled back, and that is where I thump to a halt, breathless almost beyond sense. I try to angle my arm around Ptolem's neck, to hold him as he had Tarik, and am disappointed to find both that my arm is too short to do so, and also that Ptolem is delighted that I actually tried. He yanks me around by my elbow and sets me gently on the ground in front of him. I bend over, resting my palms on my knees as Sethos always instructs me to do when I need to catch my breath.

Tarik rubs at his throat, peering down at me with his one eyebrow raised in a bit of bewilderment. "And I thought you were so adamantly against violence."

As the breath is still knocked from my lungs—my ribs had connected with Ptolem's shoulder—my response is panting that sounds like the nuanced communication of the Wachuks. Finally, I'm able to breathe in a whole breath, and it feels like I've been given a second chance at life itself. An exhilarating life where I can play as a boy, too. "And I thought you were strictly against having fun." Too many words. That was too many words, and my breath is stolen once more.

From his lofty height, Ptolem bends all the way down, farther than me even, and looking me straight in the eye, says, "I've never been attacked by a girl before. I've always wondered what it would be like. Thank you, Mistress Sepora. Now I can move on with my life knowing."

Tarik bellows his laughter while I try to think of something clever to return to the amused guard. He can speak to me this way, of course, because right now I'm Mistress Sepora, not Princess Magar of Serubel. I am the servant Tarik's friend; we are both about to set out on a mission in the name of the king. I must admit how vastly refreshing it is to be spoken down to. So vastly refreshing that I waste my precious just-gained breath on laughing, too, and it takes several moments of coughing and sputtering after that to settle my lungs.

After I've sufficiently recovered from the trauma of assaulting Ptolem, Tarik extends his hand to me and Patra uses that as her signal to rise and join us. Ptolem picks up his shield and spear—which I hadn't even noticed he'd discarded—and walks with us out into the sunlight.

"Be careful today, Tarik," Ptolem says before we board the simple chariot that had been called for us. Tarik takes the reins from Ptolem and then pulls me up into the wooden carriage.

"What's amiss?" Tarik asks after I'm settled.

"Stay clear of the Strays is all."

"The Strays?" I ask.

Ptolem nods, handing Tarik a satchel full of what I assume is food and water. "That's what we're calling them. The ones who don't quite know how to behave themselves anymore."

Tarik sets the chariot in motion, calling over his shoulder, "We're out to find some Strays, actually, Ptolem. Don't wait for our return."

After we're outside of ear's reach, I elbow Tarik. "We're *meant* to be searching for the Strays? Why? Why not wait until they come to us at court?"

"I want to see how they act outside of an audience. And we must figure out where this curious madness is coming from."

I try to hide my excitement when I say, "We're going to visit Cy?"

He gives me a sidelong glance. "Don't we always? But first, the Bazaar."

WE FIND THE MERCHANT CANTOR HAGGLING WITH a Middling woman over a silver necklace sparsely decorated with turquoise beads. His good-natured smile never fades, even as his patron throws up her hands at him in frustration. Tarik darts his eyes at me, and with a nod, I silently agree to move closer to get a better listen. Patra stays between us as we approach Cantor's booth and pretend to inspect his wares. People are wary of Patra, knowing she is the king's cat and that only he has full control of her. Still, they have seen Tarik in the markets since he was a boy and always accompanied by Patra; they are used to the idea of Tarik taking Patra on occasional walks for the king when the pharaoh wishes to exercise his cat and cannot do it himself. At least, that is what the citizens believe.

"The turquoise hardly calls for such a price," the woman is saying.

"I understand your concerns, Mistress," Cantor deflects, laying the piece back in place upon the velvet lining stretched across a plank of wood. "The turquoise is just an accent, and I do not charge for it."

"Pride of the pyramids, then what *are* you charging me for?"

"The piece is unique, we can all agree on that, Mistress. But it's the silver that I must fetch a higher price on, I'm afraid. It's in its purest form, you see."

She shakes her head, bouncing her long black curls around, giving them a life of their own. "You act as if the silver were spectorium. Show me a piece with fresh spectorium, and I'll pay you twice as much as you're asking!"

Cantor laughs, and remarkably, the woman's face softens a bit.

"Mistress Vera, you're a most challenging negotiator. Who else but me could appreciate the value in that? And you know how grateful I am to have your business. But with this piece, I must remain firm." He leans in closer, and I find that both Tarik and I do, too. Cantor sighs dramatically. "You see, my little Itya made it, and I mustn't sell it for less than what I would pay for it to get it back."

Tarik raises a brow at me, and my eyes widen. Cantor has just told a lie.

Mistress Vera's shoulders slump, her mouth twisting guiltily. "Well, why didn't you just say so, Cantor?" After a long pause, she pulls gold coins and a small chunk of blue spectorium from the stringed purse at her wrist. "Here. And tell little Itya I paid the extra sum for the exquisite workmanship."

As she turns to leave with her new necklace, Mistress Vera acknowledges us with a nod—it would be considered rude for her not to, as we are clearly royal servants of the Falcon King. I feel a bit scandalized on her behalf and wonder how many people Cantor has taken with this story. My pity stops cold, though, when the mistress's gaze drips down the length of Tarik and back up to his face, allowing a small smile of appreciation to spread across her features. Tarik is oblivious, or rather, Tarik is very good at appearing oblivious; he returns her smile with a tight one of his own, then places a hand at the small of my back and steers me toward Cantor, who waits for us at the front of his booth.

Against my will, I grind my teeth, wholly aware of the inconvenient jealousy uncoiling in my stomach. It's nonsensical, I reason, to be jealous over Tarik. We've already had our rise and fall, and there are so many sound arguments to be made in favor of not feeling anything at all toward him. I just wish one of them would come to mind at the moment.

"Cantor, old friend," Tarik says, grinning at the slippery merchant before us. "When did you come in possession of a daughter named Itya? I ask on behalf of the Falcon King, of course. He would want to offer his congratulations." Dishonest selling of goods is punishable in Tarik's court. A merchant who makes his wealth from ill-gotten gains could be taxed as little as the amount he swindled, or if he makes a habit of it, as much as his entire booth and livelihood. Tarik tends to be easier on the honest ones who confess straightaway, but the ones who refuse to speak the truth, he punishes severely. He once told me that such merchants, if left unchecked, are like a festering wound to the economy of the Bazaar. If he allowed it to take place, he would allow the demise of commerce in Anyar.

Cantor chuckles. "I did not say Itya was my daughter. I did not say who Itya was at all, in fact. So then, the Falcon King could not possibly tax me on a technicality."

Tarik picks up a golden ring with a giant square ruby in the middle of it, absently turning it over and over in his palm. I can see on his face that he has already brushed the matter aside. "The Mistress Sepora and I are here to investigate the Stray who caused a scene in the Bazaar a few days ago," he says. "I understand it was a mere few booths down from you?"

Cantor nods. "It was. At first, I thought the fellow to be jesting. But then he began to get angry." The merchant scowls. "He upturned the tables, and thieves took their share of Luka's wares, scrabbling in the dirt for all the jewels while Luka could do nothing but guard his person from the lunatic." I wonder if Tarik sees what I see, that Cantor is at this moment imagining himself in the same position and finding the idea repulsive. Funny that he should condemn thieves, after what he's just done to the Mistress Vera.

"Have you noticed an increase in this kind of behavior?" Tarik says, setting the ruby ring back down and scratching at his jawline, running his fingers along newborn stubble.

Cantor's lips form a thin grimace. "Everyone has. Some are not as brazen as the Stray at Luka's booth. Most are quiet, resigned to talking to themselves or scurrying about mysteriously, as if the rest of us are out to run them through. They disappear, you know. Their minds, I mean. Hollow as the pyramids, they are."

"Can you think of any reason why this is happening? Is it contained to just the Middlings? Do you notice the Superiors acting this way as well?" But Tarik already knows the answer to that question; on the way here, he'd told me about all the council scrolls he'd rifled through. The only class not affected thus far has been the people of the Baseborn Quarters, and Tarik said he suspects that is only because they tend to keep to themselves. Rarely are the Baseborns present in court at all—not even to file a complaint against a higher class. Anku says it's because they have their own way of governing themselves. I'd decided not to tell Tarik that, in case such a thing could be viewed as treasonous or other such nonsense Rashidi was bound to come up with. I wonder if Rashidi and I will ever tire at this game of tolerance we play and actually become friends.

In any case, why is Tarik asking questions to which he already knows the answers? I'm instantly reminded of a few nights ago, the evening of our engagement procession. He'd already known about Bardo but preferred that I tell him anyway. Is he, in some roundabout way, testing Cantor the way he tested me? And—what would Cantor stand to gain from hiding such knowledge?

"I'm afraid you'll have a somber report to give the Falcon King, Tarik," Cantor says. "The madness has no preference between the Middlings and the Superiors."

Tarik nods. "My father once told me that adversity can cause such a madness in people. That sometimes, people are unable to handle their lot in life, and they lose touch with themselves over it. What do you make of that?"

Cantor shrugs. "I suppose I could agree with that. Though I can't fathom how that could come into play here. Life is as it's always been. Births, deaths, marriages, and annulments. Selling, buying, eating, and drinking. Nothing out of the ordinary, if you ask me."

"Perhaps the citizens of Anyar are worried about something? Perhaps, for instance, they're worried about the Quiet Plague? Or perhaps they're worried that the Falcon King is not capable of executing his royal duties?"

Cantor, of course, has no idea how personal Tarik's line of questioning is. Only I notice how Tarik's voice carries with it an underlying turmoil, something unsettled at the core. I wonder how long he has been doubting himself as king. And I wonder if it has anything to do with me.

Cantor's face melts into a fatherly smile, full of reassurance and comfort. A smile I've never seen on my own father's face. "I'm quite certain that is not the case, Tarik. The people love the Falcon King. They always have. I'm afraid you'll have to look elsewhere for this source of adversity, if it exists at all."

I'm grateful to Cantor then, because Tarik visibly relaxes, no doubt hearing the truth behind the merchant's words. The people do love Tarik. And he is a good king. After all that has happened between us, there is no denying that. He loves his people, makes sacrifices for his people. It's not healthy for him to begin doubting himself now.

Still, the truth is, Tarik may be correct about the people and their burden of worry. But it has nothing to do with his ability—and I can't allow him to think it does. "Perhaps," I offer with a small smile, "the people are not happy with his choice in queen. After all, he is planning to wed the daughter of his longtime nemesis. It can't be an easy thing to accept."

That Tarik does not disagree bothers me. But Cantor merely laughs off the suggestion. "Mistress Sepora, where would you conjure up a notion such as that? Many of the citizens of Anyar have watched the Falcon Prince grow up and turn into the fine Falcon King he is. We all had hoped he would have an advantageous marriage someday, and now of course, we're even more elated that with his arrangement, he has secured his own happiness. He and the Princess Magar seem quite enchanted with each other, if the engagement procession was any indication. Not to mention the peace that will arise from an alliance of our kingdoms. What more could we ask for?" he says, nearly incredulous.

If I open my mouth at this point, I will surely stutter. Exactly what kind of impression did I give during the engagement procession that day? *Enchanted* with each other? Surely this merchant is turning Stray. Sethos had said something similar, but I'd dismissed his words as incessant teasing.

Tarik scowls down at me before looking at Cantor again. Crossing his arms and clearing his throat, the king says, "So the Princess Magar. The people approve of her?"

"If our wise Falcon King approves of her, then certainly the people will."

"The people don't know her," I cut in quickly. "And they've hardly seen the pair together to make any assumptions about them."

"Ha!" Cantor slaps the top of his thick leg. "Perhaps love is a difficult thing to sort out in our own minds, Mistress Sepora. But recognizing it in other people is quite the easy task. Those two royals are as in love as you and Tarik are."

"Er, Cantor, that's not exactly—" Tarik begins, shaking his head.

"Tarik and I aren't—" My tongue trips over the words.

"That is to say, Cantor," Tarik sputters, "our friendship is a mutual—"

"Respect," I finish for him, not unaware that my cheeks are so hot, steam is most assuredly emanating from my face.

Cantor bellows even louder, and the crowd behind us glances over curiously. I feel their eyes switching from Tarik to me, and I hear their whispers despite the breeze and the distance between us. They think we're negotiating with Cantor for marriage jewelry. And a few of them think we are well matched.

"Very well, then," Cantor says. "You have a friendship. Which of course means that the two of you haven't kissed, hmm?"

Saints of Serubel, but my face is melting. Tarik's is, too, by all accounts. One of us has to spew the lie, though. One of us has to put an end to this intrusion into our privacy.

"Of course we haven't kissed," I say as Tarik says, "Only once."

I glare up at the boy king. He shrugs, looking squeamish under my scrutiny. "Well, we did," he says finally, looking at Cantor. "And, it was quite the disaster. We vowed never to do it again."

Cantor raises a brow at me. I nod, baffled as to what exactly I'm admitting to. "You know," the merchant says, adapting a wizened tone, "first kisses are almost always a disaster. Kissing is an acquired skill, something that takes time to master. Why don't you give it another go?"

I feel my jaw slacken. Tarik and I exchange panicked glances.

"That is not necessary," Tarik says. "If the inclination presents itself again, I'm sure we'll . . . manage."

Cantor chuckles. "You may go inside my tent for privacy."

"Perhaps another time," Tarik says, already grabbing my wrist to pull me away from the booth. "We're here on official business of the king, after all."

Cantor's gut-shaking laugh can be heard all the way down the row of tents as we hastily pass them by.

12

TARIK

CY LEANS BACK IN HIS SEAT, HIS FACE TWISTED in a scowl. It's not an expression Tarik wants to see from his brightest Healer. "It could just be a coincidence that they've all been treated for the Quiet Plague," Cy says. But he doesn't believe it, Tarik can tell. "After all, the Quiet Plague has struck far and wide in Anyar. There are few who *haven't* been affected by it."

Tarik folds his hands on the wooden table between them. Cy makes a good point. "What else could it be? The nefarite? It's the Great Judge, after all."

"You're suggesting that the nefarite brings out the worst in people?" Cy ponders over this, drumming his fingers along the armrests of his chair. "I wonder how one would test that theory."

"But if someone is truly good, wouldn't it enhance the good in someone as well?" Sepora offers. "Surely not everyone is inherently evil or irrational."

Tarik nods. "Possibly. But my court would not be filled with complaints of good deeds. I only see the terrible and absurd presented in the scrolls. I've no idea of anyone acting excessively kind."

A silence settles over the three of them then. It is unlike Cy, Tarik thinks, not to babble on over possible theories and solutions; either the boy Healer does not think it to be a healing matter, or he simply has nothing to offer in the way of help. Tarik has come to rely on Cy for problems such as this, and he must temper his disappointment by remembering that Cy's healing abilities are limited to what he has experienced in his thirteen years.

"Perhaps you could take the matter to the other Master Healers," Tarik suggests softly.

Cy straightens in his seat. "Of course." If he feels slighted, he does not let on. "We've only now begun to understand how the mind works in relation to the body. Perhaps this illness of the mind we're seeing is actually an illness of the body?"

Tarik nods. "We must broaden our understanding of what is happening, I think. The Falcon King would much rather send the Stray court cases to the Lyceum for treatment rather than prison for sentencing. See that you have a place to receive these new ones, and that they are studied in excess and well cared for. The palace is willing to fund any added expenses for this, of course."

"I'll call the council of Master Healers immediately with this new request. How else can I be of service to the king?"

"He will send word if he requires more of you, friend."

Sepora sighs, standing. "A madness, a plague, and an impending war. The king and his queen have much on their plate at the moment. Perhaps a grand wedding ceremony should be delayed until some of these issues are resolved."

Despite the new developments with the Great Council, Tarik is happy to hear that Sepora considers the problems of Theoria as her own problems; there is no malice behind her words, only a sense of exhaustion. Too, it is her words that speak to her preference. Sepora would avoid a lavish ceremony if she had the choice. But Rashidi is set upon the thing, and Tarik cannot bring himself to stay the efforts of his old friend. He gets the feeling the adviser is not doing it for Tarik and Sepora, but rather for King Knosi, who would have wanted only the best for his son. And besides, his father was always one to uphold Theorian tradition.

Still, a grand wedding amid all of this does seem cumbersome. Surely his father would have understood that. And, a grand wedding at all seems unlikely at this point. As it is, he is not looking forward to the ride home with Sepora this evening. He'll confront her about her lies, her deception about the other Forgers. Perhaps he should put it off. Perhaps he should wait until he knows what the Great Council will do.

Fool! Whether or not the council comes through as requested, his future queen still keeps things from him. Who knows what else she hides?

Cy perks up, bringing Tarik's attention back to the matter at hand. "Perhaps the people need the wedding, Mistress. So that in chaos, they may find a bit of happiness."

"I'll try to view it that way, Cy," Sepora says graciously, taking Tarik's hand and guiding him out of the chair. She yawns. She is tired. He is tired. Perhaps tonight really is not the night for confrontation. But if not tonight, then soon.

Tarik nods. "It has been an interesting day. I think the Mistress Sepora requires a nap."

"I think you might be right for once," she returns, yawning again in the back of her hand. "Cy, you'll excuse us, won't you?"

The boy Healer smiles. "Of course. Please give the king and Princess Magar my highest regards."

IT IS ALMOST DARK WHEN THE TWO OF THEM RETURN to the palace by chariot. As the sun sets behind them, the palace seems to give off steam as the dying heat of the day makes mirages of water ahead of them in the desert sand. As they approach the servants' entrance, Tarik notices immediately that something is amiss; Ptolem, who should be off duty by now, stands at attention with two other guards.

Tarik and Sepora exchange glances as Ptolem halts the horses short of the entrance, his rigid body language signaling to Tarik that he has been waiting for them for some time, his news urgent.

"Greetings, Tarik," Ptolem says awkwardly. He does not like to address his king so casually in front of the others, though Tarik is sure that the guards there now do not know that they are watching their king dismount the chariot with his future queen.

"Hello, friend," Tarik says, offering Sepora his hand. She takes it, not taking her eyes off of Ptolem.

"The Falcon King bids your presence forthwith. It seems an ambassador from the kingdom of Hemut has arrived in your absence."

Ah. So it begins.

Tarik nods, clapping Ptolem on the back. "I trust the king has sent for Prince Sethos from the Lyceum as well?"

Ptolem shakes his head. "Rashidi may have, but I've not received such instructions."

"I'm sure the Falcon King will want Prince Sethos to accompany him in greeting the Hemutian ambassador this evening. Please send him an urgent correspondence on behalf of the king that his presence is required. In the meantime, Mistress Sepora and I will report to the Falcon King directly."

Ptolem, relieved to receive his instructions, hurries away without so much as a farewell.

Once inside the kitchens, Tarik pulls Sepora aside. "We are to greet our Hemutian friend this evening, as King Ankor has been kind enough to send an ambassador instead of an army. Let your servants know you're to be presented in your finest, but in all haste."

Sepora nods solemnly. "Are we ready for this?"

"I'm afraid we have to be."

ONCE SETHOS IS RETRIEVED AND EVERYONE IS gathered in his day chambers, Tarik signals for the guard to escort the ambassador from Hemut in. Upon her entering, Tarik can tell he has a difficult conversation ahead of him. Perhaps Ankor did not send an army, but rather he sent war in the form of one person.

The ambassador, introduced as the Lady Gita as is the custom in Hemut, is around the age of Rashidi, has gray wispy hair, and wields a long glass staff that looks like an enormous icicle. She doesn't need it for walking as Rashidi does, Tarik notes, as she carries it instead of leaning upon it. She could run a man through with such a thing and by her expression, she is considering doing just that.

"Welcome, Lady Gita," Tarik says, taking care to keep his voice neutral. "I do not think I've had the pleasure of speaking with you before."

"You haven't," she says, taking a seat next to Sethos, who is now crammed between the ambassador and Rashidi. Lady Gita is dressed for a winter that will never come to Theoria, but which is the constant companion of Hemut. With Hemut's daily blizzards and icy terrain, it is no wonder that she wears the skins of animals and the furs of many more, most of which are white and used as a trim for her floor-length coat. Tarik wonders how she could layer herself up so against the heat of his deserts without sweating to her death.

It is with these layers that she fidgets now, adjusting each one to her liking while she ignores all present company and the matter at hand. Tarik cannot tell if she does so out of true concern for her appearance, or if, as he suspects, she is keeping them waiting on purpose, to show that she means to start the conversation on her own time and terms. He wonders if this is how Rashidi acts when he visits other kingdoms and highly doubts it. However, if the visits were to address a slight or insult a kingdom had delivered against Tarik, he's quite sure Rashidi would have his own way of showing his acute displeasure.

Even now Rashidi grows impatient, switching his staff from one hand to the other. Tarik suppresses a grin. Sepora sits straight and composed beside Tarik, shoulders squared and chin lifted, her regal ensemble giving her a sort of untouchable appearance. Her composure is a show, he knows. As for Sethos, he snarls in his chair, arms crossed, eyes lifted toward the ceiling. He did not have time to change from his Majai attire; Tarik suspects it is his pleasure to show up to the occasion underdressed and sopped in sweat.

When the Lady Gita is sufficiently situated, she gives a small, sharp nod to Tarik, reminding him of a cobra ready to strike. "Shall we begin, Highness?"

"Of course, Lady Gita. Please proceed."

"Allow me to be frank, Highness. King Ankor is highly displeased with the correspondence you sent regarding the current happenings in Theoria. In fact, a caravan has accompanied me on my visit to return the insulting gifts you sent along with your message."

"I have never heard of gifts referred to as insulting, Lady Gita," Tarik returns dryly.

"King Ankor is not interested in gifts, Highness. He is interested in a husband for the Princess Tulle."

"Which I have offered him as well."

The lady exhales sharply. "I'm sure Prince Sethos would make a fine husband, Highness, but you can see where my king would be disappointed with a prince, when at first he had secured a king."

Sethos snorts. Lady Gita cuts him a dire look—as does Tarik. Sethos may be dressed as a Majai, but he will behave as a prince of

Theoria. Perhaps Tarik should have made that clear before allowing the Lady Gita to join them. Sethos can be as unpredictable as the ever-changing desert winds, and his open dislike of Tulle will only complicate matters. This must be a careful conversation indeed.

Tarik glances at Rashidi, and while he clearly disapproves of Sethos's conduct, he is still either unable or unwilling to offer Tarik help in the matter. After all, for the most part, Rashidi agrees with what the Lady Gita says. He has always been opposed to Tarik going back on his word to marry Princess Tulle. Tarik wonders how difficult it had been for Rashidi to have secured the arrangement in the first place, and if that has to do with his resistance to speaking up on his king's behalf now.

Tarik regards the Lady Gita for some time. He cannot admit to his feelings for Sepora, that he had made a decision with his heart instead of with sound reason; it would make him appear weak, and what's more, foolish. But perhaps there is something he can say that may pacify King Ankor. He had discussed it with Rashidi at length, but his adviser was convinced it was a poor line of reasoning for the throne. Still, out of stubbornness, Rashidi had not offered any alternative explanations, and so Tarik must go with the least provoking one he has.

"I'm afraid my hands are tied in the matter," Tarik says. "You see, unbeknownst to me, while Rashidi made arrangements for the engagement with Tulle, the Princess Magar was secretly living in my palace as a servant. When I became aware of this fact, I immediately sought to rectify the situation to avoid insult to King Eron of Serubel. Surely you can see how offensive it would seem to him that I kept her as a servant."

Lady Gita actually gasps, her gaze oscillating between Tarik and Sepora several times, which, to Tarik, is a very good sign. She finds the situation at least a little scandalous, which may garner him some pity from Hemut after all. At last, Lady Gita settles her focus on Tarik again, eyes narrowed. "And how did this come to be, exactly? How were you not aware that the only princess of Serubel lived under your own roof?"

"The details are unimportant, I think. The resulting insult to Serubel is what ultimately led to my decision," Tarik says firmly, hoping he sounds inflexible on the matter. After all, the details make him appear solidly as a dolt. Sepora was not only a servant in his palace, but arguably his closest one, and not a single member of his court nor his highest adviser had noticed. Though it seems unbelievable, Tarik doubts even King Ankor would recognize Sepora were the circumstances the same in his kingdom. Sepora herself admitted to rarely being seen by visitors and ambassadors in Serubel, having been kept busy with Forging.

As he predicted, the Lady Gita will not be placated nor intimidated by his refusal. "The details are paramount, Highness, if I am to relay the situation to King Ankor with any sort of satisfying explanation."

The Lady Gita is nothing if not persistent.

"The details are not mine to tell, Lady Gita. The Princess Magar—"

"I ran away from home," Sepora blurts, cutting him off. "It was a foolish, youthful decision to do so, of course, but I was convinced of my reasons for it. During my travels, I was intercepted by a pair of vagabonds who sold me into the king's harem, you see." At this, she blushes. It is a genuine one, reaching down her neck and disappearing into the fabric of her top.

The words, and her reaction to them, settle over the room, and her meaning becomes clear. She means to imply that Tarik has already taken her to his bed—and that he must make up for the scandal by taking her as his wife. He shifts uncomfortably in his chair, heat pooling in his own cheeks. Sepora is risking her reputation in order to pursue peace between the kingdoms. A queen who was once a mistress in the king's harem. It is a clever ploy, and possibly even a necessary one, but Tarik still chafes at how the five kingdoms will view her after this information is distributed. And this kind of outrageous news will spread far and wide. He is not pleased with her deception at the moment. And he would not want to see her reputation destroyed.

King Eron will not be happy. Even Rashidi grimaces, no doubt turning over in his mind how to control this new damage to the throne. It had looked bad enough that she had been a servant in his own palace without him being aware of it. Now he has taken her to his bed without knowing who she was?

Still, with this half-truth brought to light, his decision to wed her is irrefutably necessary. Why come to his aid now? He'd half expected her to agree with the Lady Gita, offering to cancel the wedding herself. But Sepora has proven that she is dutiful.

Dutiful to a point, at least.

"I see," Lady Gita says quietly, her expression softened. "I admit, that is quite the conundrum."

"Yes," Tarik says dryly, "it is."

Lady Gita drums her fingers against the chair's armrest. "Child, why didn't you come forth before it happened? Why didn't you inform the king at once who you were?"

"I did not think His Highness would believe me," Sepora says. "I didn't know what a Lingot was, let alone that the Falcon King was one of them. I was thought dead at home, you see. My own parents believed that. And can you imagine how outrageous it would have sounded to the Falcon King? Also . . . well, I thought perhaps I was being punished for running away. That I deserved it."

Pride of the pyramids, but is she actually tearing up? Tarik is quite certain his future queen is graced with two gifts: Forging and lying. He cannot help but be impressed, despite the outlandish picture she paints for Lady Gita just now, who absorbs her revelations as the desert sand mercilessly soaks up even the smallest droplet of water.

In fact, Lady Gita considers this for a long time, twirling her glass staff between her fingers in contemplation. Finally, she looks at Tarik, her face pinched into a scowl. "King Ankor is not an unreasonable man. When he learns of this, I'm sure he will see the desperation of the situation. He does, after all, have a daughter of his own. If he were in the same predicament, he would demand that it be righted immediately."

"You must pass on my extreme gratitude for the king's understanding," Tarik says. "And please, do return with the gifts, as they truly were not meant as an insult." Still, most of his gratitude should lie with Sepora. In great sacrifice to herself, she has single-handedly salvaged a potentially irreversible difference between Theoria and the powerful nation of Hemut. But for all his Lingot abilities, he cannot be certain of her motivations. Is she acting out of duty as future queen? Has she truly accepted that she will one day share in rulership of Theoria? Or does she, as she always has, simply wish to save lives and prevent war?

Lady Gita nods. "As you wish, Highness. But I did not come all this way to return to Hemut without a husband for Princess Tulle. It would seem our discussion must steer in a different direction altogether."

"Of course. My brother is a great warrior and a fine prince of Theoria. We would spare no expense with the wedding, in view of the circumstances. If it is amenable to King Ankor, Prince Sethos and Princess Tulle would reside in the palace, as is the traditional Theorian custom. She would want for nothing, I assure you."

This seems to please Lady Gita. Tarik wonders at her relationship with the princess. He senses an underlying fondness for Tulle. And who could blame her? In all his dealings with Tulle of Hemut, she'd been sweet and kind. Sethos's dislike of her stems, of course, from *her* initial rejection of *him*. When they had all been children, he'd plucked some flowers for her from their mother's gardens, and Tulle had accused him of ruining the natural beauty of them. Sethos, naturally, had been dejected for days on end. Even at that young age, he'd grown accustomed to pleasing the opposite sex with very little effort. He had not taken well to being rebuffed at all.

"And what of spectorium?" the lady continues. "I assume your alliance with Serubel has opened up trade with them once more?"

This is unexpected, and Tarik takes a moment to collect his thoughts. Bardo and the other Forgers instantly come to mind, but he pushes the idea away as quickly as it arises. He'd promised Sepora that he would not force the boy to Forge, and he has no intention of forcing the Great Council's hand. Not when they seem so powerful in their own right, and not when they've been so gracious as to hear him out. No, spectorium must be taken from the table. "Actually, we are moving away from the use of spectorium. We have resorted to using fire instead, in most cases, for light and for power. As a kingdom, we are choosing not to rely on a finite resource for our way of living any longer." Which is true enough that Tarik doesn't feel guilty in admitting it. It hasn't been the easiest of transitions, but slowly and surely his citizens are making do.

Lady Gita huffs. "We do not have that advantage, Highness. Remember, our structures are made of ice. Fire is not practical for our needs. We require spectorium, and plenty of it. Our supplies have run dangerously low."

Tarik is certain that only he notices Sepora's small intake of breath. She is worried again about spectorium falling into the wrong hands. She is most assuredly thinking of Bardo, as Tarik did. Does she think of the other Forgers as well? Surely she does. Tarik feels his jaw harden.

King Ankor may not even know of spectorium's use in cratorium, and if not, Tarik is eternally grateful. Ankor prides himself on his powerful army. Having cratorium will inflate not only the strength of his massive forces, but perhaps even his curiosity in using it as well. Still, the Hemutians are not known to abuse their power. Generations of royal Hemutians could well have set out to overtake all the kingdoms already but have never chosen to do so.

He will assure Sepora of this fact later. Besides, she can take comfort that Sethos's marriage to Tulle will unite the kingdoms of Theoria and Hemut. There would be no need to create a weapon like cratorium.

There would be no war.

Still, he cannot—will not—force Sepora nor Bardo to Forge. He must make this Sepora's decision, for more than just consideration for her feelings. He must know if she trusts him. He must get his answers sooner than later. "As Princess Magar oversees the trading of spectorium with Serubel on Theoria's behalf, I will leave this decision in her capable hands." In her capable, deceptive hands, is what he wants to say. But that conversation is for later.

She cuts him a look that could slice through nefarite. Yet, she offers a gracious, if not counterfeit, smile to Lady Gita. "I will take this request into consideration, of course. But as you may be aware, our spectorium grows scarce. The Falcon King is wise to say it is a finite resource. It would also be wise, I think, to consider other alternatives for providing light. Perhaps we should both consider turning to Wachuk for answers. I've heard rumors that they've mastered a way to slow a fire from burning—to make it less destructive."

Though a mere rumor, Tarik had heard of it as well from one of his informants only days ago. How Sepora could have learned of it he doesn't have a clue as she had not been with him at the time of the report. Apparently, as the rumor goes, the women of Wachuk have found a way to cool fire without losing its power altogether. That it can be touched, but burns as brightly and twice as long as regular fire. His informant could not validate the rumor, and what's more, did not believe it. But now that it has been brought into negotiations of peace with Hemut, Tarik will need to investigate the truth behind it.

Lady Gita is not appeased, though she nods solemnly. Tarik can tell she respects Sepora, despite her hesitance to yield spectorium— and despite the blow Sepora will now take to her reputation because of her earlier admission. "We have heard the same report from Wachuk," Lady Gita says finally. "We have already sent representatives to that kingdom to learn more." After a long moment, she sighs. "I will return to Hemut with this new turn of events." She looks back to Tarik. "I feel that my king will want a prompt marriage. When may I tell King Ankor they will wed?"

Sethos jumps to his feet, startling all present as his chair topples over behind him. His nostrils flare, his eyes wild. Tarik is wise enough to dread whatever words his brother carries on his tongue.

Sethos points at the Lady Gita. "You can tell King Ankor that I would sooner wed a hairless mule than his upstart daughter!"

"Sethos, enough!" Tarik bellows even before his brother is finished, but Sethos won't be quieted. He points his accusing finger at Tarik now.

"Everyone else may bow to your wishes, but I'll not allow you control of *my* life! I'd rather spend the rest of it in shackles than be tethered to that shrew."

Lady Gita is on her feet as well, her staff shaking in her hands. She moves faster than an old woman should. "This is outrageous! I'll not allow you to insult Princess Tulle with such viciousness." She glares at Tarik. "A fine prince of Theoria indeed! He has no respect for his own king, and even less for his future bride. When King Ankor hears of this, I can assure you there will be dire consequences. And to think I almost fettered the good Princess Tulle to the likes of that appalling brute!"

"Sethos," Tarik growls, "you will apologize at once."

"Sethos, please," Sepora pleads, "do calm down."

"I won't," he says with venom, and in that moment he resembles an enraged bull ready to strike at anything that moves. He has a savage look about him, his manner unstable. Sethos has reached his temper's threshold. During all the negotiations, his brother has sat quietly without so much as a snide remark—a sign Tarik should not have taken as comfort. He knows there is no reasoning with his brother at this point, the way there is no reasoning with a scorpion, once provoked. He must remove his brother from the room before all is lost.

Lady Gita whips her outermost coat behind her and taps Tarik's desk with her staff. "There will be no wedding," she says, her ire and shock tightening her lips into a white line. "And no alliance. You can be assured of that. Prepare yourself, Highness. Prepare yourself for what is to come!" With that, she sweeps out of the room, taking all hope of peace with her.

13

SEPORA

MY BEDCHAMBER IS THE ONLY PLACE I FEEL SAFE visiting with my mother. The castle is abuzz with the way Lady Gita had stormed out this afternoon, at the way she'd mounted her great white bear, then spat upon the dirt beneath them both before she vacated the palace grounds, her guards barely able to keep up with her. Right away, Mother had summoned me to my chambers, eager to hear all that had taken place.

Even now, she sits across me in the seating area near the balcony, eyes wide with horror. With one hand, she covers over her gasp. "He *refused* to marry Princess Tulle? And insulted her to her own ambassador?"

"I'm afraid so," I tell her. I desperately want to defend Sethos to my mother, but the words elude me. I know Sethos has a temper, and he's always made it clear that he did not want to wed Tulle. I had always assumed, though, that he would do what is best for Theoria. After his outrageous display just hours earlier, how can I assure Mother that Sethos has good intentions? Even I don't believe that anymore.

Mother rubs her temples with her fingertips. "This will not do.

Oh, this will not do at all. Don't you see, Magar? This will mean certain war."

"Yes."

"Where is Sethos now?"

"Tarik has called for his imprisonment. I haven't had a chance to speak with him about it."

"What is there to speak of? He blatantly disobeyed his king and started a war in the process. The Falcon King is right to jail him."

"Sethos is his brother," I say, astonished. "And a prince of Theoria. He does not belong in chains." Although right now, it would not bother me to see Sethos given a lesson in humility. For all his arrogance, I thought he had at least a fraction of reason within him.

Still, I cannot be too hypocritical. I have made plenty of brash decisions, decisions that affected a great number of people. Decisions that could be considered selfish.

Mother sniffs. "Sethos did not seem to care about that fact when he was so busy looking after his own needs and not the kingdom's. The Falcon King rules with a strong mind. You'd do well to emulate him, Magar." She leans forward, pulling her thick braid around and caressing it with her fingers, unaware of how her words sting. Still, it is not lost on me that this is the only sign of fidgeting my mother ever shows. "Your father will take advantage of this situation. He will insist that it is only logical that you Forge. That our kingdoms arm themselves with as much cratorium as we can produce."

"He may be right," I say, defeated. "Hemut is not weak. Its army is vast and well trained."

"You must not give in, Magar. Wars have been fought—and won—in the past without the need for cratorium. This will be no different. Theoria has their powerful Majai force. Serubel has a suitable army to complement them. No, Forging is not the answer."

I stand, walking to the balcony. Despite its size, my bedchamber seems to be closing in on me. I had hoped to confide in Mother about Bardo. Now I see that there is no need. I must Forge. Yes, the united forces of Theoria and Serubel may be able to defeat Hemut. But cratorium will end a war much sooner—and with fewer casualties. Fewer Theorian casualties. Fewer Serubelan casualties. This is what Father will say.

This is what Tarik will be thinking.

Oh, how I hate Sethos at this moment.

"You cannot carry the weight of this on your shoulders, child," Mother says. "Let the kings discuss this. Let us see what they decide. Your Falcon King is wise and respects that you do not wish to Forge. After they have spoken, then we will determine what *our* next course of action will be. I will speak to your father. You mustn't worry, child. All will be well."

"Yes, Mother."

But I alone possess the power to make all well again. And Sethos has forced my hand.

14

TARIK

TARIK WAS NOT EXPECTING TO FIND SEPORA waiting for him in his bedchamber, and especially so late in the evening. She had been particularly quiet at the evening meal as her father ranted on and on about how they should be preparing for war with Hemut, not even attempting to mask his suggestions that Sepora should be forced to Forge. Wise Queen Hanlyn did little to calm her husband, as it was plain that he would not be placated, and especially not openly, for others to hear. The entire meal had been exhausting, and Tarik had thought Sepora would retire early after having been subjected to the ordeal. Even Tarik had wished to do so.

Yet here Sepora stands, leaning upon the threshold of the arched balcony entranceway, hands folded in front of her, her feet bare and her hair let down in all its glory. She is here to speak privately of the day's events, he knows. He wonders if they will someday make this a ritual, performing their duties as required during the day and confiding in each other at night. He fervently hopes it will be so. But so much of their future rests with her, and she can be as volatile as her father at times.

"I thought you posted Lingots at your door, Highness," she says. "You assured Rashidi and me that you would."

"I did, Princess."

She pushes off the wall and seats herself in the chair closest to her. "I told your guard that you had requested my presence. He let me in immediately."

"It's as it should be. I'd instructed my guards to let you in, under any circumstances."

"Oh." She ponders over that for a moment. He wishes she would say something, so that perhaps he could discern her thoughts, but she seems determined to keep her reflections to herself. She has come to know him and his ability to read her well—and has learned to adapt even better. It is bittersweet, he finds.

"To what do I owe the pleasure of your company? I'd thought you'd be sound asleep by now."

She sighs. "Would you be able to sleep after all that has happened?"

"No."

Shaking her head, she leans back in a way that Tarik discerns as a sort of finality. Her next words confirm it. "I have reached a decision about the matter of spectorium."

Tarik seats himself across from her and tries not to appear as tense as he feels. He had not been aware that she had been deciding anything on the matter of spectorium. That she is even reconsidering her stance of Forging must be a good thing. A small hope settles on his heart. Perhaps he will not have to confront her after all. Perhaps she will tell him of the other Forgers. And perhaps it will be enough to forgive her. "Go on."

"If anyone is to Forge, it will be me," she says. "It is my duty as the queen. In any case, it isn't likely that Bardo is ready to take on such responsibility. It is unlikely that he can control his ability enough to be of use to Cy, and what's more, in the creation of cratorium. When you are inexperienced, it can sometimes be difficult to summon spectorium at your whim. If Forging must take place, I will be the one to do it."

She speaks of Bardo and of herself, yet no mention of the other Forgers. A bit of his optimism disintegrates.

Still, Tarik is more than a little surprised at her mention of cratorium. He'd felt sure that she would stubbornly refuse, even now, as she has all this time. But Hemut is not to be trifled with. Neither he nor Sepora needs his leading commander to remind him of this fact. His father always instilled in him the belief that Hemut was powerful, and every effort was always to be made to keep the peace between them.

If only Sethos had been privy to those conversations.

But now, when Sepora speaks of duty, it is easy for his shock to give way to understanding. Out of duty to Theoria, she ruined her reputation today. She is becoming the queen he had hoped she would be. But what of the wife he so desperately wants?

With her promise to Forge, she speaks the truth. He just hates that she delivers it with the enthusiasm of a dead animal. And her omission about the others is as good as a lie. He cannot allow himself to forget that.

"Thank you," he says simply, matching her colorless tone.

"Now that it is settled, we need to talk about my father. And the war with Hemut."

"Yes. We do."

"Wars have been won without cratorium," she says quietly.

So, her submission in the matter of Forging was not the same as her permission to make cratorium of it. He sighs. "Commander Morg is anxious to produce it and I can't say that I blame him. Rashidi pressures me each day to make it a priority."

Sepora rolls her eyes. "Of course he does. I would expect nothing less." Tarik wonders if the animosity between Rashidi and Sepora will ever end. To say it would be a relief would be an understatement; their bickering and differences of opinions seem to pull him in opposite directions sometimes. Both are precious to him. Both are valuable to the kingdom. But both want different things. Rashidi wants Sepora to Forge. Sepora wants Rashidi to eat his own walking stick.

Why must he always choose between them? *Should* he choose between them? He doesn't know anymore.

"Hemut is strong, Sepora. A swift end to the war means more lives saved. If we used cratorium from the start, we would defeat them with few casualties. Fewer Theorians die, fewer Serubelans. Is that not what you want?"

"I think you misunderstand my request," she says. "It is not the war I'm concerned about. It's my father I don't trust. Giving him access to cratorium would be a mistake."

"You think I don't know that?"

"Then what will you do?"

He presses his lips together. He and Rashidi have discussed the matter at length. As long as King Eron keeps up his pretense of peace, there is nothing he really *can* do. Withholding cratorium from Eron's armies would offend him and give him a reason to turn on Theoria. In the midst of a war with Hemut, that would be disastrous. *Not* withholding the cratorium would give Eron the *means* to turn on Theoria. It is a difficult thing to contemplate. "I'm not sure yet."

"How long do you think we have before Hemut attacks?"

"Lady Gita will be arriving home to tell Ankor of the news in a matter of days. It will take at least a week to assemble his army, and another few days to move it to Theoria. The heat may slow them, but not much."

Sepora scowls. "That is not a long time."

"It could be longer. But given the insult, I think he will rush straight to our boundaries."

"And how long will you keep Sethos imprisoned?"

"Until I feel better." And the matter is not up for discussion. The very mention of his brother makes his blood simmer. Even now, he clenches his jaw to refrain from uttering expletives Sepora is not meant to hear. Sethos has endangered the entire kingdom. Still, Tarik knows he himself is partly to blame. Himself, and his father, King Knosi. He gave Sethos too much freedom, too much leniency. Tarik hadn't wanted to upturn his brother's world after their father died, but he should have slowly begun to rein him in, adjust him to the life of a prince. After all, Sethos cannot shun his duties forever.

Yet, that is exactly what he has just done. And now Tarik must deal with the consequences.

"I'd rather not discuss my brother at the moment, if it's all the same to you."

Sepora looks as though she would say more but crosses her arms instead. She studies him for a long time. It's a maddening habit of hers of late, to consider him without expression, without so much as a clue to what she could be thinking. No doubt Master Saen has taught her many effective ways of eluding a Lingot. And apparently Sepora is a zealous study.

After an endless silence, she says, "I will begin Forging in the morning. But for now, I think it's wise to keep this from my father. Perhaps even my mother."

Tarik is more than surprised to hear this. Thus far, Sepora has shown a certain loyalty to her mother that, until now, he had deemed unbreakable. *What has changed?* And does her mother know of the others? *Ask her, you dolt.* But still, he cannot. Cannot, or will not. "You think your mother will side with your father in using it?"

"No. But she advises me not to Forge out of fear my father will take advantage. If she finds out that I—it's just that I do not want to disappoint her, if you must know."

So. She is going against her mother's wishes in order to aid him. It is more than he ever could have asked for. No, not more. It's precisely what she should have done to begin with. The same bitterness settles over him. He will not thank her for something that should have been her duty all along. And he has more than that to discuss with her. "I think you're making a wise decision." It's all he can offer her at the moment.

She stands. "We must protect Theoria. And in doing so, I'm protecting Serubel as well." She looks at him sideways. "It is another secret we must share together. You must tell Rashidi not to open his flytrap of a mouth about it, too."

"And what will I tell Rashidi about the others?"

She tilts her head. "Others?"

"Yes, Sepora. The other Forgers in the Baseborn Quarters. What will I tell him of them?"

The color leaves her face as water from a broken vessel.

He runs a hand through his hair. "So. You did know about them. You knew, and you didn't tell me, even when I asked. You remember our engagement procession? You remember me asking if you kept anything else from me?"

"I . . . I did not remember at that moment of the other Forgers."

It is the truth. Pride of the pyramids, at least she did not lie to his face then. But what about the time that has passed since? He finds it difficult to believe that when considering whether she would Forge for him, she did not also think of them. "You have kept this from me. How long have you known?"

She takes a seat again and folds her hands in her lap. "Since before I knew I could trust you."

"Are you so sure you trust me at all, Sepora? Not once did you think of the other Forgers since our engagement procession?"

Sepora removes her gaze from his and fixes it to the stone floor. "I did not feel that mentioning it was necessary if I was going to Forge."

"It was necessary for our trust, Sepora. And now I'm afraid that has been irretrievably broken."

Her eyes fly toward him. "What are you saying?"

He inhales, still not ready to utter his next words. "I'm saying that our engagement is off. You may tell your parents on your own time; I'll not force your hand in that. I will play the part until you have told me otherwise. I will make a diplomatic announcement to the kingdom when the time is right. But we will not wed. I'll not have a wife I cannot trust."

Just as quickly as her color had drained from her features, it returns with an ire he has not yet seen. Her cheeks fill with blood, her eyes near slits glaring up at him. "You allowed me to make a fool of myself today in front of Lady Gita. You allowed me to ruin my reputation, to humiliate myself, all for the sake of your glorious Theoria. And now this?" She shakes her head. "You are not the king I thought you were."

The painful truth, as she believes it. She sweeps up and out of the chair.

And then she is gone.

15

SEPORA

A PLUMP TEAR SLIDES DOWN MY CHEEK, PAUSING
momentarily at the tip of my nose before plummeting to the pillow beneath my head. I pull my blanket up over my face as a shield
against the midnight moonlight spilling in from the balcony in my
chambers. In my old servant's quarters, I had only one entrance to the
balcony; the cloudless sky and moonlight did not bother me so much
then. Now I have five entryways to the balcony, and the sheer tapestries
do little to block the luminous orb from interrupting my sleep.

Ha! The moonlight indeed. It is laughable to blame my sleepless-
ness on the glow of it this night. Not when my mouth is full of salt
from tears licked from my lips, my nose runny from uncontrollable
sobs, and my pillow soaking with the mess of all of it.

No, tonight the blame lies with myself. Myself, and Tarik.

He toyed with my heart while I toyed with his trust. Who is the
worst offender? I cannot be sure. But what I do know is that Father
will be inconsolable, Mother will be disappointed, and . . . really, who
else matters at this point?

The entire five kingdoms, I tell myself.

And all because I opened my mouth to appease Lady Gita on

behalf of Theoria. To the five kingdoms, I am now a concubine, a tarnished princess with nothing to offer. Mother will be thrilled when I tell her. Father will be murderous.

Oh, Mother. I'd soiled my name for the sake of preventing war earlier, when I'd implied that Tarik had already taken me to his bed. I just could not bring myself to tell her of my shame. Even now, a blush tickles my cheeks, a blush so hot I feel it may evaporate my tears altogether. All the five kingdoms will hear of this. All the five kingdoms will view me as a harlot first, a princess of Serubel second. That is, if Father will have me back. Even if I marry someone else by some miracle someday, my guests will certainly be thinking of it. Perhaps even speaking of it when I turn away. Entertaining foreign kingdoms, their ambassadors, will be a nightmare.

No one has ever said such things of Mother, I'm sure. And what will she say when she learns of it? Surely Mother would have come up with a hundred other reasons why the Falcon King must wed me. Mother would have handled Lady Gita the way a Majai handles a bow and arrow or a sword: with skill and ease and grace. And when she tells me what I *could* have said—and oh, she will not refrain from putting me in my proper place and listing alternatives as if she were listing chores for a servant—I'll feel even more embarrassed about what I've done today.

And what of Tarik? He had not even thanked me tonight for agreeing to Forge, much less made mention of the sacrifice I made earlier in his day chambers. Of taking responsibility for *his* impulsive decision to call off the union with Princess Tulle. Doesn't he realize what it meant for me to say those things? Even Rashidi seemed horrified at what I'd done, yet Tarik held an expressionless face, as if I'd spoken of the weather or the fabric of the tapestries.

Confusion and hurt vie for my attention as I turn over in my bed, away from the taunting moonlight. Never before have I wished more to be a Lingot. Tarik can sense my lies, and if I'm not careful, even my thoughts from body language alone. It is not fair. None of it. I have never felt so broken as I feel now, not even when I had to flee my home in Serubel to a life unknown. At least then I had my self-respect. Now I have nothing. And worse, I probably have no one. No allies to come to my aid. At this moment, I am alone.

Still, I am not the weakling I was when I left Serubel and fled to Theoria. I am brave. I have done brave things. And I will be brave about this. It is my duty, my—

The covers are suddenly snatched from my body and I let out a startled scream. Hovering over me is a Theorian guard, one I've never seen before. His broad shoulders block the moonlight shining in from behind him, his face a shadow before me. "You'll need to come with me, Princess," he says gruffly.

"Why? What has happened? Is the king all right?"

"Get up."

Something is not right. A guard would not speak to me so. Not now that I am to be queen. I try to roll away, to the opposite side of the bed, but he grabs my arm. Before I can scream, his fist connects with my mouth, and I immediately taste blood, feeling it trickling down my neck.

"I said get up."

But standing now is impossible. The room spins, and I feel myself sway upright in the bed. Without warning, I am struck again.

The moonlight fades from my vision.

16

TARIK

SEPORA DOES NOT SHOW FOR THE MORNING MEAL, and Tarik cannot help but feel immersed in guilt. He'd allowed her to leave last night without addressing her very real sacrifice in taking the blow for his own rash behavior the day he'd arranged to marry her. He had not acknowledged or praised her for making such a great effort to keep peace between Theoria and Hemut. And somehow a simple "thank you" had seemed so very impossible for him to give her for her decision to Forge, yet now so necessary.

Still, he refuses to regret his decision to call off the engagement in the end. She has fought it from the beginning. Deemed it a mere duty, if even that. Was he not just doing her a favor by relieving her of her obligation?

He'd been awake all night thinking of her, and how hard it must have been to submit after having put up such a fight to prevent the creation of cratorium. And then he'd chosen to call off their engagement, after such a trying day for both of them. He could have been more careful with her feelings. He could have been more careful period. *What must she think of me?*

"Highness," the Queen Hanlyn says gently, "if it suits you, I will be happy to awaken Magar to have her join us. I'm sure she has just overslept. It is a habit of hers, I'm afraid."

He well knows that. When she was a servant, she was tardy more often than not when it came to her morning duties. But perhaps she has not overslept; perhaps she is still nursing wounds inflicted last night. If that is the case, it wouldn't do for Hanlyn to interrupt her. He'd told Sepora it would be up to her to inform her parents. He'd meant that.

King Eron snorts, using his spoon to scoop out a portion of citrus cut in half on his plate. "The child has always preferred sleep over breakfast. But then, she always kept late hours. I wonder what she was up to last night." He looks pointedly at Tarik, who shifts uncomfortably in his chair. It was not proper for her to await him in his bedchamber last night. Has Eron been spying on him, then? He will have to warn Sepora to be more mindful of others who may be watching. That is, if she will ever speak to him again.

All at once, the doors to the dining room burst open and Sepora's servant, the one called Cara, hurries to Tarik's side, followed by two guards whose scowls turn Tarik's stomach for a reason he can't explain.

"Your Highness," Cara says, breathless, "I'm sorry for interrupting your meal, but the Princess Magar has gone missing, and we suspect foul play."

Tarik stands, sending his seat flying backward and toppling over on the marble floor. "Foul play? What do you mean?"

"She wasn't in her bedchamber this morning, Highness. The covers were strewn about, as though a struggle had taken place. And Highness . . . there was blood on the pillow."

Hanlyn gasps, covering her mouth with the back of her hand. Eron stands, leaning on the table for support. "Blood?" he roars. "Who would dare to—"

"We've initiated a search of the palace, Highness, and of the grounds," the guard behind Cara informs Tarik. "So far we've turned up but a single set of footprints beneath her balcony leading to the wall of the palace, too big to belong to the princess. Beyond that, there is nothing."

Tarik is both relieved and furious that a search has already begun. He should have been informed the moment she was found missing.

"There is something else you should know, Highness," the guard says, his face grim.

"Go on."

"The guards posted at her door have been murdered. Their throats slit."

Tarik strides toward the door, breaking into a run and calling over his shoulder. "Go to Commander Morg. Inform him of the situation and tell him that no stone is to be left unturned in the city until she is found. No citizen is to enjoy any privacy on this day while the princess is missing. Cara, send for Rashidi. Tell him to meet me in my day chambers at once. King Eron, Queen Hanlyn, you may join us, if it pleases you."

IT IS NIGHTFALL BEFORE COMMANDER MORG REPORTS to Tarik's day chambers, his expression somber. Tarik's heart turns over in his chest. "You didn't find her." At this, Queen Hanlyn wrings her hands. The action is distracting, as it seems to fuse many different motions into one.

"I'm afraid not, Highness," Morg says, tucking his hands behind his back. "Unfortunately, we have every reason to believe she has been taken. None of her personal belongings nor clothing are missing. Her Serpen is in her stable." Morg eyes the pillow on Tarik's desk; Tarik had it retrieved from Sepora's room. "And the blood . . ."

The blood is what worries Tarik the most. And the murdered guards at her door. If the trained guards could not defend themselves, how could Sepora? She would stand no chance against a skilled assassin—especially an assassin who could take down two Majai together without stirring a commotion.

Eron pounds a fist on his armrest. "And how could such a thing happen? Have you no sense of security here? And of course, you know who has taken her."

Tarik is startled at this. Morg whips his head toward the king as well. "We are working to determine that, Highness," Morg tells Eron.

Eron snorts. "Is everyone in this room daft? The Hemutians have taken her. Of course they have." He cuts his glare to Tarik. "*Your* brother insulted them in every way possible. We assumed they would wage war. I'd venture to say, this is their retaliation instead."

The truth, or what Eron believes to be the truth. And Tarik is beginning to believe it, too, for it makes sense. King Ankor has quite the temper, but he is a cunning ruler. A war would cost him much, while abducting Sepora, the future queen of Theoria, would deliver an insult on the most personal level to Tarik. If Ankor's daughter has no husband, Tarik will have no wife.

"Morg," Tarik says, standing. "Gather every Majai in the kingdom and prepare them for a sunrise departure to Hemut. King Eron, I assume I have the full support of your army as well?"

"Indeed," Eron says. "And *I* assume we have full access to the means to make cratorium?"

Cratorium. The word is spoken with obscurity surrounding it. It is a risk, giving Eron the explosive. Sepora would not approve, and by the way Queen Hanlyn's eyes have grown wide, she does not approve, either. But Sepora is missing, and taken by someone who is not afraid to cause her bodily harm. That is not something he can bear. Releasing cratorium to Eron is a risk he will have to take. "You may have your cratorium," he says sharply. "Just make sure that it is pointed toward the Hemutians, King Eron."

Eron scowls. "I'm sure I don't know what you mean."

"I'm sure that you do," Tarik counters.

Tarik had not noticed that Rashidi had stood as well, until his adviser places his hand on Tarik's shoulder. "Highness, may I have a word?"

"If you're going to suggest that we do not wage war against Hemut for their crime, then no."

Rashidi sighs, indicating he had been about to suggest that very thing. "Think of Princess Sepora's safety," he says quietly. Tarik hates when he says things quietly. His father, King Knosi, always said that it is those times that Rashidi is being his most reasonable self, that if he is quiet, he is brilliant. Against his will, Tarik acknowledges that he would do well to listen to what his adviser has to say now, even if it is not what he wants to hear.

"Yes?" Tarik growls, pinching the bridge of his nose.

"Please consider, Highness, that you do not know where they will keep the princess. If you start a full-on war with Hemut, you could injure her with our attacks. It is unlikely that they would do much to protect her, if they mean to deliver an insult. Indeed, they would get the highest of satisfactions if it were your own army that killed her."

Killed her. Bile rises in his throat, and he swallows several times to push it back down. The idea that Sepora could die makes him dizzy. Disavowing their engagement is one thing. Thinking of her death and losing her forever is quite another. Slowly, he sits back down, unable to meet anyone's gaze for fear they'll see his alarm. King Eron would see it as a weakness to be so unsettled at a time when his wit is most needed.

"What's more," Rashidi continues, "we do not have proof that the Hemutians have taken her. All we have is that pillow, two dead guards, and footprints in the sand. Our enemy has not made himself known to us just yet."

"We already have an enemy in Hemut," Eron says angrily. "Lady Gita made sure to impress that upon us before she left."

Rashidi nods humbly. "That is a good point, King Eron, yes. But perhaps if we looked at the matter more closely, we might find more than one possible motive behind the abduction. For instance, I find it curious that a Hemutian warrior would know precisely where the Princess Sepora's bedchamber was. Also, I think it odd that he could slip through the palace without being detected. The Hemutians are not a small people."

At this, Morg nods, thoughtful. "I've spoken with my officers and their men. None of them saw anything amiss last night."

Oh, why must Rashidi be so reasonable at such an inconvenient time as this? Just moments ago, Tarik had wanted to destroy the room with his bare hands, declare war on Hemut, and secure King Ankor's head on a pike prominently placed on the palace wall for all to see. An extreme reaction, he knows. And now Rashidi would have him calm down. Blast it all.

Tarik looks at Morg. "Recruit the Master Saen from the Lyceum. Inform her of what's taken place. You will question each man in your guard again, in her presence. Detain anyone she mistrusts for further questioning by me personally."

"Of course, Highness."

"That's it?" Eron blusters. "You will waste time interrogating your household while my daughter could be moving farther and farther away from us as we speak?"

"It is not a waste of time to investigate further before declaring war on a powerful kingdom without the least bit of proof," Tarik says. "Rashidi is right to be cautious, and as Sepora's safety is my utmost concern, I wouldn't even think of attacking until we have located her."

"This is outrageous!" Eron spits. "But what more could I expect from a boy king?"

"Eron!" Queen Hanlyn exclaims. "Do forgive him, Highness," she pleads with Tarik. "He is merely upset at the turn of events."

This is what she knows is a lie. King Eron had meant to be provoking.

Tarik rises to his feet in a calculated slowness. "You are a guest in my kingdom, King Eron. I trust you will comply with my wishes in this matter by not inciting a war we may have no business fighting as of yet. In the meantime, I must speak with my brother." Tarik strides to the door without ceremony. "You may all let yourselves out."

"Sethos?" Rashidi calls after him. "But why?"

Tarik turns back for the briefest of moments. "Sethos owes me an immense favor," he says. "And I'm going to collect it."

17

SEPORA

THE REPUGNANT SMELL OF FISH AWAKENS ME. The white cloth over my face is not so thick that it inhibits the sunlight from shining through in small patches, nor does it block out the scent of the mound of fish lying next to me. My jaw aches incessantly and my teeth feel rattled, but to make a sound now might not be the wisest of choices, as I can make out six looming shadows standing near me in the stifling heat of the sun. Besides, even if I wanted to, I could not make an escape; I'm bound tightly at the feet and my hands are laced together behind my back. And so my only option for learning more about my circumstances lies with my listening as closely as possible.

The consistent sound of water being pushed about is the only noise I hear, which must mean we are moving along the River Nefari, possibly by rowboat. The men who have taken me are not of the conversational sort; no one offers a word to one another. I have no sense of how much time has passed; perhaps since they are quiet, we are still within the boundaries of Anyar. Perhaps I could scream and gain someone's attention. By now, Tarik will be looking for me. Mother will be looking for me.

Yet I fight against the urge to make a sound; I'm stiff and uncomfortable and I long to stretch. Also, I'm low on energy, which means too much time has passed since I've Forged. Soon it will begin leaking from my palms. Much time has passed.

I'm confronted with the fact that if we've been moving along the River Nefari since early morning, we are no longer in Anyar at all. I have no idea if we head north or south, and I've no idea why I've been taken. Even as I try to contemplate it all, my vision becomes blurry, my thoughts even more obscure.

Just before I lose consciousness, one of the men speaks. "Cover her with more fish. There's a boat just ahead," he says gruffly.

Only, he doesn't speak in the Theorian language.

I've been taken by Pelusia.

18

TARIK

TARIK FINDS IT IRONIC THAT SETHOS'S "PRISON cell" is nothing more than Sepora's old bedchamber when she was but a servant in the palace. However, the great wooden door is now kept locked at all times with no fewer than four Majai guarding it. Inside, a great wall of thick needlelike thorns and thistles, plucked from the Valley of the Tenantless, barricades his brother from straying to the balcony outside where he has been known to traverse the palace walls as skillfully as a lizard might.

There is, of course, a true prison outside the city of Anyar where Theorian criminals are kept, either for the duration of their sentence or until the day when they'll be pitched from the Half Bridge arrives, and that is where everyone save Rashidi thinks Sethos stays. But true prison would only serve to feed Sethos's ego. He would emerge a hero among his Majai brethren, a true survivor to have stayed among Theoria's worst, securing admiration instead of shame for his crime.

No, it is better, more insulting, to keep Sethos in the pampered confines of the palace, where he will suffer the humiliation of a soft punishment, for he hates the palace, and what's more, he will be ashamed to even call his time served "imprisonment" at all, when he sleeps in worse conditions while living at the Lyceum—a mere cot in a room with dozens of others and three tasteless meals a day. A bedchamber in the palace is something his Majai brethren would tease him about, were he to mention it to them. In fact, Tarik thinks to himself, he will make it a point to inform his brother's friends at the Lyceum just how lavish his "cell" really is.

Tarik approaches the four guards at the door. "Unlock the prisoner's cell," he tells them, and one of the Majai actually has the audacity to smile at the command. "Yes, Highness," this Majai says, pulling the necklace with the key from around his neck and turning it in the door. "The 'cell' is now unlocked, Highness."

Tarik smirks as he enters the bedchamber. Sethos will never live this down. Tarik need not even start the rumor itself. He's quite sure that by the end of these guards' shift, it will be widely circulated just how horrible a sentence the prince has served.

When Tarik enters, the chamber is dark and needlessly rank. He finds he must step around piles of excrement, the smell of ammonia almost overtaking him. It seems his brother prefers to live in squalor rather than use the perfectly intact lavatory in the far right of the room. It is born of a two-year-old's tantrum, Tarik knows, and it is evidence of his supreme stubbornness. No doubt their father would be proud.

Tarik, however, is not amused.

He finds Sethos sitting in a chair beside his canopied bed, knees drawn to his chest. "Highness," Sethos says in a mocking tone, "to what do I owe the pleasure? Have you come to personally serve me my evening meal? How thoughtful."

Tarik stands against the wooden pole of the canopy and crosses his arms. "I've no time for banter, brother. Sepora has been taken, and by an unknown enemy."

Immediately, Sethos jumps to his feet. He is shirtless, which reveals several deep scrapes and cuts along his torso. He had attempted to squeeze through the thorn barricade after all, and his efforts had left him a bloody mess. Tarik could not be happier.

"Taken?" Sethos utters an oath under his breath. "When?"

"Last night."

"Last *night*? And you come to me only now?"

Tarik recognizes this is a blow to his brother's pride. Sethos cares for Sepora and her safety, and had once been entrusted with it—before his outburst in front of the Lady Gita. "Generally I do not confer with prisoners who've committed treason against Theoria."

Sethos rolls his eyes. "You have not come here to speak of mundane politics, Tarik. Tell me what has taken place."

Sethos is right, of course. Now is not the time to reopen discussions of his brother's misdeeds, not with Sepora missing and in danger.

Tarik sits on the bed—first ensuring that Sethos had not soiled that too out of spite—and sighs. He tells his brother of the details of her abduction, of the blood on the pillow and of the slain Majai, of the footprints leading to the palace walls, then disappearing on the other side of it. It does not take Sethos very long to think on it before he says, "Ankor."

"That is what we thought at first as well. But we have no proof, and—"

"Declaring war might endanger Sepora."

Tarik is surprised, and impressed, at his brother's insightfulness. He has always been clever, Sethos, but has never really been inclined to use that talent for much good—except where his Majai training is concerned. "Yes."

"When do I leave?" By this time he is pacing the room, running a hand through his already disheveled hair. His voice does not mock. His eyes are sharp, his stature tense.

"I want you to handpick a small party to take to Hemut and

locate Sepora if she's there. The idea is discretion. In and out, without detection. Bring her back safely to me, brother, so that I may officially declare war on King Ankor. Go tonight to the seamstress and have her fashion your men something warm." Tarik is quite sure it is not a good idea to mention he had broken the engagement with Sepora, lest Sethos attack him on the spot. Besides, it is best for all to believe that they are still engaged—he had, after all, left it up to Sepora's discretion in disclosing it.

"All we need is our weapons."

"You'll freeze, Sethos. The snow is deeper than a man is tall."

"The Hemutians think it a secret that they keep archers in the woods along their southern border. I'll borrow something cozy from them before it gets too much colder on the other side."

Tarik sniffs. "Attacking their archers does not sound discreet."

"Dead men are always discreet."

"If you cannot find Sepora, Sethos, we cannot declare war on Hemut."

"If I cannot find Sepora, brother, it's because she isn't there."

The truth. Sethos will not return without Sepora. He will infiltrate every part of Hemut until she is found. There will not be a nook or crevice in which he doesn't investigate. And when he finds her, and she is safely in Tarik's arms again, he will see to it that Hemut is nothing more than a memory to the rest of the kingdoms.

19

SEPORA

MY EYES WILL NOT FULLY OPEN, BUT ONLY FLUTTER occasionally, revealing bits and pieces of the room I'm in. The ceiling is all wood and of a grain I do not recognize. Beneath me is a bed that is not uncomfortable, but irritatingly soaked through with warm water. There is a fireplace at the edge of the room, whose heat I do not feel. My jaw hurts, and I know from my experience with Chut and Rolan in the Dismals that not only are my lips dry, but the bottom one is split open. And for all the energy I have, I cannot move; I am tethered hand and foot to the bed, spread-eagle on my back.

But, Saints of Serubel, why can't I open my eyes?

Instead of dwelling on it, though, I focus on my other senses. There is someone or something shuffling about the room. After a few moments, I realize it is a woman, and she is humming a song I've never heard. She tinkers around with metal of some sort, making an awful noise that echoes through a room that must be mostly empty, for nothing seems to absorb the sound. "Who are you?" I demand, yet my voice is too shaky to be anything but pitiful.

"Ah, you're awake," she says amiably. She speaks to me in Serubelan, but her accent tells me that she is not from there and at the moment, I can't sort out where I've heard it before. "I've come to administer your treatment," she says. "And of course, to clean you up before it settles in."

"Settles in? Clean me up? What's the matter with me?"

"Why, you've wet the bed, Princess."

"*I've wet the bed?*"

"Indeed, Princess. With spectorium. It has leaked from your hands and ruined the linens."

Spectorium. I've lain in this bed long enough that my body expelled spectorium on its own. That will be at least three days' time. "Where am I?"

Yes, where am I that someone knows what happens when I prolong Forging—and more important, that I am a Forger in the first place? Why does this woman treat me as though she knows me personally, not just that I am a Forger? I'm vulnerable now, yes, but I'm also feeling very handled at the moment.

I do not like to be handled.

"All in due time, Princess," she says. I hear her rustle around some more, and then the sound of liquid pouring into a pot. "I've a sponge here and soap, with boiling water that needs to cool. When it does, I'll give you a good scrubbing. You'll feel much better then."

"Whoever you are, you need to release me at once. I am a princess of Serubel, and future queen of Theoria. If you return me now, the Falcon King may exercise leniency on you." Of course, I'm *not* a future queen of Theoria anymore, but if Tarik has kept his word, no one knows that quite yet. And if I'm being honest, I can't be certain that he would come after me, under the circumstances. Still, I'm proud that I sound more authoritative than I feel, what with being tied to a bed and having messed myself with spectorium—something I haven't done since I was a child. I wonder what I look like, lying here in a glowing pool and giving orders in such a condition.

The woman chuckles in a way that suggests she knows exactly who I am, and exactly what the penalty will be by keeping me here, but is not concerned in the least about any of it—and is not impressed by the power I'd hoped to infuse into my tone. "You must calm down, child," she says soothingly. "No harm will come to you here."

"Then why am I tied up?" Not that being tied up actually hurts, but it does make one feel particularly defenseless against any such harm. And it does make one feel like a prisoner.

"The bonds are for our safety, not yours, Princess." She tinkers around closer to me now, almost at the bedside. Her movements sweep the scent of roses into my nose. Roses, and food. She is cooking something in here. Something that smells delicious. My stomach growls in want, and the woman chuckles again. "I'm making lamb stew. It's a special recipe handed down through generations of my family. I'm sure you'll enjoy it."

While the idea of eating sounds glorious, I ignore her attempts at being kind. "You're protecting yourself *from* me? Whatever for?"

She is close now. I hear her set something down upon perhaps a table next to my bed. "We understand you've had the benefit of training with the Majai and your ability to Forge weapons from nothing is well known. Aside from that, you tend to thrash about when you receive treatment."

My ability to Forge weapons is not well known. Only those closest to me are privy to that information, and I do not recognize this woman's voice from a stranger's at the Bazaar. I feel bare and vulnerable, as though all my secrets have been uncovered. I might as well be lying here naked. I must have been at one point; the clothes I wear now cover the lengths of my legs and arms, cinching at my ankles and wrists. This is not what I wore to bed however many nights ago. Someone has changed me while I was unconscious.

"Why can't I open my eyes?" And did she just say *treatment*?

Have I been mortally injured? I test my jaw and find that it has mended well since I first found myself on the boat in the River Nefari. Oh yes, the boat. I've been taken by the Pelusians. That is where this woman's slight accent comes from. If I put up such a fight as to be wounded, I don't remember at all. There are no bandages on my face, no cloths wrapped tightly against my skin anywhere. Still, my eyes will not open. Somehow, though, this doesn't seem as important as before.

The woman clicks her tongue in what she must think sounds like a comforting noise. "That's it. Nice and relaxed you'll be soon."

"Why? I do not want to relax." I'm aware that my arguments are abrupt and even childish, yet I can't quite get my bearings enough to offer more resistance.

"Ah, but the calming serum we gave you will ensure that you are. It will help you rest during your treatments."

Calming serum. I've been kidnapped, re-dressed, and drugged. This is sounding all too familiar. "I do not need to be treated. I feel fine." If arguing is the only way I have of being difficult, so be it. Surely I should be difficult, for the principle of the thing. With or without the calming serum.

I can almost hear her smile when she says, "That's a silly thing to say. Everyone wants to be relaxed." She is even closer now; I feel her leaning over me. She tugs at the leather strap at my left hand, and does the same to my other limbs, ensuring they are all secure. "Now, be very still, Princess. I'm going to administer a needle to your right arm." She touches the crook of my arm then, tapping it with the pad of one finger. "This vein here is your best, I think. You'll feel a small pinch, I'm afraid. Oh, I do wish you were still sleeping. You wouldn't feel the pain of the cure if you were sleeping."

Pain. The way she says it makes me wish I were sleeping, too. "Cure? What cure? Have I fallen ill? Am I wounded?" Saints of Serubel, but why won't she answer my questions? I remember the giant man hovering over my bed in Theoria, the way his fist connected with my mouth. I don't remember any more harm done to me during my bouts of consciousness. "If I've been injured, I've a right to know!" Not that this woman cares about my rights, obviously. But perhaps if I can appeal to her apparent caregiving nature . . .

"No!" she says, gently brushing a bit of hair out of my face and tucking it behind my ear. "You're in perfectly good health, child. That lip of yours will heal in no time. You'll see."

"Then what cure do you speak of?" I've never heard of curing someone who wasn't ill, and it's at this point that I begin to doubt I'm awake at all. This must be some sort of vivid dream, which is why my eyes won't open. I'm simply not ready to wake up yet.

I'm ready to believe this, that it's a dream, until I feel her hand at my arm and the needle when it pushes into my vein, startling me. After that I feel a liquid oozing into my bloodstream. And the burn. It makes a scalding trail through my body, and I imagine the gleaming molten liquid the silversmith in Serubel uses to shape swords, and I cry out as the intensity increases and spreads everywhere. "I do not need a cure," I tell her, my stomach tightening with agony, "if I am not ill!"

"This is not for any ailment, child," she says mildly. "This is the cure for Forging."

It is then that I vomit all over myself.

PART TWO

20

TARIK

TARIK PUSHES THE FOOD AROUND HIS PLATE, unable to bring a morsel of it to his mouth. It has been ten days since Sepora's disappearance and his nerves are frayed beyond repair. He'd thought that perhaps taking his evening meal in his chambers would solve the issue of his not eating of late, as he cannot stomach the company of King Eron for another moment, and Queen Hanlyn has grown so quiet that she's barely a comfort to either Tarik or her own outraged husband. But it is not the quality of the food nor the exhausting task of entertaining Sepora's parents that keeps him from his meals.

It is that Sepora herself is in danger, perhaps hurt, and he can do nothing about it until Sethos returns with a report from Hemut. He has such mixed feelings about Sethos's absence. On the one hand, his brother's prolonged visit to Hemut means he truly is searching every part of that kingdom for Sepora. On the other hand, pride of the pyramids, but what could be taking his brother so long? He is normally fast and cunning and shouldn't he be home by now with a report, which would be worst-case scenario, or with Sepora, which would be the best possible outcome? Is he deliberately taking his time to punish Tarik for imprisoning him in the first place?

Tarik can only hope that if his brother is taking his time in returning, it's because Sepora is safe in his keep and not because he himself has been captured by Hemut.

21

SEPORA

BAYLA OPENS THE DOOR TO MY CHAMBER AND slides in with a tray of food that smells wonderful. She saunters to the small table set with two chairs opposite the room and eases the tray down as if it were filled with porcelain dining ware instead of plainly carved wooden bowls and spoons. They do not trust me with anything but spoons, with anything but wood.

And they shouldn't.

Anything sharp and I would secure my release from this place— at least that's what I want to think. They discovered that the first day three men untethered me from the bed and I Forged a blade faster than they could close their open-hanging mouths. It must have been shocking that a girl who was supposed to have been cured of Forging by then had wielded a sword of spectorium against them.

Fools.

That's when I learned I was in a castle. As I had bounded down the hallway like an untamed Theorian cat, I took in my surroundings as best I could. I passed windows that peered out onto a vast sea. I turned corners made of salt stone. I toppled servants dressed plainly but with clearly embroidered emblems on their collars.

Royal emblems of the kingdom of Pelusia.

Bayla confirmed this once I was captured again and dragged back to this wretched room without windows.

Bayla. I cannot get a grasp on the woman. She's friendly enough, when she's not "treating" me for Forging. Even now, while she's sweeping the chamber, she chatters on about her grandson, about how much I'd enjoy the weather outside if I'd simply behave long enough to be escorted to the gardens, and how delicious I'll find the soup she's brought from King Graylin's famous kitchens.

I glance about the room, my mood growing all the more sour as she dusts the mantel over the fireplace. It's the only real source of light in the room, and they keep it going day and night, for the northern ocean breeze seems to breathe in between the cracks of the salt stone. The chamber is clean and simple, but it is not meant for esteemed guests, which Bayla keeps insisting I am to King Graylin.

Until they unbound me just this morning, I'd insisted any "guest" would take exception to being secured to a bed—and an uncomfortable bed at that. And so I sit on the disagreeable bed, unbound but well guarded nonetheless, for three heavily armed guards stand just beyond the door. If Bayla so much as raises her voice, I'll be overrun with swords and daggers and whatever else Pelusians use as weapons.

Guest, indeed.

The last time I saw King Graylin, I was a girl of twelve and he was a *real* guest at our royal table on a rare visit from Pelusia. Aldon had told me Graylin had been a foreign prince who'd married the Pelusian queen to secure an alliance between Pelusia and Brezland, a kingdom far north of the five, and when the queen died, he was so saddened that he never took another wife—and never returned home, wishing to stay behind in Pelusia to ensure his beloved's kingdom did not go to ruin at the hands of her next of kin, a greedy cousin or something of the sort. He'd fathered a daughter with the queen, a girl of my age at the time, and talked lovingly of her, telling me she and I would be great friends had he brought her along.

In any case, King Graylin had seemed kind and gentle during his visit, and ultimately boring to a twelve-year-old girl, but certainly not of the nature to kidnap a princess right before she would wed perhaps the most powerful king in all the five. Surely he knows retribution is coming. As soon as Tarik discovers where I am.

If Tarik discovers where I am.

If Tarik *cares* to discover where I am.

Tarik. I wonder, endlessly wonder, what he must be thinking. What he must have surmised happened. Does he think I've run away? What else could he possibly be thinking? What else is he to assume, except that I'm too ashamed to face my parents with the news of our broken engagement and that I've fled for good this time. I push that thought aside and try to think of other, less selfish things. What of the guards outside my door back in the Theorian palace? What must my parents be thinking? Are they worried, or do they, too, assume I've run away?

Still, my mind strays back to the Falcon King. Will he marry Tulle after all? Rashidi will almost certainly have talked him into it by now. And if so . . . if so, then what is it to me? The Falcon King and Theoria are no longer my business. He made that abundantly clear the night I was taken. So what, then, will become of me, if I am to escape Pelusia?

Will I return to Serubel, a tarnished princess whom no one will wish to marry? If I'm cured of Forging, will I even have a place in the Serubelan castle, or will Father disown me altogether? And what of Mother? Blast it all, but I have no time to be a prisoner!

"You took me at a most inconvenient time," I tell Bayla as I stand so she can make my bed, tucking the corners tightly in place. "And all for nothing. Your treatments are not working." As I say this, I produce a ball of spectorium in my hand, allowing it to float between my palms and light up the room. Once it cools, I walk it to the mantel and set it there, basking in the glow of white illuminating the chamber.

Bayla is not impressed. She shakes her head and beats upon my pillow until it takes shape once more. "It will work. Have patience."

This is how each of our tiffs begins. "I don't *want* it to work. You'd think me fighting you each and every night would be proof enough of that." I've tried to reason with Bayla. I've tried to tell her of the Quiet Plague, of the need for spectorium so that Tarik can protect his kingdom against Hemut. For her part, she acts sympathetic. But each night, she has me tied to the bed and injected with a burning liquid as I scream in pain.

And each morning, I wake up and Forge her a brand-new figurine made of fresh spectorium. This morning it was of herself. Right down to the apron she wears. She ignored it as she tended to my room. I have never been so infuriated by politeness in all my blasted life.

It is almost time for treatment, I can tell. I seat myself at the table and lift the bowl of soup to my mouth, not caring to use the spoon. Bayla is right; the soup is delicious. Yet I know the food is laced with a sedative and something for pain; Bayla has told me as much. But the coward in me takes it anyway, because on the nights that I don't, the agony of treatment is far worse.

Tonight, though, Bayla does not make the usual *tsk*ing sound at my manners at the table as I gulp down my water and tear the bread apart with my teeth. In fact, she has grown eerily quiet, taking a seat on my bed and watching me closely from across the room. She folds her hands in her lap, her shoulders squared, as if she's waiting for me to make the first move.

What the first move should be, I haven't a clue.

Curiosity gets the better of me. Curiosity, and the overwhelming feeling that I should run. Bayla is never silent. "You're pleasantly quiet this evening," I tell her around a bite of bread. "To what do I owe the peace?"

She grimaces and I'm instantly sorry for my insult. Bayla is not my enemy. King Graylin is. She is just my keeper. She is just following orders. I could be more kind. I recall how soothing her voice is when she's trying to comfort me during the pain. She doesn't want to hurt me. She thinks she's helping me. She thinks she's being a good servant.

I hate feeling any sort of amity toward her, though. It seems wrong, yet it feels worse to treat her badly. I try to think of what Mother would do in this situation.

I couldn't fathom Mother being in this situation.

"I'm sorry," I say. "That was unkind."

She gives me a rueful smile, one that makes me feel like a swine. "Think nothing of it, Princess Magar. I know you've become impatient during your stay with us."

There she goes again, implying that I'm a guest. Is she a simpleton, or just intensely loyal? Either way, I throw my hands up in frustration. "There is no talking to you."

She sighs. Patting the bed space beside her, she gives me a meaningful look. "Come sit, Princess. King Graylin has decided it is time you know why you are here."

I eye her suspiciously. Is this a ruse to get me to the bed so that my treatment will begin? If I sit, will the guards immediately rush in and overtake me, tethering me to the posts? She must read my thoughts, because she says, "There will be no treatment tonight, Princess. You have my word."

Her word. I mull that over for a moment. She hasn't led me to believe she's a liar. She tells me when I'll be receiving treatment. Even when she knows I'll lead the guards on a chase around the chamber, gouging and kicking and screaming and Forging scalding bombs of spectorium to throw at them, she still gives me warning when it's time for treatment. She waits patiently while I thrash about on the bed until I succumb to the sedative, if I've chosen to take it. With supreme gentleness, she tells me when the needle will go in, and she coos words of comfort when I writhe in pain. I do not have to be a Lingot to know that when Bayla speaks, she means what she says. It's just that she's never offered to speak of why I'm here before.

I slowly take the seat next to her on the bed.

She grasps my hand and pulls it into her lap, gently rubbing it consolingly. I wonder if she does this to her grandson when he's on the verge of a tantrum. I wonder if I am on the verge of a tantrum. I suppose it depends upon her explanation, though I can't imagine anything will justify kidnapping me and keeping me hidden from the people who love me.

So I don't expect it when she says, "Your mother arranged for your escape from Theoria, Princess Magar."

"*Mother* did this?" I'm not so sure I can trust Bayla after all. Mother would risk a war between her beloved Pelusia and Theoria? The Falcon King would not, could not, let this go without retaliation. Perhaps I am no longer to wed him, but Mother does not know that. It would be his obligation to avenge his name. No, Mother would never risk that. Bayla must be lying.

Yet she nods enthusiastically. "She wished to save you from your unwanted marriage, and to protect you from your father's reach. To protect the *spectorium* from your father's reach."

My father's reach. The spectorium. An unwanted marriage. I close my eyes against the striking realization that what Bayla is saying makes perfect sense. Because she knows too much about my mother's intentions to be making it up. Mother sent me away from

Serubel in the first place to protect the spectorium from my father's reach. Of course, she'd never imagined how badly I could manage to jumble things up.

"Why did she not tell me of her plans?" Because this is a new behavior on Mother's part. She always tells me, guides me, on what to do next. Abducting me without warning seems out of nature for her.

Bayla pats my hand once more. "She knew you were determined to help your Falcon King, that you had resigned yourself to becoming his queen. She knew you wouldn't come willingly. She knew you would Forge for him eventually. She couldn't let that happen. Not with your father in such close proximity."

Tears sting at my eyes. *She knew you would Forge for him eventually.* Was it not exactly what I'd promised Tarik just moments before he called off our engagement? It hurts that she had no confidence in me. But it pains me much worse that she had no cause to. And Mother has been in control of the situation the entire time. It must have taken her weeks to make these arrangements, to convince King Graylin to be her accomplice. And she didn't trust me with the plans. She didn't trust me with the truth. She didn't trust my ability to make the right decision.

Even after I had fled my home kingdom and sacrificed so much at her request.

But is *this* the right decision? Shouldn't my own choices be left up to *my* decision? Because as it stands right now, Mother has treated me as a pawn just as the two kings did in arranging my marriage in the first place.

Rage seeps through me, burning hotter than any treatment ever could. Bayla tenses beside me. "You mustn't be angry with her," she says gently. "She was only thinking of you."

"She could have told me. She could have made me privy to her schemes. She should have consulted me before having me beaten, stolen from my bed, and kept captive in a dank and solitary holding cell."

"If you would behave, you could be moved to a proper guest chamber."

"Why did she have me taken so brutally?"

"She had to make it look like a proper kidnapping. She had to make it look authentic to the Falcon King. And, of course, to your father." *A proper kidnapping.* No, Tarik does not think I've run away from my circumstances yet again. He thinks I've been taken.

"Don't you realize what she's done?" I say, standing. "She's made it look as though the kingdom of Hemut has taken me!" What else is Tarik to assume? With the way Lady Gita stormed out of the palace in the wake of Sethos's outburst, it all but reeks of a retaliation from the ice nation.

Bayla shakes her head. "Your mother is wise. She would not let that happen. I'm sure of it."

I peer down at her, really looking at her for the first time. Her eyes are too confident for a mere servant. "You *know* my mother?"

"Very well, Princess Magar. I attended her when she was but a child."

"Why is King Graylin helping her?"

She shrugs. "They are fast friends. And he doesn't want a war between all the five kingdoms any more than she does. Taking you was the only way."

I rub a hand down my face. "Does King Graylin know that there is a plague in Theoria? That only spectorium can cure it? Or did my mother fail to disclose that to him?"

Bayla nods solemnly. "He does, Princess. And he has found an alternative treatment for it as well."

Treatment. I am so very sick of that word. "The same way you've *treated* me for Forging? I do hope you jest." I fling the words at her like daggers. She takes them in stride, standing to pace about the room. She wrings her hands. I've shaken her composure, but what did she expect? That I would take this news with joy and relief? That I would suddenly stop caring about the people of Theoria? That I would believe in Graylin's ability to help when Theoria's brightest citizens remain helpless in healing their own kingdom? "Besides," I tell Bayla, "if there is such a treatment, why has he not offered it to the Falcon King already?"

"He will exchange it for your freedom, Princess Magar."

"Exchange it for my freedom?"

"It will be an offer the Falcon King cannot refuse. Release you from your vow to wed him in exchange for the means to save his people."

Release me from my vow to wed Tarik? Ha! King Graylin has a merry surprise awaiting him, then. I'm just about to inform Bayla that our vow has already been broken but think better of it just before the words leave my mouth. Tarik may not want me anymore. But his people still need the cure for the plague. I cannot ruin that for him. But I'll not take Bayla's word for another thing. "I demand to speak with my mother at once."

"I'm afraid that's not possible. She is still in Theoria helping to prevent war with Hemut."

"How noble of her," I spit.

Bayla takes a seat on the bed again and peers up at me. "You're angry that she didn't involve you in her plans. But she only wants what is best for you, Magar. You must understand that. She doesn't want you to be trapped in a loveless marriage the way she was. She doesn't want your father to start a war with all the kingdoms. She wants only your safety and your happiness."

"And who says mine would be a loveless marriage?"

The servant cocks her head at me. "You care for the Falcon King?"

"And what if I do?" What if? Tarik and I have our differences. But to deny that I love him still would be a lie.

"I find it odd that you would, after all he has done to you. Kept you as a servant, vowed to wed another while making you believe he had feelings for you. Jumped at the chance to have your spectorium as soon as your father attempted to make amends."

Oh, how I long to lunge at this woman who knows so much, this woman who is so confident. And of course she would see things in that light. After all, I had thought the very same thing.

"Your mother says the Falcon King is a Lingot, that he can discern a truth from a lie. Yet, that does not stop him from lying himself, Princess Magar. Surely you must realize all he has to gain from wedding you. And what do you gain? Where is the benefit for you?"

Oh yes, Tarik has all this to gain from marrying me. Except that he has no use for me as a queen now that he has the other Forgers. And he has no use for me as a wife if he can't trust me. There is nothing I can do to change those things now.

Is there?

This woman may know my mother, but she has no idea of *me*. What's more, she has no idea what has truly passed between Tarik and me. Even my mother could not know. Bayla only knows what my mother has told her.

Yet her words are far-reaching, for they play on my own fears. Have I truly lost Tarik for good this time? Does evidence of my broken heart appear on my face even as I try to stifle the anguish within me?

Where is there benefit for you? A loving husband who will treat me with respect, for one. I know that if I had been honest, he would have been a kind and thoughtful husband. *What else?* A kingdom that seems to hold a measure of adoration for me. *And?* A chance to prove myself as capable a queen as my mother.

Yet . . . Yet. Bayla speaks the words of my mother to me now, I'm sure of it. My mother is a very capable queen. How much of this should I take into consideration?

"And so, Princess Magar, your mother thinks it's wise to cure you of Forging. It has no value to you. Your ability carries with it only a burden, one that Queen Hanlyn wishes to relieve you of."

It is true that Tarik had much to gain from wedding me. It would be true for any man who approached my parents with the same offer of marriage. That in itself is reason enough to keep my ability to Forge. For *without* it, and *with* my new reputation, I will need all the help I can gather in order to wed someone else one day. Of course, Mother could not possibly know all these things, as she didn't bother to consult me before stealing me away into the Theorian night.

Still, the people of Theoria need spectorium. But if what Bayla says is also true, that Graylin will give Tarik the cure for the Quiet Plague—and that Father will no longer have the means to create cratorium—why not at least pretend to be willing to give up my ability? Surely I can somehow hide my Forging, let them think I'm being cured. I've hidden it before, many times.

"But your treatment is not working," I counter, deep in thought. "Perhaps you should try something else." Something less painful. And hopefully, equally ineffective.

"No. This treatment is not working, that is true. But there is another way."

"What other way?"

She pulls out a chair at the table, folding her hands upon the smooth wood. "The treatments we have been giving you were meant to weaken the organ that creates the spectorium. Now we know that it doesn't work that way. The organ must be removed."

"Organ?" I think of all the organs Aldon taught me of the body. To my knowledge, none can be removed without consequence. I shudder. It does not go unnoticed by Bayla.

She nods solemnly. "Our Healers have determined where the spectorium comes from. It is an organ that only Forgers have, that ordinary people do not. We can remove it for you. We can remove your burden, Princess Magar."

Is my Forging truly a burden? I have always thought so—until now, when it could be taken from me by force. Nothing else will be taken from me, I swear it. No one will make my decisions for me any longer. Not Tarik, not Mother, nor Father nor King Graylin. Not even the good-natured Bayla. No matter how noble their intentions are, others do not have control over who I am. Tarik may not want me for his wife, but the people of Theoria need a cure. If all the Forgers in the Baseborn Quarters cannot make enough spectorium to keep the plague at bay, then maybe Graylin's cure can.

And so I will play along with Bayla. With my mother. With King Graylin. And I will return to Theoria with the cure. After that, I will make my own fate.

I look at Bayla, who has been studying me closely. I wonder what she sees. "How can I trust that you have the cure for the Quiet Plague?" I ask.

Bayla stands, striding to my bed and crouching down on her knees, which crack with the action. There is a sharp scraping sound, and she grunts as she pulls something from underneath me. When I see what she has in her hands, I gasp.

It is the Serpen art from my bedchamber in Theoria. "Your mother sends this as proof of her devotion to your well-being. She said you would understand its meaning upon seeing it."

And of course I do. Mother must have removed it herself, because no other servant in the palace would do so, as Tarik's own beloved mother had it placed there before she died. It is a sign that she approves of my being here. I had only ever spoken to her of the distasteful art, a design we both abhorred because of the horrifying way that the

Serpen must have been stripped of its scales. It is a symbol of unity, this art. That Theoria does not fully understand me, but that my mother always will.

Or, at least, that Mother thinks she fully understands me. But I've just begun to understand myself. And I will be a puppet for no one.

I do not look away from the artwork when I say, "Tell me more about this organ of mine."

22

TARIK

TARIK DOES NOT TAKE COMFORT IN THE FACT that Cy is without a clue as regards the madness overtaking the kingdom. Each day, there are more and more reports of Strays upturning normal lives, daily routines, the goings-on of a once-functioning Anyar. Tarik walks along with Cy through the courtyard of the Lyceum, full of the less violent strays, and although Tarik has come as the Falcon King this day, heavily guarded, he doubts his face paint hides the disappointed expression he wears when witnessing firsthand what his citizens are becoming.

Some talk to themselves, some bicker with each other over nonsensical things, some sit at the fountain and rock back and forth as though they've lost the will to stand. "And where are the aggressive ones being kept?" Tarik asks as they pass a man licking his hands so fiercely that his fingers have become prunish and wrinkled at the tips.

"As much as I hate to say this, Highness," Cy admits with a grimace, "they are being detained behind locked doors for their own safety and that of the kingdom."

"The *kingdom*?" Commander Morg says as he strolls behind them.

Cy nods. "Some of their madness is not born of lunacy, but of conspiracy. They speak openly of overtaking the throne."

Startled, Tarik places a hand on Cy's forearm, but Cy seems hesitant to bring his eyes to meet his king's. "And how seriously should we be taking this threat?"

"Seriously," Morg answers, a scowl darkening his face. "Madness is one thing; treason is quite the other."

"But they are one and the same, I'm certain of it," Cy says. "They must be treated as patients, not criminals."

Morg snorts. "This is not a decision for a boy Healer to make."

"*Master* Healer," Tarik corrects. "Cy is a Master Healer, and I will take into consideration his opinion in the matter."

"My apologies, Highness," Morg says, but he still looks at Cy as though the Healer himself is in need of medical care. "Madness or not, we cannot allow these delusions to leak into the minds of the strong, giving them ideas that perhaps the throne *is* weak."

"Which is exactly why these people are being detained," Cy snaps.

"But how many are not being detained?" Morg presses. "How many roam the roads and pathways wreaking havoc on the reputation of His Highness?"

Tarik cannot help but agree. Ill though they are, their threats are very real. It is the most inconvenient time to be preparing for war with Hemut. Tarik lowers his voice when he says, "Send soldiers throughout Anyar disguised as mere citizens. Find these ones who escape detention, and bring them in to receive treatment." He turns to Cy. "You do not care to treat ones without consent, I know. But this is a royal command. You will treat every Stray you come across the best you know how."

Cy is clearly alarmed. "But nothing has truly worked, Highness. All I can do is treat symptoms until the cure is found."

"Do what you can." Tarik shakes his head. "Cy, do what you *must*."

It is not an unfair thing to ask, Tarik thinks. After all, Tarik is doing what *he* must, which is to keep up the pretense of being a king sound in mind. Day in and day out, he pretends to pore over scrolls and correspondence all the while withering inside that Sepora has not yet been found and returned safely to him. *But returned to me for what? Did I not call off the engagement myself? Will she not be leaving with her parents as soon as Sethos returns with her from Hemut?*

Yet his decision to disavow their engagement had not been a hasty one. He'd considered it at length, and decided in the end that he could not, and would not, have a queen nor a wife he could not trust.

It is the worst feeling in the world, he thinks, as they leave the Lyceum and head for the palace.

To be in love with someone you simply cannot have.

23

SEPORA

BAYLA INSISTS THAT IF I'M TO HEAL CORRECTLY, I must get up and walk immediately after the surgery. The pain will be shooting and fierce, she says, and dizziness will overtake me. The stitches in my stomach will become puffed up and angrily red, but Bayla assures me the salve administered by her Healers will ward off infection and keep the true pain at bay.

That is, of course, if I were truly going to have the procedure done to remove my gallum—or my Forging organ, as it were.

But my days spent with Bayla are now a back and forth with her about whether I'm ready to go through with it (I'm not) and whether she might tell me more about the cure for the Quiet Plague. (She won't.) I feel like a snake charmer of Theoria playing the flute for a cobra that will not be charmed. Between our combined stubbornness, I'm convinced we could rule all the five.

"Without Forging, how will I ever recover my energy?" I wonder more to myself than to her. It is good to keep up curiosity and a pretense of open-mindedness, lest she force my hand completely. But while I still seem to consider, she still seems to give me time to ponder.

She lets out a small chuckle and pats my hand. "I suppose you'll have to gain energy like the rest of us, through robust activity to keep the blood moving."

"Robust activity sounds horrible," I tell her.

"You've not been enjoying the walks about the castle? Perhaps we'll stay kept in your room once again." The threat is empty, but it turns my stomach just the same. The newfound freedom of Bayla accompanying me on tours of the grounds and castle has been refreshing to say the least. She is still difficult to read, though. I'm not sure if I've gained her trust or if she has guards stationed at every route of escape.

Even now, we bound up a circling stairwell outside a tower wall, and while I could easily fling myself inside the open windows and flee, I pretend as though I don't even notice they're there. After all, fleeing now would not secure me the cure for the plague. And I'm not leaving until I have it.

"Once we reach the top," she says jovially, "I have a surprise for you."

"A surprise?" I try to sound excited, but it is likely another breathtaking view of the ocean or a tray of delicious scones prepared on the order of Graylin himself especially for my delight. I grow weary and bored of being treated so nicely, now that I comply so easily with the wishes of my captors. I even miss arguing with Rashidi and sharpening my wit through debating on kingdom matters with Tarik.

No. I must not let my thoughts stray to Tarik yet again. What we had has been gone for a long while now. I must work to control my feelings toward him, now more than ever. I'll have to face him one last time when I deliver the cure to him. And then I'll have to walk away.

My gut clenches even as Bayla is chirping about, oblivious to my sour turn in mood.

"Yes!" she is saying. "And it's a shame that it is a surprise at all, truth told." She scoffs. "Your mother should have taught you of it, if

I do say so myself. Did she teach you nothing of the Pelusian way of life?"

Actually, she didn't. In fact, it seemed a sore subject with her mostly. When I asked questions about her home kingdom, she'd always respond with a distant look in her eyes that Pelusia was a part of her past and not worth discussing. My tutor, Aldon, touched on Pelusia as part of our history and culture lessons, but he never mentioned the capability of their Healers or even that King Graylin's kitchens were famous for their regular turnout of fine delicacies. On the topic of the other four kingdoms, Aldon had been an endless fountain of knowledge. I'd always just assumed that Aldon did not know much of Pelusia, for if he had, he certainly would have taught me more.

Now, I think it's worth noting that my mother could have instructed him to neglect teaching me about Pelusia. But why, I couldn't say. Perhaps she didn't want me pestering her with questions and making her long for the life she left behind. Which, as a curious child, I certainly would have done.

Realizing I haven't yet responded to Bayla's question, I say, "I'm sure Mother preferred to embrace her new way of life rather than dwell on the past. She's very set on being a good queen."

Bayla smiles at that. "She's always been an obvious ruler, even before she was chosen by King Eron to become his wife. She had a superior way of dealing with her peers, even when she was very small."

I can believe this about my mother. I cannot imagine her crying at all or being bullied by other children. Still, she is not an overpowering wife to my father. She knows when to step down. Or rather, she *chooses* when to step down—for the time being. I used to think her a waif. Now I think her brilliant.

Brilliant and ruthless.

A bit of bitterness stings at my eyes. For all her strength, she did not stop Father from beating me when I wouldn't Forge. It had been difficult not to resent her for that, for her appearing as a coward ever bending to my father's will. Still, she did help me escape, even if she hid the fact that she had been my accomplice all along. I wonder what Father will do when he learns of this latest turn of events. When he learns that she stole me away in order to remove my Forging abilities. He may well seek to execute her. No, my mother is not a waif. She simply chooses when to be courageous and when to appear helpless.

My mother is cunning.

When we reach the top of the tower, Bayla serves me breakfast in a stunning courtyard overlooking the northern sea. The beaches below, made up of rocky sands and broken shells, take the first hit of morning tide, each strike of foamy wave pushing forward and receding back into the ocean. Even the breeze seems to cater to our out-of-doors meal, cooling our hot eggs and boiled grains. I pull my cloak around me for added protection against the chill imbued in the wind. It is nice to be outdoors, and even lovelier that my things are being moved from my windowless chamber to another wing where I'll have a balcony and proper sitting area.

It seems Tarik is right; I have a gift for deception.

I think of my sitting area at home in my bedchamber. At home in Theoria, that is. Eating out of doors in the sunlight would be a stifling experience, even with the servants fanning me with large fronds of palms. I imagine that is why the grand dining room is the innermost chamber of all the palace, the coolest and shadiest place to escape the heat. With its vaulted ceilings to give the hot air a place to go, the dining room is by far the most temperate place in the palace.

Bayla gives me a curious glance. "Daydreaming again, are we?"

"I do miss Theoria," I say shyly, taking a sip of the pomegranate tea she'd brought along for our meal.

"You must get that thinking out of your head, Princess. You must prepare yourself for the fact that your Falcon King *will* trade you for the cure." She does not say it unkindly. She doesn't have to. The words are daggers in themselves, no matter how they are delivered.

"I know he'll not choose me over the cure for his people." Of course, not for all the reasons Bayla must be thinking. "He will have no choice but to accept the terms King Graylin offers," I say with a sense of finality and acceptance I don't quite feel yet.

"You care for this Falcon King, don't you?"

Blushes have a way of answering for you, I find. Mine is profuse. Yes, I'm still in love with Tarik. Yes, I still care for him. But one day, that will not be so. Time will pass. My feelings will subside. I'm sure of that.

She chuckles. "Oh, my dear. Then why have you not told your mother this? Your mother is under the impression you want out of the marriage."

And why would she think otherwise? I never once gave her the impression I had feelings for Tarik. I never once told her that I had stayed by choice, and not because I could not escape Theoria. "I did, once. Want out of the marriage, I mean. Things have been complicated between Tarik and me. We have had our differences."

"You think?"

I grin. "Are you a determined spinster, Bayla? Prejudiced against a happy marriage?"

But she ignores my jab. "If you truly care for him, I'm sure your mother will understand. Perhaps she'll convince Graylin to offer the cure for the plague as a wedding gift, instead of as an exchange. After your procedure, of course."

A wedding gift. What wedding? is what I want to say. "Perhaps" is all I offer instead.

"Your mother is not unreasonable, you know. But that is enough of this talk. I promised you a surprise today. And now I'll show it to you."

At this Bayla nods to one of the servants who had been attending us for our morning meal. The servant leaves for a moment, and then comes back with a large bowl of soapy water. Surely we are not meant to bathe in this crisp morning air! I'm desperately hoping this is not some morning ritual Pelusians have, to catch their death of cold by means of an outside bath.

Bayla instructs the servant to remove our dishes from the table. She then sets the bowl of water in front of me, sloshing a bit of it onto the tablecloth. Bayla smiles down at me, clearly excited about what will come next.

"You see," she begins, "Pelusia is a mystery to all the other kingdoms, only keeping to itself and not caring to mingle with the rest. Is that correct?"

"Yes," I say. Pelusia has never been one to trade or even visit other nations. The citizens are quite snooty, in the eyes of many. I do not say this to Bayla, for she is quite proud of her kingdom.

"Incorrect," she says triumphantly. Then she cups her hands together, scooping up the sudsy water and submerging her face in it, scrubbing violently as though she were covered in soot from hairline to chin. She turns away from me then, grabbing a cloth strewn over a chair, and dabbing at her face to dry it.

When she turns back to me, I gasp.

Bayla has scrubbed away her face. That is, Bayla now has a new face. A young face. The face of a girl who could not be older than me.

Before I can say anything, she begins removing her clothing. With wide eyes, I watch as she peels away her dress and apron, and with it rolls of womanly curves to reveal that underneath, she is quite petite and skinny, wearing the same kind of servant's attire, only this clothing fits her nicely, showing a trim waist and much smaller breasts. Lastly, she pulls her gray-haired bun from atop her head and lets her blond curls fall down the length of her back.

Bayla is no grandmother.

"You see," Bayla says, her raspy voice not matching her appearance now. "We do mingle with other nations. They simply do not know it." She clears her throat. "Excuse me, Princess Magar." From her bodice she retrieves a vial of liquid, and plucking off the cork, downs it in one swallow. "There," she says, her voice sounding youthful and fresh. "That's much better."

I blink up at her in disbelief. "You're . . . you're a young girl."

"Well," she says, taking a seat next to me at the table. "I'm not as young as I look."

"But . . . why?"

"King Graylin thought you would be more comfortable being attended by an older, more experienced woman."

"No," I say. "Not that. Why do you *disguise* yourself within other kingdoms?" And how? How did she make her face appear decades older than it was? Even now, there are still leftover wrinkles near her ears where the water did not touch. Bayla never existed at all. Is Bayla even her real name? And, of course, she couldn't have attended to my mother when she was younger. She may not have a connection to my mother at all.

I stand, stepping away from the girl before me. "You speak of how Tarik can lie to me, and all the while that is exactly what you have done."

"I lied to you about nothing. I just never revealed myself to you in my true form."

I shake my head. "You couldn't have attended my mother when she was a child. You lied about that."

Bayla nods, pursing her lips. "Yes, you're right. I lied about that. It was my grandmother who attended Queen Hanlyn when she was a child. My grams was very fond of your mother."

"How old are you?"

"Sixteen, Highness."

I can believe that. "Why did you fool me in the first place? Why didn't you reveal your true self?"

"I thought it would be an amusing way to show you the Pelusian gift of disguise."

"Amusing for whom?"

She smiles as three servants with stiff, swishing dresses sweep onto the courtyard carrying trays of clay jars and glasses of what appears to be paint. They remove the breakfast fare from the table and place their new load upon it. There are strips of a fine, gauzy cloth beside the jars and a big pot of steaming water emitting a foul smell. I crinkle my nose as the wind catches it and sweeps it toward me.

"Amusing for us both. Tell me, Princess Magar, who would you most like to poke fun at?"

Rashidi, easily. But I'm not sure I should admit this to young Bayla. Insulting the Falcon King's highest adviser might be disrespectful. I shouldn't do it.

"Rashidi," I say with glee.

She bites her lip. "I'm afraid I don't know what he looks like." Then she claps her hands happily. "So then, that means you must drink the bonce potion so that your mind tells your body what to look like!" She gives me an apologetic look. "Oh, but I must warn you. It's made with the brains of the Façade Fish. It won't taste very good. One could call it disgusting, in fact."

So, I'm to sample the steaming pot of Façade Fish brains. Blasted marvelous. "Façade Fish?" I ask, trying not to look at the pot, somehow still hoping it will taste like the shepherd stew Tarik's kitchens make every few days.

Bayla nods. "Oh yes. The Façade Fish can make itself appear as anything in the ocean. Rocks, sand, even other fish. We use the scales in our paint, but they won't work unless you ingest the brains, which prompt the scales to act upon your thoughts."

"You're jesting."

She laughs. "I know ingesting brains is not ideal, Princess Magar, but surely you've been eating stranger foods in that barbaric Theorian kingdom of yours."

I've never heard Theoria called barbaric before. Even Aldon had taught me that Theoria was the center of higher learning and innovation and that its citizens thought of Serubel as barbaric for teaching their women how to fight. Pelusia was never mentioned as a rival of Theoria in medicine or modernization and I wonder again if that is because Aldon didn't know it, or my mother required him to hold back in telling me. But why?

Besides that, I wasn't suggesting Bayla jests about eating brains—camel brain is a delicacy in the palace and one that I nearly drool over when my plate is set before me. It's the idea that the brains of the fish and its scales still act together, long after the fish itself is dead. I'm intrigued, and I bet Master Cy would be, too.

"Are you ready to try for yourself?"

Crossing my arms, I take in the paint and gauze and fish brains before me. "Why would you teach me to do this?"

"Your mother thought it would help you pass the time here, while she sorts everything out back in Theoria. King Graylin is beside himself for keeping you in that tiny room for so long. I'd bet he'd give you a tour of the palace himself were you to ask."

"You're not afraid I would disguise myself and run away?"

Bayla looks surprised. "Run away? Back to your Falcon King,

who used you to get what he wanted? Away from Pelusia and back to a kingdom inferior in every way?" She blinks. "The thought of you wanting to leave hadn't crossed my mind."

Bayla is both clever and deceptively innocent at the same time. Reminding me that I'm returning to a man who might have used his power to manipulate me and my feelings for him is a low blow from her. But return I must, to deliver him his cure. And it wouldn't hurt for Bayla to know something else, for these small jabs at him hurt all the same. "I love the Falcon King," I tell her quietly.

Her eyes widen, the way I'd expected them to. I would never have told the old Bayla that I love Tarik. The old Bayla might have looked at me with scorn and perhaps pity, her eyes full of experience of many loves lost and a hardened heart in her old age. Yet this Bayla is younger than me. This Bayla might not even know the stomach-swirling experience of a first kiss or the rush of catching her beloved looking at her when he should be paying attention elsewhere. This is where Bayla is innocent. And I must make her understand that returning to Theoria, and soon, is important.

"How could you love him after what he did?" she says, her voice full of wonder and devoid of any judgment.

I pull out the chair next to me and indicate she should sit. She does so, and with the interest of a child about to learn how to skip rocks along the river for the first time.

"It was difficult," I tell her. "So difficult. But what I've come to know about love is that it's a sticky thing, like a spiderweb. You can remove it mostly, but there are always a few strands that stay behind for the spider to rebuild. Love is a web that never truly lets you go." It feels good to admit this to someone. It feels good to acknowledge that while I cannot have Tarik, I can still feel something toward him, as painful as it is.

"And if the Falcon King does indeed trade you for the cure?"

"Then I will allow it. The Falcon King would be happy. I could go on with my life, and Mother will have the satisfaction of knowing she was right all along, I suppose." I say these words as I think them, not realizing Bayla is hanging upon my every thought. I look at her now, and her eyes have glistened over.

Bayla is a romantic at heart.

"Suppose the Falcon King does still want you. Will you go against your mother's wishes?"

"My mother's wishes are that I not be used as a pawn. If the king still wants me over the cure—which is highly unlikely—then I won't be a pawn, I will be marrying for love. I can't imagine her wishes would contradict that outcome." Oh, how can empty words hurt so very much?

Bayla smiles at me, though, taken in by my grandiose tapestry of lies. By this time, she has leaned in close, resting her chin on her palm and eyeing me wistfully. I laugh. "Perhaps your mother needs to be looking after *you*, before some servant boy sweeps you off your feet."

An instant blush reveals to me that one already has. "What is his name?"

"Pontiadi. He's the king's messenger boy. He's eighteen, Princess Magar, and has lips softer than the petals of a rose."

I grin. "Bayla! I do hope you hide your kisses from prying eyes."

"Not even a Beholder could find our secret hiding spot."

"A Beholder?"

"Yes," she nods, still blushing. "Beholders have extremely good vision. They can see things from far away and tiny things and the like, but they also notice details. Details that ordinary eyes cannot see."

"Like what?"

"Well, when I had dressed up as my grams, a Beholder would be able to tell who I truly was. They would see the fine details in the paint, even the powdered scales would reflect back at them." She picks up a handful of sand from the ground and shows it to me in wonder. "You and I see sand. Perhaps our eye catches the bigger grains at times, and we can point them out. But a Beholder? A Beholder can see *each* grain of sand, no matter how tiny. A Beholder could count them, if asked. Even the hairs upon your head, a Beholder could count."

I think of our Seer Serpens and how beneficial it would be to have a Beholder mounted atop one, or at the very least, examine the smoke given off by the eyes when burned. "How many Beholders are there?"

She shrugs. "In Pelusia, there are many. They enjoy the king's company often, as they are one of his biggest assets and he wishes to keep them happy so that they stay. Many are lords and ladies, given titles to keep them rooted here in Pelusia."

There is much I have to learn of Pelusia and its King Graylin. "Show me," I tell her abruptly. "Show me how to make the paint. I'll eat the brains. Make me look like Rashidi."

24

TARIK

TARIK IS IN HIS DAY CHAMBERS WHEN RASHIDI bursts through the doors, hands thrown in the air in frustration. It's an impressive show of physical fitness on Rashidi's part, since he's usually bent at the neck and using his staff as support for walking. Now he extends his staff along his arm, pointing at the door in outrage. "This is what you get when you send a dolt on a secret mission, Highness!"

Sethos abruptly appears in the doorway pulling behind him a hand attached to an attractive girl with fiery red hair. A very familiar girl with fiery red hair. A fiery redhead that has no business being in Theoria, given these circumstances, and especially wearing such scanty Theorian attire.

"He wishes death upon us all!" Rashidi says, sweeping his hand toward Princess Tulle dramatically.

Tarik grits his teeth. "I'm sure my brother has a very good and levelheaded reason he has brought Princess Tulle back with him from Hemut, and I'm sure he'll tell us this very reason before he draws his next breath."

Sethos smirks, pulling out a chair for Tulle to be seated in across from Tarik's marble desk. As he takes his own seat, he crosses his legs and plunks his feet on the table, getting comfortable for what will no doubt be a long story filled with stupid decisions and ending with how Princess Tulle came to be wearing the clothing of a concubine.

Tarik pinches the bridge of his nose, leaning back in his own seat, as Rashidi wanders around and around the three of them, groaning in outrage. "Get on with it, then," Tarik tells his brother. "Where is Sepora?"

"Not in Hemut," Sethos says. The truth, or so Sethos believes. Which means his brother turned the place upside down looking for her. "Tulle does not know where she is, either."

Tarik focuses on Tulle, examining her facial features before he asks, "Princess Tulle, as a Lingot I must ask—do you know where Sepora is?"

She offers an apologetic smile. "I'm afraid I do not."

The truth.

Tarik relaxes, not realizing he'd tensed for the question at all. "Now that we've gotten the most important matter out of the way, please tell me if my brother harmed you when he took you. If he did, I'll see that he's punished for it. Severely."

Sethos rolls his eyes while Tulle's smile brightens. "He didn't take me. I asked to come with him."

Oh, of course. Of course, this would be Sethos's way of punishing me for throwing him in prison. Sethos has seduced Princess Tulle right out of her home kingdom and into . . . well, into his harem, so it would seem. Tarik had heard rumors that Sethos kept a harem, but the rumors always struck false to him. Now, he's questioning whether his Lingot abilities failed him.

He turns to his brother. "You will return Princess Tulle to Hemut at once."

"Incorrect," Sethos says, almost bored.

"Remove his tongue!" Rashidi screeches from where he's settled across the room. "Cut it from his head!"

"Do calm down, Rashidi," Tarik drawls. "At least until I can decide if this is a family affair or a kingdom matter."

"They are one and the same, Highness," Rashidi says, linking his hands together in illustration. "One and the same."

Tarik turns back to his brother. "Suppose I don't have your tongue cut from your face for refusing a direct order. Suppose I listen to your reasons for refusing a direct order. Suppose I even humored you and let you speak without interruption. Will I regret it?"

Sethos smiles. "You will be most delighted, actually."

"Do tell, then."

"Princess Tulle and I have decided to wed."

Tarik wipes his hand down his face. Things are not this simple with Sethos. In this way, he is like Sepora. Always doing what is required, mostly anyway, but in the most intrusive and roundabout way that could possibly be thought of. "May I be the first to offer my congratulations, or has King Ankor already had the pleasure of doing so?"

Princess Tulle winces, but Sethos takes her hand in his and pats it gently. Rashidi and Tarik exchange a look. Sethos is not treating Tulle as though he'd rather wed a—what was it? Oh yes, a hairless mule, he'd said to Lady Gita. No, he's treating her as though he's very much in love with her.

And if Tarik's Lingot abilities do not fail him now, Sethos is indeed.

Splendid. Just splendid. Tarik presses his fingertips together to keep his hands from wringing his brother's neck. "Am I to assume that King Ankor did not give his permission for the two of you to flee Hemut together, then?"

"Not exactly," Tulle says. "But he knows I'm here."

"Yes," Sethos chimes in cheerily. "They were unable to catch us once we reached the forest, as it were." He gives his beloved a rueful smile before turning back to Tarik. "So, uh, I'd say now would be a good time to start making the cratorium and preparing for war. Since Sepora isn't there, and all, no need to hold back. I'm sure Morg would concur in this matter."

Tarik locks eyes with his brother, but issues an order to Rashidi instead. "Rashidi, please escort our esteemed guest Princess Tulle to the most lavish chamber available and staff her so that she is without want for anything. I'm sure she is tired from her journey and will want to make the most of a bath before the evening meal. Meanwhile, Sethos and I will discuss . . . wedding plans."

Rashidi gives Tarik a scowl that could wither a man to dry bones but gets hold of himself before offering a gracious hand to Princess Tulle. "My dear princess, I do apologize for the most unusual way you were brought before the Falcon King. You'd think we in Theoria were without manners, but that simply isn't the case . . ." he's saying as they trail down the hall.

Sethos grins at Tarik. Tarik crosses his arms. This is to be a game, then.

"For the entirety of your miserable existence, you've loathed that girl," Tarik begins. "And now you would marry her, when doing so in this way forces Hemut to war with us?"

"If you must force me to admit I made a mistake, then fine. I made a mistake. I'm in love with Tulle. Although loathing and loving are very similar in nature, I think" is his brother's reply. "It can be confusing at times to sort through. If Sepora were here, I'm sure she could attest to that."

"Sepora isn't here, brother, because you've failed to return her to me."

Sethos rolls his eyes. "I cannot cover all the five kingdoms at once, can I? You sent me to Hemut. She isn't there. Where else shall I look?"

"I think I may know the answer to that," calls a voice from the door. They are both startled to find Ptolem standing quietly and patiently at the door. "Forgive the intrusion," he says, "but the guards allowed my entrance."

As they should; Tarik had given Ptolem authority to enter his day chambers without obstruction. He has proven most useful of late.

"Come, Ptolem," Tarik says. "Tell us what news you bring."

Ptolem strides to the marble table separating Tarik from killing his brother and places a tiny rolled-up scroll upon it. It is so tiny, in fact, it would be difficult to write on it with any kind of precision. "What's this?" Sethos asks, unwinding it before Tarik even has a chance to reach for it.

Ptolem straightens his chin. "Prince Sethos, this scroll was intercepted by a boatman on the Nefari this afternoon. It was attached to an infant Serpen no longer than my forearm." With this, Ptolem lay the dead creature on the table where the scroll had been. It's barely thicker than a quill used for writing and almost the color of the sky.

"That would be difficult to see," Tarik muses. "Nothing more than a sliver of color in the sky. It could probably have been mistaken for an insect." And they had not been looking for insects. They had been looking for birds. For people. For servants coming and going in the night.

"Hmmm," Sethos says, reading. "It appears to be correspondence between Queen Hanlyn and King Graylin in Pelusia. And I quote, 'My work here is almost done. How fares Magar? I will arrive within the week.'"

Tarik feels his nostrils flare, a burning heat filling his cheeks, a bitterness coiling in his stomach. Hanlyn had not grown quiet out of worry for her daughter. Hanlyn had been so somber, so unusually economical with her conversation in order to hide the lies her words would surely reveal.

"It is time I had a talk with Queen Hanlyn and her adoring king," Tarik says through grinding teeth. "Bring them to me at once."

A SOLID HOUR PASSES BEFORE ERON AND HANLYN can be rounded up together and herded into Tarik's day chambers. Eron and Hanlyn sit in different attitudes as a servant goes about the room lighting candles, for the evening has reached them—a sign that the hottest season of the year is over and that cooler weather will soon be upon them. Eron sits with agitation and restlessness while Hanlyn folds her hands in her lap and studies Tarik with a fixed expression of surprise. Both reactions ring true to his abilities.

A flustered king and an aloof queen. A confusing pair to be sure.

Confusing, if Tarik were not a Lingot. "King Eron, did you know that Queen Hanlyn has been behind Princess Magar's disappearance since the beginning?"

Eron's eyes grow wide as he beholds his wife, raking his eyes down the length of her. He gives out a sharp laugh. "Hanlyn would never defy me in such a way. Look at her, boy, she quivers at the accusation."

Tarik laces his fingers together, studying Hanlyn calmly. She does tremble, but not in fear. She is angry. Her eyes burn with it; her mouth tightens with it. She has been caught. Tarik is curious how she will handle it. Will she be as smooth and graceful as she always is? Will she fling insults at him, hiding her guilt to her husband? Because Eron's words ring as true as sunrise; he has no idea of his wife's duplicity.

"What do you have to say of yourself, Queen Hanlyn?" Tarik says, locking eyes with her.

She inhales sharply and turns to her husband. Placing a hand on his, she says, "I've respected the Falcon King and his way of ruling." Surprisingly true. "But I fear I've given him too much credit, where credit was not due. He lies to you now, Eron. And we must not allow him to get away with this atrocity. He accuses us of kidnapping our own daughter. Where is the sense in that?"

Ah, so she is twisting his words to include Eron in the insult. "He accuses us." "We must not allow it." She is falsely appealing to him as a united pair, further proof that she acted alone. Her lies may fool her husband, but they fall strikingly false on Tarik's ears.

"Why have you been keeping her in Pelusia?" Tarik barks, of the dance she creates with her words. "Order her release, and I will spare your life."

"Her *life*?" Eron says, standing. "Have you gone mad, boy? You have no authority to make such threats!"

"She is a guest in my home and has stolen away my future queen after you yourself made the arrangements to wed her to me. Have you forgotten my Lingot abilities? Have you forgotten that the truth does not escape me? For weeks, I have heard you lie to me of lasting peace between Theoria and Serubel, how you'll only use cratorium against Hemut. For weeks, I have endured your sneaking about the kingdom, sending your men to size up Kyra for its Scaldling venom as though my own guards were blind to their visits. You've been planning an attack from the comfort of my own palace. Oh yes, I know all of it. But you made no formal action against me, and so I did nothing. Yet now your own wife has taken Sepora. Give her back to me, or I'll execute you both."

Eron's face has grown the kind of red one gets when one has eaten something excessively spicy. "Execute us? How dare you accuse my wife of such treason and now you threaten our very lives? You'll not live another day, boy, I'll see to that! Falcon King or not."

"Guards!" Tarik bellows, and ten file in, seizing the king and queen from their chairs and holding them until further instruction. "King Eron, I hereby charge you with conspiracy against me, negating the arrangement of peace between our kingdoms. Queen Hanlyn, I charge you with the kidnapping of the future queen of Theoria, Princess Magar."

Sethos materializes from behind one of the guards, eating an apple. Around a mouthful, he says, "Tell me, brother, how satisfying was that? Power suits you, I think."

"Do shut up, Sethos."

During the commotion, Patra had relinquished her warm spot near the balcony and now nuzzles Tarik's hand with the tip of her nose. He acknowledges her with a few strokes, and she sits at his side, her head nearly reaching his shoulder. She is alert, he knows, but purrs into his leg as if to comfort his unraveling temper.

And unraveling it is. Queen Hanlyn has still not confessed to her part in taking Sepora, and it looks like she might not. Perhaps if she hadn't completely escaped his attention in the lengthy search for Sepora, he wouldn't be as angry with her. But somehow she managed to elude him, the way Sepora can sometimes elude him, and he wants to know how. He remembers the blood on Sepora's pillow and wonders—hopes—that it wasn't real to begin with. Surely this woman standing before him who seemed so courteous and warm at his table each and every meal could not have harmed her own daughter.

Could she?

Right when he would ask her that very thing, another person bursts through the door—Cy, his Master Healer. It takes both the young boy's hands to hold the pyramid made of fresh spectorium, a pyramid so large, it sheds a pale light on the entire room, drowning out the yellow of the candles.

"Your Highness, look!" Cy exclaims. "Fresh spectorium. It was on the steps of the Lyceum, more than I've seen in months and months!"

Tarik groans. The Great Council could not have chosen a worse time to show their extreme generosity and loyalty to the Falcon King. Now Eron and Hanlyn will know there are more Forgers. If the outcome of their trial—and there must be a trial to show the other kingdoms he does not simply murder his guests on theory alone—does not result in imprisonment, and they are set free, the citizens of the Baseborn Quarters will be in danger from them. He must now take additional steps to protect them.

Sepora will not be happy when he secures her release. She'll view it as a betrayal. After all his talk of trust, and now this, the accusations he flings at not only her father but especially her beloved mother as well. But did Sepora not betray him in the first place, keeping the other Forgers a secret from him all this time?

Pride of the pyramids, why must things always be so complicated?

It was a foolish thing, to take his attention away from King Eron, for somehow the man has freed himself from his guards and lunges at Tarik with one of their swords. Even Sethos cannot save him now. Time seems to stand still as the blade slides closer and closer to his heart, and his reflexes, he knows, are not fast enough to dodge the blow.

But Patra's are. She meets the king's lunge, catching his forearm in her jaws and snapping the very bone. Eron screams in anguish— until Patra springs at his face, her guttural growls ferocious as she mauls him.

"Patra, disengage," Tarik commands, but his cat has gone wild. Sethos draws his sword, but hesitates, clearly at a loss for what to do, no doubt warring with his dislike for Eron and his love for Patra. Tarik shakes his head at his brother; taking his sword to Patra would be useless at this point, for the king's lifeless body slumps to the floor.

Patra backs away from him then, putting herself between Tarik and the rest of the guards, even Sethos. Cy crouches in the corner covering his head with his hands, his pyramid of spectorium all but abandoned. Actually, where is the pyramid of spectorium?

And where is Queen Hanlyn?

Tarik and Sethos seem to realize her absence at the same time. "Find the queen," Sethos barks, sheathing his sword behind his back and stepping over Eron's body. "And someone clean up this mess."

Five of the guards dispatch, and five stay to do Sethos's bidding. Tarik strides to Cy, picking him up from the floor and brushing off the imagined dust from his small body. "It will be okay," he tells the boy Healer. "Patra was just protecting me."

"I've never seen a cat do that before," he says. "I mean, I know they're trained to . . . to . . ."

"Yes, well, I've never had the occasion to need her for that. Now, let's go to my bedchamber and discuss your findings, shall we?"

"Y-y-yes, Highness. Of course."

Patra follows behind them, her tongue smacking the blood from her face as she walks. Over his shoulder, Tarik calls to his brother. "Sethos, set out for Pelusia at once."

25

SEPORA

PERHAPS I COULDN'T QUITE RECALL RASHIDI'S every detail when I'd Cloaked as him a few days before, because my result had been mixed. His scowl I perfected, though, and Bayla and I had such great amusement poking fun at his expressions and my perceptions of what they all meant. Since then, I've had scads and scads of practice.

Perhaps I should feel guilty in not putting up a fight to escape anymore. But there is something salutary in my staying here. Of course, I've had to consistently deter Bayla from forcing me to have my gallum removed, but for now, she seems determined to talk me into it with gentle suggestions, and as long as I keep up the appearance of considering it a little more each day, she seems content to let the matter wait. And each morning after breakfast and our serious discussion of the surgery, I'm allowed to play with the Cloaking paint.

Today, since Bayla left to attend to some castle matter, I've already impersonated two servants and a seller of wares I saw from the castle wall far below us. Him, I probably did not perfect, because I couldn't take in all of his features. I'd wondered what a Beholder might have noticed from so far ahigh. The pores of the seller's chin? Each eyelash pointing this way or that? Nose hairs, even? Still, I imagined what *I* thought he looked like, and that is how he appeared when I had finished my work.

As I admire my reflection in the full-length mirror before me now, I'm thoroughly impressed with myself. It's by far the best execution of my efforts. My eyes appear hollowed out, as though bags had deflated beneath them, my lips appear thin and testy, and my eyebrows are bushy white, with the help of some added hound hairs and a touch of candle wax to keep them in place. Growing up, I remember our servant Testra allowing me to sneak into my mother's wardrobe to dress up in her clothes, but in retrospect, those times were not nearly as fun as this banquet of paint and costumes and bonce potion, even the smelly aroma of Façade Fish brains lingering about the veranda.

Next, I've decided to impersonate Bayla herself. When she brings me my evening meal, she'll be shocked to find that she's bringing it to herself. I'll use the colored oil to soften the white in my hair, making it the golden blond her tresses are. And if I squat ever so slightly, I'll be just as short as she. She should be proud. Skilled at Cloaking, that girl is. And ever the skilled teacher, if I do say so myself.

Still, as easy as I thought it would be, it takes me the better part of the remainder of the day to perfect Bayla. And, as the hours pass, and my food arrives by a different servant altogether—who doesn't even care to look up at who she's serving—I begin to worry about what is keeping my jovial companion. Is this one of her many games? Does she want me to look for her? The thought excites me, to run amok in the castle without a chaperone. On the days we tour the place, I've taken in many details and hidden them away in my memory, in the case that I do need to actually escape. But I've also come to admire the expanse of the thing, the history here, and the fact that Pelusia trades very much—just not with the other four kingdoms. They prefer the goods and services of the mysterious northern kingdoms, who reside across the enormous ocean that separates us all. And they've built ships large enough to stock for the months-long journey it takes to reach them—that I learned when Bayla took me to the docks on the shoreline.

Perhaps my search for Bayla will take me back to the docks and to the briny air and the chilled wind and the odor of dead fish being sold at market. I pull on my own slippers—the only giveaway that I'm not, in fact, Bayla, and head for the door.

For the past three days, she has tested my skill in spotting Cloakers. I've not quite gotten the hang of it yet, but she can spot every one in the castle and outside as we walk along, to the point where I've wondered if she herself is a Beholder. Some Cloak themselves to appear more attractive. Others, beautiful women, Cloak themselves to appear plain so as not to garner so much attention for themselves. Still others Cloak themselves just for the fun of Cloaking, and it is these that we search the castle grounds for, and they for us. It is a childish game, I know, but one that keeps me busy until I hear word from Mother. The last correspondence I received told me that the king is worried for me, but that is to be expected, and not to be anxious, but to remember who I am, a Serubelan princess, and to stay strong—and of course, to keep considering the matter of surgery.

To say the least, I feel guilty that I am having fun while Tarik must handle the conundrum he's in, but I'm comforted in knowing that Mother has it all in her capable hands, even if Tarik does not know it. Mother will not let the kingdoms go to war any more than I would allow it.

Still, if Tarik were missing, I would be worried sick, and inconsolable, even though he called off our wedding. Is it wretched of me to be wasting the day at play while he wonders what has happened to me? But I can't allow the hope that he still cares to nag at me too much. I must get over this hope of mine, that there will ever be anything between us again. He might be worried, but he'll have other matters to attend to that will keep him distracted, I'm sure. He cannot be too worried for a princess he no longer intends to wed.

I push those thoughts aside as I wander the castle Cloaked as Bayla, looking at each servant I pass but, most important, smelling them. I receive many odd glances, of course, but I've come to realize that Bayla always smells of roses, and while she may be Cloaked as someone else, she most definitely will still *smell* like Bayla. Well, Bayla and bonce potion.

I pass a door closed almost shut, but stop in my tracks. There is candlelight coming from inside—and while I don't smell roses, I hear the unmistakable voice-song of Bayla. I crack open the door just a bit and find my mark, arms wrapped around a much taller boy with dark hair and features. A handsome boy, who, by the intimacy of their embrace, could be none other than Pontiadi. I begin to ease back out of the doorway, fully meaning to let these two finish their private moment together. But something Pontiadi says halts me cold.

"You mustn't tell the Princess Magar."

That is when I lean in closer, until I'm sure they'll glance my way and catch me.

Bayla shakes her head. "I cannot keep that from her. It isn't fair, Ponti!"

He strokes her golden tresses, obviously troubled by her frustration. "Sweet, who are we to decide what is fair? We are but servants in this castle. It's the king's decision. We cannot interfere here."

"And what if it were us, Ponti? What if someone were trying to separate *us*? What if someone were trying to marry me off to another? Wouldn't you want to know?"

Marry her off to another? Saints of Serubel, what is happening?

"I would not allow any man to touch you."

"She *loves him*, Ponti. She told me so herself. She loves the Falcon

King. She doesn't want to marry a northern prince. She cannot go from being a pawn of her father's to a pawn of her mother's. I won't let that happen!" She stomps on his foot, but he holds her tightly, only grunting with the pain.

"If you tell her, she'll flee. We'll both be in trouble then," Ponti reasons, but Bayla's tears are affecting him, I can tell.

"She is my friend. I won't betray her loyalty."

"And what of us? The king will send me off in his army, and I'll ne'er see the likes of you again."

"Did he say *why* she's to marry Prince Bahrain?"

Prince Bahrain? I've never even heard of this person. Mother certainly never mentioned him in her letters. Does she know that Tarik has broken our engagement, then? Is that why she's arranging another marriage for me? I feel a small betrayal at that; Tarik had promised I could tell my parents on my own time. Perhaps he figured my disappearance had changed that, especially if he thought I had run away.

Bayla pushes Ponti away, her head lifted high. "The Falcon King won't stand for it, the same way you wouldn't stand for it."

"The Falcon King will stand for it, because he'll be gaining the cure for the Quiet Plague. He'll let her go, and gladly. He'll call off the engagement, once tempted with it. Any good king would."

So Mother doesn't know?

"Then come with me," I say, stepping fully into the doorway and out of the shadows of the hall. Ponti gasps, looking from Bayla to me. I've done a superb job of Cloaking her; even he can appreciate that. "Come back with me to Theoria and make things right. The Falcon King will not turn you away. I will not turn you away. You'll be punished for nothing."

Ponti pushes Bayla behind him. "You do not know what is happening here, Princess Magar."

"You're right, I don't. Explain it to me, then," I say evenly.

Bayla pinches him in the side and he groans. "Stop that, Bayla. You know I must take her to the king at once. The king will know what to do with her."

"Do you know how to fight, Ponti? Because she does. She's been trained by a Majai."

Ponti looks up and down the length of me, considering. "She could have lied about that."

My instant smile has him reconsidering. Finally, he says, "I should call for the guards. I should call for them right now and end this—"

"I'm afraid the guards will not be able to help you at this moment," a familiar voice calls from the door behind me. Sethos steps in, a sword in each hand, and a tired expression on his face. I don't miss the fact that there is blood on both the blades. "They are . . . indisposed."

He looks at me and then to Bayla. "Which one of you is Sepora? I don't have all day, so I'll just start slicing the both of you."

"You're a dolt," I spit. "And you won't harm them, or I'll harvest your eyes from your head."

Sethos smirks. "Good, I've found you. Let's get a move on, then."

He grabs my arm and hauls me toward the door. I dig my heels into the floor, but his strength is too great and we are heading down the hall within seconds.

"Stop!" I plead. "Graylin will kill them if he finds out they let me escape."

Sethos sighs. "You're not escaping. Obviously, you would have done that already, had you any sense. You're being kidnapped, and to my great amusement, against your will. Now let's hurry before I have to actually kill someone. And if you make me knock you unconscious, you'll be deliberately starting a fight between my brother and me, and you know how I'd love that."

"Trust me when I say your brother couldn't care less." Finally I snatch my arm from his grasp.

He narrows his eyes to near slits. "My brother has been worried sick about you for almost two weeks. Much has happened, Sepora. Do not try my patience. I'm tired and hungry. Also, I'm hungry."

"Your brother has no business worrying for my safety any longer. He called off our engagement before I was taken."

Sethos stiffens. "You lie."

"He didn't tell you?"

"Guards! We have an intruder!" Ponti calls from the doorway.

Sethos sighs and stalks toward Ponti, knocking him on the head with the hilt of his sword. Ponti slumps to the stone floor in a heap. Bayla is about to scream, but Sethos is at her side, holding his hand over her mouth. "I heard everything. The Falcon King will exact vengeance from Graylin the minute he hears about this nonsense of marrying his bride off to another. I suggest you both flee Pelusia before that happens." He nods to Ponti's figure on the ground. "If you scream now, though, I'll slit his throat. Maybe not today, maybe not tomorrow. But I'll come back and find him no matter where you go. And I always get my mark."

Bayla is sobbing beneath his hand, but she nods vigorously in understanding. "Good."

He strides back to me and and snatches my hand, dragging me forward again. "See? Everyone can be reasoned with. Except perhaps you, I think."

"You're unbelievable."

"All the same, it's good to see you. I can't wait to tell you all of the news." He climbs up into an open window that barely fits his large frame. Looking down, he nods. "The haystacks are still there. We're jumping, I'm afraid. They'll have found the other guards by now and be looking for us."

"I'm not jumping."

"You're sure? Because throwing you out would greatly amuse me." He reaches out his hand for me.

I look at it, sucking in a breath through my teeth. "I can't do it."

"Pride of the pyramids, take my hand and let's go."

"Can you knock me out, the way you did Ponti?"

He rolls his eyes. "Give yourself something to tell your grandchildren and jump, Sepora. You jumped from the Half Bridge, why not from a steep castle tower? Besides, we really must be on our way. My future wife awaits my return in Theoria, and I'm dying to get back to her."

"Your future *wife*?" My eyes must be the size of saucers.

"I'll tell you everything. As soon as you jump."

There is a commotion coming from down the hall, and the sound of men's voices echoing toward us. I'm in the window before I know it, looking down at the wagon with hay in it. "You're sure we won't die?"

"Of course," Sethos says, grinning.

And then he picks me up and tosses me out.

26

TARIK

RASHIDI WAITS WITH TARIK AS HE PACES THE floor of his day chambers. It had been announced to them both an hour ago that Sethos had returned with Sepora, and they would arrive at any moment to report to him. The entire palace seemed frenzied as a swatted bee at the excitement of the princess returning. Tarik is not sure if it is out of happiness or out of curiosity that the servants bruit about at the return of Magar, the future Theorian queen, but as Ptolem reports it to him, everyone wonders what her reaction will be to her father's death. It is a good question.

Tarik closes his eyes at the thought of having to tell Sepora of her father. Perhaps Sethos has already told her. It is a long journey on foot to Pelusia, but Ptolem said they'd disembarked from a skiff on the Nefari just before the Half Bridge. Sethos has had time to make Sepora aware of all that has happened. Whether he did or not, Tarik couldn't say. Sethos is not very good at serious talk. And he is not very good at comforting.

The door opens then and a very tired-looking Sethos and a very passive-looking Sepora enter the day chambers. To Tarik's surprise, Rashidi pulls out a chair for Sepora and urges her to sit. He chides himself for not doing the same. Both Sepora and Sethos look as though they've endured much. Sethos is covered in blood and dirt, and Sepora, after Tarik's closest scrutiny and relief, merely dirt. She is clearly dressed in servant's attire and he wonders what his own servants must have thought about their future queen being brought to them in near rags and dragged around the palace in such a state.

They will think Pelusia has much to pay for.

And they would be right.

Sethos waves off Rashidi when the older man lifts Sethos's arm and inspects a gash on it. "It's fine," Sethos assures him. "But if you're concerned, friend, please call for as much food and water as can be found at this late hour in the kitchens. We're starved half to death. And where is Tulle? I wish to see her."

Tarik does not miss that Sepora's stomach grumbles. She doesn't seem to care, though. She sits straight, and without expression. If she is trying to throw off Tarik's Lingot abilities by not speaking or telling her emotions with body language, she is doing a most excellent job of it.

Tarik seats himself across from them as Rashidi gives instructions to the guards outside the door. When Rashidi has rejoined them, leaning against the wall by the balcony, Tarik looks to his brother. Sethos is easy to read, even in the dimming candlelight. He is tired and irritable and not happy with Tarik. In the corner of the room, Patra flicks her tail. She watches Sethos and Sepora closely. Ever since the incident with Eron, she has been more cautious of Tarik's visitors. He hopes her affection for his brother and Sepora will return soon. It had taken a few days for her to warm up to Rashidi again.

"You are both unharmed?" Tarik says quietly.

"Of course. Physically, anyway." With this, Sethos sneers.

"Physically?" Rashidi says. "In what other way could you be harmed?"

Sethos glances up at the adviser then cuts his eyes back to Tarik.

"It would seem the Falcon King owes you an explanation as well, Rashidi. Perhaps he would like to enlighten us all on why he is no longer engaged to Princess Magar of Serubel."

Rashidi pushes away from the wall. "I beg your pardon?"

"Tell him, Tarik. Tell him what has occurred."

So. Sethos is angry, either with the fact that Tarik called off the engagement, or the fact that he neglected to tell him of it. He does not need to look at Sepora to know her expression has not changed. Still, Tarik is surprised when she speaks up.

"Sethos, I believe I did disclose why he called off the engagement, and why he did not tell you about it. In fact, I believe we discussed it several times, including during the entire journey to the palace from the Nefari." Her words carry fatigue and a bit of exasperation. "What I would like to know is, why would a king send for a princess to whom he is no longer engaged, and whose parents he no longer entertains as guests in his royal household?"

Tarik leans back in his chair and crosses his arms. Sethos knows of the nulled marriage, and Sepora knows of her father and mother. Of course they exchanged information on their voyage. That was to be expected. And Tarik knew he would need to explain things to the both of them, but he did not expect an ambush as soon as they arrived. He had imagined a more private setting for each of them, and one in kind for Rashidi. But it seems his brother is intent on being shifty; his mouth is set in a way Tarik knows well.

It is set in a way that suggests he will expire before he lets the matter lie.

A knock at the door relieves him of an immediate answer, and as the servants set down two trays of cheeses, meats, and breads, and pitchers of water and wine, his mind works doubly hard to come up with answers—answers that do not make him sound, as Sethos calls him, like a lovesick whelp.

He did not actually think when he sent Sethos on his way to Pelusia to retrieve Sepora. It had been reflexive to get her back, like blinking when something is in one's eye. It wasn't until his brother was well on his way that he considered the consequences of his actions. All that had occurred to him was that he knew where she was and wanted her returned safely to him, and immediately so. Of course he did, because he loves her. But Sepora is right to question why *the Falcon King* would be bothered with the task. Why *the Falcon King* would have any more interest in her at all, since she is no longer to be queen of Theoria.

And he doesn't have an answer. Not a true one, anyway.

What he does have, though, are questions. And that will have to suffice for all of them for now. He waits for several long moments, watching Sethos and Sepora attack the fare as though they'd never before seen food. Rashidi, for his sake, stares at the floor, careful to hide his own feelings from Tarik as well. It does not sit well with Tarik that everyone in this room feels betrayed by him at the moment.

Finally, Sethos takes a long drag of water from his chalice then slams it on the table. "So then, where were we? Ah, yes. Your unique situation of not being engaged to one Princess Magar."

"Stop calling me Magar," Sepora says around a bit of bread. "And stop being so official. You are brothers. You can talk about it in your own time. Don't lose your temper for my sake. I've already told you, it doesn't matter in the least to me."

That last bit is a lie, and Tarik feels as though he has been run through with a sword. So, they both must suffer from his decision. But he must stand by it. It was made as king, and not as doting lover. He is relieved that she is dropping, for now, her questions for him about the matter. By her demeanor, he even doubts she will bring it up again. With Sethos, though, he can tell he will not be so lucky.

Amid the hurt, she says, "You need to tell him what my mother is planning. It affects us all far greater than any lost marriage vow."

Sethos glares at Tarik. "It seems the queen of Serubel was planning to rule all the five, and doing so from the comfort of your own palace. Really, Tarik, I expected much better from your so-called spies." He glances at Rashidi. "No offense to you, friend."

Rashidi nods. "Tell us what has happened."

"Well," Sethos begins, lacing his fingers behind his head, "while I was gallivanting around Graylin's castle, I heard the king and Queen Hanlyn—how she beat me to Pelusia I'll never know—in his throne room speaking quietly to themselves. They were discussing the matter of getting married, and of marrying Sepora off to a Prince Bahrain of Nunsdem, of the northern kingdoms, so as to strengthen an alliance with them. And, of course, the lost opportunity of murdering you and overthrowing Theoria while it is weak with the Quiet Plague and in a state of war with Hemut for abducting Magar."

"Stop calling me Magar," Sepora interjects nonchalantly, taking another bite of cheese. "Go on, though."

"I was just repeating what they said. Anyhow," Sethos says, as if he were not interrupted, "they figured once Theoria was defeated, the rest of the four would submit to them, seeing as they planned to attack Hemut while Hemut was busy attacking us."

Tarik shakes his head. "How did Queen Hanlyn hide this from me? I'm a Lingot. I should have detected this undercurrent of animosity."

Sethos slides a glance at Sepora. "It seems a certain gift for deception runs in the family. And besides, did you ever directly ask her if she intended to overthrow the kingdom? She did a fine job at suggesting Eron was responsible the entire time."

"Her suggestions were not lies. He did not have good intentions toward Theoria, marriage alliance or no," Tarik says. "She did use that to her advantage, it would seem."

Just then, Tulle opens the door and rushes to Sethos, embracing him with all her small frame will allow. He reaches up and pulls her into his lap, giving her a mighty kiss on the lips. Sepora's eyes nearly pop from her face. Tarik suppresses a grin. She'll need to get used to this sort of behavior.

Or will she? Will she even stay, after all that has happened? Even as his mind works to find reasons for her to stay, his reason screams that she should not. But where will she go that she should be safe from her mother? And—will he ever reconcile his heart to his mind?

Sepora clears her throat, looking from the infatuated pair to Tarik. It is awkward for them both, he wants to tell her. The affection Sethos and Tulle show for each other is not unlike the affection he and Sepora once shared. "Yes, well," she says, "you were aware that I confided much in my mother while she was here."

Tarik nods.

Sepora lifts her chin. "What I did not say was that she discouraged me from Forging for either you or my father. I can only believe that it was to make your forces weaker from lack of spectorium when the time came for war. While I was in Pelusia, she sought to remove my Forging abilities."

"*Remove* your Forging abilities? Is that even possible?"

"According to Graylin's Healers, it is. According to them, I have a gallum. And when removed, I lose my ability to Forge."

"And you *agreed* to this?"

"Of course not."

"What did they do when you tried to escape?" But he regrets the words as soon as he speaks them. Because if she was tortured, he will travel to Pelusia this very night and strangle King Graylin himself.

Sethos pulls his attention from Tulle just in time to laugh. "Escape?

Surely you jest. When I found her, she was playing dress-up with her maidservant."

Tarik looks back to Sepora. "You didn't try to escape? You . . . you stayed there of your own accord?" He cannot help but raise his voice. He had worried this entire time, to near death, when she had not even tried to escape? What's more, she had apparently been enjoying herself. Had she no regard for his feelings?

"I . . . I found out my mother was the reason behind the abduction and I . . . trusted her judgment."

"You trusted her judgment even while she was trying to remove your Forging abilities? Even as she was trying to change who you are?"

"Forging is not who I am," she says, standing, and making Patra uneasy. He cuts his feline a look of warning. She yawns in dismissal. But Sepora does not notice Patra. Sepora is on the verge of a rampage, Tarik can tell. "And at the moment, my mother seemed like the only person in all the five who cared for me at all! She never fully disclosed all she had planned. I didn't even know she was in Pelusia! But that is not why I didn't try to escape. I needed to stay because—"

But the door is thrown open once more.

27

SEPORA

PTOLEM BURSTS THROUGH THE DOOR. "YOUR Highness," he says, breathless, "Strays have overrun the palace. You must flee now. There is no time to waste!"

My reason for staying, the cure for the Quiet Plague, falls flat. "Strays?" Sethos says, standing, but not releasing Tulle from his grasp. "How did they get by the Majai guards?"

"Some of them *are* Majai, Prince Sethos," Ptolem says, the blood draining from his face. "The force that overtakes the palace now is Majai, Healers, Superiors, Middlings, all of them. They have come for the Falcon King's head. We must get you out of here, both of you!"

Rashidi is the first to spring to action. I am surprised by the new life brought to his bones, the sense of urgency in his normally calm, collected voice. "The hearth," he says, ushering Tarik and Sethos and Tulle, each royal by one arm and Tulle by extension, since she is still attached to Sethos, toward the hearth at the end of the long room. "There are secret passageways that run through the palace. We must get inside, quickly!"

I watch them all shuffle toward the hearth. Rashidi forces down a hidden lever in the mantel and the entire back wall of it slides to the right with a great grinding sound. I'd always wondered why a palace in the middle of the desert would have need of a hearth. Theoria never gets cold enough for a hearth. But yet there are hearths all over the great palace. Hearths, and obviously, secret passageways connecting them.

Sethos looks back at me, and yells, "Pride of the pyramids, Sepora, now is not the time to dawdle. Come now!"

But as I watch everyone pile into the passageway and disappear, following their Falcon King to an uncertain fate, I stay grounded in place. I do not belong in that tunnel with them. I do not belong in this palace. I do not belong in Serubel, under the cunning hand of my mother, or in Pelusia, under the despicable intentions of King Graylin.

I am now a girl who does not belong anywhere. Why the Falcon King brought me back here I do not know. But going with him now is not the answer to anything.

Yet Sethos is at my side in an instant, throwing me over his shoulder, even as I protest. "Leave me be, Sethos!" I say angrily. "I can make my own way out."

"I see the look upon your face, Sepora. You've no intentions of making your way anywhere. Now stop writhing or I'll knock you over the head myself!" But we're already in the passageway, the door sealed behind us before his words are finished.

I'd forgotten how very fast Sethos is.

PART THREE

28

TARIK

TWENTY-SEVEN.

This is the third time Tarik has counted that there are twenty-seven fresh spectorium lamps lining the inside chamber of the Great Council's meeting place. One lamp for each column in the round room. Four good-sized guards at the door. Nine Council members. Two Theorian spies ready to report. The Majai commander Morg, along with Tarik's ornery younger brother, who grows excessively bored at meetings filled with reason instead of bloodlust and who longs to spend time with his future bride, who sits silently and composed next to him, and an old adviser who is well suited to negotiate and coexist with a Great Council.

And precisely one Princess Sepora.

One Princess Sepora whose eyes are still sharp silver or glistening silver, depending on her state of temper. One Princess Sepora who has adjusted well to living in the Baseborn Quarters during the Stray rebellion, adapting the long braided hair of her Serubelan brethren and the tanned skin of someone who works for their share during the day, much to the chagrin of the Council.

One Princess Sepora who puts forth just as much effort as Tarik not to make eye contact.

Tarik pushes that thought aside as one of the spies steps into the talking circle of the room. Out of respect, this young Lingot spy, Potipher, a friend of Cy's, should be facing the Council to make his report, but every so often, he glances at Tarik. It is not a secret to the spies that Tarik is the Falcon King, but in case of other spies who favor the Strays, he is never to be addressed as such.

Not while his life, and that of his brother's, are in danger each day the rebellion thrives.

"I have made contact with Master Lingot Saen," Potipher is saying. "She is not a Stray, and is happy to be of service to the Falcon King." Truth, Tarik knows. Not only did Saen pass this young one's test, but the third-party information also passed his knowing ears.

Tarik gives the Council a slight nod. Not that the Council does not already have a Lingot of their own.

"It is reported as well," the spy says, "that the Serubelan army left behind so hastily by Queen Hanlyn in her escape after Eron's death has been freed by the Strays. Her army has joined forces in keeping the palace secure from those who would support the Falcon King. We believe the queen is still in communication with her forces. We do not know if she does so from Pelusia or from Serubel."

Out of the corner of his eye, Tarik notes that Sepora lifts her chin. She does this whenever her mother is mentioned, and each time, regret swirls in his stomach. She'd been loyal to her mother, and he'd been enraged by that, had seen it as yet another betrayal when truly, what else was she to think? He'd disavowed their engagement. She had been right to trust her mother at that point.

But none of it can be helped now. They've not been able to steal a moment to speak and even if they had, what more is there to say? Now his duty is to concentrate on taking back Theoria, the way his father would. His father would not allow matters of the heart to rule at this point.

At the moment, they are trying to decide whether they should wait for Hemut's most assured attack to weaken the Stray forces, or whether they should begin preparation to force their way back into the palace and intercept the attack from Hemut to prevent as much damage as possible. Commander Morg, as always, prefers the latter option, as does Sethos.

But alas, having an opinion, and having the means to execute it, are two very different things. "The Serubelans have also secured the burnt city of Kyra," Potipher says, sealing the truth in Tarik's thoughts. Of course the Serubelans guard Kyra. Queen Hanlyn knows that Sepora was not responsible for the fresh spectorium on the steps of the Lyceum, for Sepora had already been taken by then. She will have surmised by now that Tarik has other Forgers at his disposal. She knows, too, that the only way to take back Anyar and the palace is with cratorium. That, and more than just a handful of citizens still willing to serve the Falcon King. No, that is not fair. There are more than just a handful. But how many more? That is what he needs to know.

"We simply must take back Kyra," Morg says, stating everyone's thoughts aloud.

"We are working to find all those loyal to the Falcon King," Potipher says. "It is a slow process, I'm afraid." Tarik takes that to mean that they are few and far in between. If only the Quiet Plague had not been so ravenous among his citizens. Even with fresh spectorium at his Healers' disposal to stave off the symptoms of the plague, the citizens, in their madness, are refusing treatment. Those who do not lose their minds, lose their lives.

"We need help from those who have not been touched by the Quiet Plague," Sepora says quietly, stepping into the talking circle. The

Great Council is always pleased when she speaks. Sepora has been a reluctant attendant at these meetings. Sethos says it is because she feels she has no place at them anymore. Tarik thinks it is because she does not want to have a place at them anymore.

"Please expound on that thought, Princess Magar," Olna, the Council leader, says.

"I refer to other kingdoms not at war with Theoria."

"That would leave only Wachuk," Morg says with distaste.

Sepora does not look at him. "We need warriors to overtake Kyra for the cratorium. Wachuk has those in abundance."

Olna nods. "Yes, they do, Princess Magar. But it is not my belief that we need to overtake the old city of Kyra."

Morg is already set to argue. "We need cratorium, Mistress Olna. To make cratorium, we need Scaldling venom."

"Then you will certainly need to speak your piece with Wachuk, Commander Morg," Olna says, squaring her shoulders. "For they have Scaldlings. I believe *that* is more important than old venom dust in an ancient city."

"Did you say *Scaldlings*?" Sepora says. "*Live* Scaldlings?"

Olna nods. "Indeed. Centuries ago when we were first captured and set upon building the great pyramids of Theoria, we brought with us Scaldlings from the great war. Our ancestors were permitted to keep them, as their fire-breathing abilities had been removed. As our people came to adjust to the desert way of life, we realized that we had no need for Scaldlings, that feeding them was a burden when we could hardly feed ourselves. We began to breed them, and to sell them to the royals of Wachuk. Since that kingdom worships fire, they were very willing to trade with us for food. While we no longer have Scaldlings here, I'm positive that the Wachuks have kept them. They would not let a breed of fire-breathers die out as we did."

Tarik steps into the circle, his mind reeling. "This was many, many years ago. Does the Great Council still have a standing relationship with Wachuk?"

"We do. But you must consider, we have nothing to trade them at the moment. Nothing that would be of value to them. You have no control over Theoria's goods, and they do not have need of spectorium. You cannot simply ask to borrow their Scaldlings. They are partners in trade, not friends."

Sethos steps into the talking circle then, and Tarik nearly rolls his eyes. No doubt his brother means to suggest they attack Wachuk and simply take the Scaldlings. To Sethos, overtaking a nation of women warriors must be like overtaking a kingdom run by infants. But Sethos surprises them all. "I have an idea who could help with that." He strides over to Tulle and pulls her into the dirt circle. Quite unwillingly, she nods to the Council, all the while staring daggers at his brother. It's the first time Tarik has ever seen her upset with Sethos, which is a miracle in and of itself. "The Princess Tulle is whom we should send to negotiate our terms," Sethos says proudly.

"Why is that, Prince Sethos?" Olna says, doubtful. Truth told, Tarik is doubtful himself. Tulle has always presented herself as shy and unassuming—traits that struck true to Tarik. Satisfactorily negotiating with the fierce Warrior Queen Emula of Wachuk does not seem a likely feat for Tulle. In fact, it seems quite impossible.

"What I haven't told you, because frankly I didn't see it was any of your business, and by *your* business I mean my brother's, is that Princess Tulle is actually a Warm Blood."

Tarik blinks. Should he know what a Warm Blood is? He glances at Rashidi, who shrugs, clearly mystified. Even Olna seems perplexed. Sethos rolls his eyes, clearly enjoying the fact that he has confounded everyone in attendance. "You see—"

But he is cut off by Princess Tulle herself. "I am perfectly capable of explaining myself, thank you, Sethos."

Tarik suppresses a grin. Perhaps Tulle is not as shy and unassuming as he'd thought. Tulle looks at Olna. "I assume I am permitted to speak on my own behalf?"

Olna nods, curious. "Indeed, Princess. You are the only representative present at the moment on behalf of the kingdom of Hemut. We will certainly hear you out."

"Thank you," Tulle says, a bit too graciously, and Tarik is almost certain Sethos has his hands full with this one. Sethos would not find her so interesting if he did not have his hands full. "The reason Sethos did not mention sooner that I am a Warm Blood is that Warm Bloods are generally outcasts back home in Hemut. We are rare, and when we do crop up, we are kept hidden at all costs. I, however, could not be hidden. And so Father kept me out of court for as long as he could and still does to this day."

"Yes, sweetling," Sethos says, "but tell them the part where you single-handedly whipped the entire Hemutian army in the forest."

But Tulle is not as proud of this feat as Sethos is. "I was forced to subdue them, I'm afraid. To use my powers against them."

"Powers?" Tarik asks, sizing her up thoroughly and still finding her lacking in where the word "powerful" might be applied. She is, after all, a dainty little thing.

"Yes," she says, holding her open palm out for all to see. In an instant, a flame erupts from her hand. "The power I have is to create fire."

29

SEPORA

I KNEW THERE HAD TO BE MORE TO TULLE THAN what meets the eye. Over these last two weeks in the Baseborn Quarters, I'd grown quite fond of her modest personality and her innocent kindness. But I'd known all along that there was something else Sethos found endearing, something else that would hold his interest the way only Tulle does. After all, simple modesty and kindness are not the sorts of things Sethos is attracted to.

And as Tulle casts long flames about the room in a display of her abilities, I've figured out Sethos's infatuation: Tulle is deadly. No, not with a sword, and not with her tongue, but she is deadly with her flames. More deadly than even Sethos can be, if she subdued an entire army with her ability. I wonder how Warm Bloods can be outcasts at all, rather than rule the blasted kingdom of Hemut themselves.

But as Tulle put it, they do not fit in there. Their bodies are too warm to even sit on the thrones made of ice. And what's more, they do not want to fit in. Not among an ice nation, anyway. No, Tulle has been quite happy to be in Theoria and with Sethos.

Even now she is saying, "I would be honored to speak to Queen Emula of Wachuk on Theoria's behalf."

"Still," Olna says, "what can you offer them?"

"At this point, nothing," Tarik interjects, "but she will certainly have their ear."

Sethos nods. "There's no doubt she'll command their respect, if nothing else. I think it's worth the shot."

"If we have Wachuk as an ally, certainly we could take back the palace," I say before thinking. I keep forgetting I have nothing to gain in taking back the palace. Nothing to gain, but nothing to lose, either, I remind myself. I am no longer to be queen of Theoria. I will no longer reside in the palace. Perhaps I'll stay here, in the Baseborn Quarters. Still, I feel a responsibility for what has happened. The citizens would not have gone mad at all if I had Forged to treat them in the first place—or at least I don't think they would have. I think back to my time in Pelusia and to Bayla insisting then that King Graylin had the cure and was simply using it as a negotiating tool. If only there were some way we could get our hands on it. Even if I could return to Pelusia, I wouldn't know where to look.

That's when my gaze falls upon Cy. Cy, who is so unsuspecting, sitting outside of the circle taking it all in stride. Cy would know where to look, what questions to ask, how to act like a student of healing in Pelusia.

Poor Cy.

"I think we should send Cy to Pelusia," I say abruptly.

Tarik and Sethos had been going back and forth about Tulle, but her role has already been decided, so I don't mind interrupting. The chamber falls quiet, the echo of their words dying off after my own.

Tarik regards me with a scowl. Of course, Tarik always regards me with a scowl or a glare, but mostly an indifferent expression these days. I've become so accustomed to it, his look hardly registers. Hardly. "Cy? What does Cy have to do with this?"

"Everything," I say, turning away from him and addressing Olna.

"When I was held there, the servant Bayla told me King Graylin had the cure for the Quiet Plague. If that's true, we could try to secure it from them. Taking back the palace is not our only concern. The Strays themselves pose the bigger problem if they continue to behave this way. We need to put a stop to their behavior and regain control of the kingdom." There I go, using the word "we" when I know very well Tarik doesn't hold a place for me in his kingdom anymore.

And if I don't have a place in his kingdom, he's hardly likely to consider my opinion in his plans for it.

"If the Strays refuse the fresh spectorium, why would they accept whatever cure the kingdom of Pelusia holds?" Tarik says. "Why did you not bring this up before?"

I square my shoulders. "I was about to tell you this at the palace, but the Strays interrupted me."

Tarik's glare softens. I hate when he softens. It reminds me of how things used to be. How they could still be. "How can we trust that they even have a cure?" he says. "We would be fools to risk our best Healer for such a dangerous mission." His voice is full of reason—which irritates me beyond sense.

"Your Healer has been rendered useless at the moment," I counter. "He certainly has an abundance of time on his hands sitting around the Baseborn Quarters tending to cuts and scrapes. What better use of his time than to send him after the cure?"

"He's thirteen years old," Tarik says. "And clearly Theorian. He wouldn't stand a chance in Pelusia by himself. They're surely on alert for any citizen of ours coming and going from their boundaries."

"Perhaps we can use their arrogance against them." Truth told, I continue to push and offer help because this is the most the Falcon King has deigned to speak to me since he called off our engagement. I've missed parrying with him. And I can see that my arguments are forcing him to reconsider his position. "If you're worried for his safety, send Sethos with him. Sethos knows how to find Bayla. She'll Cloak them."

Sethos crosses his arms. "That could actually work. If we're disguised, we'd have run of the kingdom, and I'm nothing if not thorough. What say you, Cy?"

Cy keeps his gaze leveled at Tarik. "I'm fourteen now," he says, a bit perturbed, "and we need that cure."

Olna sighs heavily, drawing our attention to her. "But you're forgetting that even if you have a cure, the Strays aren't likely to take it."

"We'll force them to," Tarik says. "After we take back the palace."

I nod. "It's the only way."

"It's settled, then," Sethos says, slapping me on the back. I clench my teeth; the boy prince doesn't know his own strength sometimes. "We leave at dawn."

Tulle steps forward again, gently reaching for Sethos's hand. I wonder if hers are hot to the touch, after her fiery display. Even if they are, I know Sethos would never draw back from her. He's both too masculine and too smitten to ever do that.

"If we're dividing up, as it were, I think we would do well to send Rashidi to Hemut," Tulle says. "I think my father's adviser, Lady Gita, would listen to him."

"Lady Gita?" Sethos says, incredulous. "She'd sooner gut him with that icicle of hers than listen to him now that I've stolen you away!"

But Tulle shakes her head. "I'll send him with a message. She'll listen to him, I swear it."

"What message would Rashidi tell her?" Tarik says, the tension from his face abated. I try to ignore the envy stabbing between my ribs, making it difficult to breathe. It was not so long ago that he treated me with such gentleness.

"She has always respected Rashidi," Tulle says, "and she's looked after me since my mother died. If there is a way she can help, she will."

"And if she doesn't?" Tarik says. "I cannot have my closest adviser run through with an icicle."

"It is my duty to try," Rashidi interjects. "I have served Theoria all my life. I won't abandon that service now."

Tarik rubs a hand down his face. "And what am I to do while you're away? Twiddle my thumbs and hope for the best?"

"You're to trust your most loyal ensemble of servants," Rashidi says gently. "And let them serve you. Keep yourself abreast of kingdom news."

"I serve the people, the same as you do, Rashidi," Tarik says. But his face is complacent. He will stay behind.

And so will I.

30

TARIK

IT HAS BEEN ONLY A DAY SINCE TARIK SAW THE remainder of his loyal staff off to their respective missions and he is almost driven mad by the silence as the light of morning breaks into his tent. His hope for Tulle's success, his worry for Cy and Sethos, his fear for Rashidi's life—all of them have kept him awake this night.

That, and the fact that he is now alone with Sepora with few distractions to keep him occupied. Before, he would take turns consulting with Rashidi, quarreling with Sethos, and watching along as Cy tended to the few injuries and illnesses sustained by the residents of the Baseborn Quarters. Before, he could forget that Sepora labored along with the descendants of her people, learning to weave baskets and blankets, and sew tents. If he were sensible, he would keep his distance from her. He would let her labor in the day, and he would find something else to do.

But pride of the pyramids, his sense seems to vanish each time he interacts with her. It seemed a good idea, the best idea, in fact, to renounce their engagement. After all, she had kept vital secrets from him, as it were. Not only that, but she dallied in Pelusia while he risked his brother to find her.

Idiot, he tells himself. She stayed behind in Pelusia to find the cure for the Quiet Plague. She admitted only a night ago, when she'd confessed that Pelusia had harbored a cure for it. He remembered that she almost told him so the evening Sethos brought her back to Theoria. She'd been on the verge of saying it, he is sure of it. She'd shown a loyalty to the people of Theoria in doing it. If anything, he owes her an apology for assuming the worst.

If anything, he must give credit where credit is due.

Does it mean something that she showed loyalty even at risk to her person? Of course it does. Does it mean he made the wrong decision in calling off their engagement? He's not sure. He does love her yet, but trusting her seems impossible, given how deceptive she can be. How deceptive she *has* been. And isn't trust more important in a royal marriage than love? That's what his father would say. It's what Rashidi would say.

But what do I say?

All he knows is that he must steer clear of her, or the tension between them will drive him mad. If she's upset about his calling off their engagement, she hasn't said as much, not even to Sethos. Yet her own words betray her at times, even when her body language speaks differently. What does that mean? Is she as indifferent as she acts?

He shakes his head at the mess of it all. He simply must occupy his time somehow. He's been longing to go into Anyar and see for himself what has occurred. Now that his obstacles—Sethos and Rashidi—are gone, he will do just that.

He springs from the cot and runs a hand through his hair. He'll pack a satchel with food and water and make a day of it. He'll scout for Sed of the Parani and finally make his acquaintance, and then he'll visit Cantor at the Bazaar. He'll inspect the state of his kingdom firsthand. Maybe that will help him to solve the problem of how to take it back. Too, it will take him all day and into the night to return, and by then Sepora will have retired to her tent—which is, unfortunately, right next to his. There will be no reasonable need to seek out her company, though. No need to bother her after her long day of work.

At least, he hopes not.

Olna will not like it, he knows, for it's a dangerous endeavor for anyone to venture into the city, especially since they have not truly determined how many Strays there are roaming about the place. But Olna is not the Falcon King. It is not Olna's responsibility to help the innocent citizens of Theoria. And so Olna does not have a say in the matter. Besides, Cantor had said that some of the Strays are harmless. Some are given to tendencies of quiet madness, while others lean toward violence. But how many are afflicted with violence? The reports cannot confirm anything with certainty, which is why he must go himself. He is not helpless, either, of course. In past years, Sethos needed someone to practice with at home before he'd moved to the Lyceum, and Tarik had been his partner more times than not. While not a Majai, Tarik can certainly defend himself. Too, he has Patra for protection.

Tarik glances at his giant cat sleeping in the dirt next to his cot. "Patra," he says. She opens her eyes, lifting only her head to peer up at him. He can tell she's gauging whether to get up. "Let's go to the Bazaar." She well knows the word Bazaar and that it means an outing for her. Slowly she picks herself up from the ground and stretches enormously, yawning wide enough to encompass his whole head. Though she's adjusted well to the new scents and people and surroundings in the Baseborn Quarters, he senses a restlessness in her that sometimes goes along with too much time spent lounging around the palace. She hasn't been exercised in quite some time; today will be good for her, too.

He collects his things and opens the tent flap—and comes face-to-face with Sepora.

Well, not exactly face-to-face. She was passing by right at that moment, her hair pulled up into an unkempt bun and carrying a satchel of her own. He doesn't recall her ever carrying a satchel to report to her duties before.

Curious.

"Oh," she says, stopping abruptly. She licks her lips and toes the dirt in front of her, not meeting his eyes. She is, of course, hoping that he won't ask her any questions.

She'll be sadly disappointed.

"I was under the impression food was brought to you each day," he says, making a point to nod at the stringed bag thrown over her shoulder. Of course, he doesn't really know what's in the satchel, but his guess must have been close because she scowls.

"What are *you* doing?" she says, eyeing his own load.

"I asked first."

"Not directly."

"I'm asking now."

A huff, followed by the crossing of her arms. "Your interest in my affairs ended the day you called off our engagement."

She has him there. She's not really a citizen of Theoria, so he is not by any means her king. Still, his *actual* interest in her didn't end that day, merely his *official* interest did. Which means he will not be put off.

"Where are you going?" he says, ignoring her fury at his persistence.

"I said—"

"Let me be clear. You are not to leave the Baseborn Quarters. I'm not your king, but I am still king over the Great Council. If I request it, Olna will have you bound and stationed in your tent until my return."

"Return from where?"

How is he to answer without sounding hypocritical? Telling her it's not her concern would not be fair. Not when he just made such an outrageous threat. "I have business in Anyar."

"Just as I have business at the palace."

At this, his pulse quickens. "No." The palace is overrun with Strays and people disloyal to the throne. It is the last place any of them need to be until they have the means to retake it.

She laughs. The sound is bitter and full of mocking. "By the time you get to Olna, I will be gone."

He steps toward her, a bit of fear crawling over his skin. She really means to leave. And he really has no way to stop her, unless he intends to throw her over his shoulder and fight her all the way to Olna. She must realize what he's considering, because she says, "If you touch me, I'll fight you to the death."

Blast, but the determination in her voice rings true. What's more, she actually seems like she *wants* to fight him. Which is something he'll never do. "What business do you have at the palace? At least tell me that."

She studies him for a moment, her stature relaxing a bit. "I'm going to get Nuna."

Oh. Of course. That would be the one interest she has left at the palace. That would be the one interest she has at all, in fact. She has lost her father, her mother has betrayed her, and her betrothed has shunned her. She has no place in Theoria anymore and if she returns to Serubel she will be subject to her mother's rule—and her plans to marry her off to a perfect stranger.

Tarik is not immune to her losses, not nearly as much as he lets on. But in the wake of her deception, he must abandon his responsibility toward her. Still, he can't shake the unease he feels at the idea of her returning to the palace alone. And can he blame her for wanting to go? Would he not have already gone after Patra? He glances at the cat beside him. There is no doubt in his mind that he would. He sighs. This is going to be a long day indeed.

"The palace is too dangerous to navigate right now," he says. "Come to Anyar with me. We'll ask after Nuna there."

"How would anyone there know about Nuna?" She tucks a wisp of hair behind her ear as she reasons on his offer. The act is so achingly familiar to him that he has to look away.

"Palace gossip is the most valuable gossip in Anyar. Word spreads much like a sandstorm when it comes to the king and the goings-on of the palace," he offers.

She considers for what seems like an eternity. Finally, she says, "I'm ready when you are."

SED IS NOT AT THE BASE OF THE HALF BRIDGE WHEN they arrive. In fact, there are no Parani at the Half Bridge, which is highly unusual given the reports that the Strays have been executing people and disposing of them here, to be swept away by the River Nefari—surely the Parani would not waste such an opportunity to feast.

"What do you make of it?" Tarik says as they climb the hill back to the top.

"I'm not sure. There is one other place we can check. It's where he prefers to meet privately when speaking with Master Saen and me."

Tarik still cannot comprehend the idea of speaking to a Parani. But if Master Saen can use her Lingot abilities to do so, he can as well.

He allows Sepora to lead them farther north, around the big bend in the river. The water seems more shallow than usual, and the current is not as strong as it should be. Too, there is a repugnant smell in the air. "Something isn't right," he says. "The River Nefari is deeper than this until the tributaries part south of the Half Bridge."

She nods. "I was just thinking the same thing."

Once they reach the agreed-upon meeting spot, they descend to the water's edge. Sepora picks up a sizable rock and throws it in the water with a giant plunk, followed by two more. "It's how we alert him to our presence," she explains.

Within minutes, a large male Parani appears before them. "That's Sed," Sepora whispers.

"I have been waiting for you," Sed communicates through a wail of frustration at Sepora. "What is the reason for your absence?"

Awestruck, Tarik relays this to her, but turns back to the Parani, his Lingot mind racing. The nuances in the pitch of his voice are key, he knows. He must match his tone to Sed's, or the communication will be faulty at best. Tarik clears his throat. "I'm Tarik, a friend of Sepora's and a servant of the Falcon King." It feels odd, to speak without words.

Sed beats his chest with a closed fist. "The Falcon King has betrayed our kind. Why should we speak to him at all?"

"The Falcon King himself has been betrayed. Tell me all that has happened. I will try to help."

Sed glances from Sepora to Tarik. Finally he says, "Theorians hunt us down like common fish. They run spears through many young ones and old ones, the weak who cannot fend for themselves, the slow who cannot escape."

"This is not the king's doing," Tarik says. "His people have turned on him as well."

At this, Sed shrugs. "It is not my concern whether the king is unwilling or unable to stop it. It only matters that it's happening. Our pact has been broken either way. How can we trust any help the king offers now?"

Tarik takes a moment to bring Sepora abreast of the conversation. Distraught, she removes her sandals and wades into the water to where Sed has stationed himself. "Tell him that the king has plans to retake his kingdom. That all is not lost." Sed watches her closely, then looks to Tarik for the translation.

Tarik passes Sepora's request along. Sed answers immediately. "You are a brave female, and I admire you. But your loyalties lie with an incompetent king whose citizens disregard our kind. Things are no longer under my control. You are not safe to be in the water. You must leave now. I cannot protect you."

With this, he glances to his right, and as Tarik follows his gaze, the hairs on the back of his neck stand at attention. Just upstream, the calm waters of the Nefari are disturbed into a frenzied commotion. He has seen this before; it's what the water looks like when Parani swarm just below the surface, racing toward their next meal.

"Get out of the water, Sepora! Hurry!"

He flings himself at her as the water with a life of its own moves closer to them. Grabbing her arm, he jerks her out of the river and to the shore, both of them soaking with the force of his splash. Just as they reach the dry sand, a webbed hand snatches at her ankle, gripping it solidly and hauling her back to the water's edge.

With everything in him, Tarik pulls her from its grasp. The Parani snaps its teeth once, twice, hissing as it retreats back into the water. Tarik wastes no time in dragging Sepora up the hill and to safety.

They are both panting when they reach the top.

"What happened?" Sepora says, gasping for breath.

"Sed no longer leads the Parani. They kill upon sight. We cannot rely on them as allies." It's a shortened version of what Sed communicated, but it will have to suffice until his breath doesn't escape him with every word. He takes Sepora's hand, pulling her away from the Nefari and toward the Bazaar. He can't take the chance that the Parani can somehow traverse land and reach them again.

Halfway to the Bazaar, they decide to break their fast. As he chews on his dried meat and fruit, Tarik mulls over their close call at the river. Of course the Strays have broken the treaty with the Parani. They have broken peace with every law of the land. Their minds outside of reason and sense, they obviously see no need for peace and order. It is not something Tarik wanted to see. Perhaps he'd imagined an isolated chaos in the palace, or a handful of Strays running amok in the Bazaar. Things, situations, that could be contained. But the fingers of this new madness are far reaching. If Cy fails to secure the remedy for the Quiet Plague, all could be truly lost.

"Cy will succeed," Sepora says quietly. He's startled that she can read him so easily at times. He must be more mindful of his expressions. Some of his thoughts are not meant for her knowing eyes.

Especially his thoughts of her.

31

SEPORA

THE AFTERNOON SUN BEATS DOWN UPON US; walking is much slower than taking a chariot around the kingdom and we move at a treacherous pace in the heat. I don't think either of us expected it to take this long; we reach the Bazaar by nightfall, but only just.

Cantor's booth is closed in the front, but candlelight emanates from the back of his tent. Tarik calls out to him and when he finally peers out of the tent flaps, he frantically gestures for us to come inside.

"Tarik! Sepora!" Cantor says, eyes wide. "It is not safe for you here at night. What if you are recognized? Servants of the king do not fare well during these times."

Not for the first time, I think of Anku and Cara back at the palace. Are they safe? Did they escape? Do they think I've abandoned them?

And what of Nuna? If citizens themselves aren't safe, what will they do to the future queen's Serpen? Only those in the room at the time know of Tarik's renouncement of our engagement. How better for the Strays to punish their king than by punishing his queen?

Tarik places his hand at the small of my back, ushering me to the inner rooms of the tent as we follow Cantor's lead. I swallow down the panic. I have to get to the palace. The people aren't safe. The Parani aren't safe. Nuna is not safe.

"The Strays have spies everywhere," Cantor is saying.

"So does the king," Tarik replies, sitting on the carpeted floor across from his friend.

Cantor nods, grasping Tarik's meaning. "How can I be of service?"

"How do the palace servants fare?" I blurt. "What of the princess's Serpen?"

Cantor purses his lips. "Most of the palace servants are still intact, Mistress Sepora. They are put to work by the Strays who reside there; that is their only saving grace, that they are useful. As for Princess Magar's Serpen . . . I'd hoped when the royals made their escape she had taken it with her."

This brings me a semblance of comfort. Perhaps Anku and Cara are among those still deemed useful to the Strays. And hopefully, if they are, they're of a mind to take care of Nuna. Perhaps even hide her.

I feel guilty, hoping for my servants' safety for the sake of Nuna. Of course it's not all for the sake of Nuna, but it encompasses a great deal of my concern. "Have you . . . You haven't seen any Defender Serpen scales being sold at the Bazaar?"

Cantor regards me solemnly. "I have not, Mistress."

Tarik gives me a reassuring look. "They certainly would have made it to the Bazaar. Magar's own Serpen's scales would be priceless."

I nod, grateful for that consolation. Still, I have the need to see for myself. Nuna is all I have left. But I can wait. At least until I'm not under Tarik's close scrutiny.

"There are still a large number of citizens loyal to the king," Cantor says. "Not all have gone mad, you see. But they have not heard from His Highness for a long time. Some fear him dead."

"He is well and alive, Cantor," Tarik says. "How can we reassure the people of that? And that he needs their support now more than ever?"

"It will have to be done quietly. The Strays do not hold trials for those loyal to the throne. They exercise immediate execution. They are too wild to do anything with any kind of civility."

"What of the Majai? How many of their forces have gone Stray?"

"The Majai have been spread throughout the city. They await the king's command. Some have turned, but most remain intact. That is what I hear, anyway."

"I need to get word to them, Cantor. I—er, the king needs them to assemble soon."

Cantor's gaze vacillates between me and Tarik. "Before we go further, there is something I must tell you both."

A thick anticipation fills the air while Cantor fidgets the hem of his shendyt. "You see," he says, sucking in a breath, "I know who you are. I'm a Lingot myself, Highness. I've known all along."

I feel Tarik stiffen at my side. "Why are you just now telling me this?" he says, frustration coloring his tone. "Why did you not make yourself known sooner?"

"Forgive me, Highness. But I have seen you grow from a young boy to a fine man and a great king. The lie has been weighing upon me for years as you visited my booth, but I could not bear to tell you. I only tell you now because you do not know whom to trust, and if you were to find out from another source that I knew your identity, you would not trust me any longer."

Tarik shakes his head. "I cannot believe that you evaded me all this time. How did you do it?"

"I was careful, Highness. The way only a Lingot knows how to be."

At this Tarik flashes me a look, and I flush a little. I'm not a Lingot, but evading the Falcon King seems to be a special gift of mine and we both know it. Even now, I plot against his wishes without him knowing.

"I consider you a friend, Cantor. And right now, I need all the friends I can gather."

Cantor nods. "I'll discreetly spread the word. For me to do so will take at least a week, as the Majai are spread far apart for safety. You should know that the Serubelans and Stray Majai guard the palace. It will not be easy to seize it from them."

Tarik does not acknowledge this warning. I can tell he is lost in thought but his expression has taken on that indifference, the wall he uses so well. "I will send word to you in a week's time regarding our plans," he says absently. "Until then, I await news from many sources. I can't make a decision until I hear from them." Tarik stands, pulling me up with him. "Sepora and I must go. Our friends in hiding will be expecting us back soon."

Cantor stands, too, shaking his head. "You cannot leave, Highness. It's too dangerous. The Strays adore the nighttime. They come out and wreak havoc until morning. They truly are mad—and they seem to feed off of each other, roaming about in pairs or even crowds. You must stay with me. I have room for the two of you."

I'm relieved at Cantor's suggestion. As exhausted as I am, walking to the palace from the Bazaar is a much better option than walking back from the Baseborn Quarters. With any luck, I can fly Nuna back before morning. "I am weary," I tell Tarik, trying to sound as pitiful as possible. "And it is a long way back."

Tarik regards me suspiciously. My words are mostly true, but I know he detects deceit in them. Or perhaps he just mistrusts everything I say now on principle. Probably both. "I suppose we could stay until morning breaks," Tarik says, still looking at me, "but we need to leave at first light."

I say nothing. It would be foolish to agree; Tarik is already wary of me and at first light, I hope to be high above the desert, flying Nuna back to the Baseborn Quarters. Saying nothing is what is best for my agenda.

But as Cantor leads us into a separate room of the tent, Tarik's scowl suggests that to him, saying nothing was worse than lying.

32

TARIK

WHEN CANTOR SAID HE HAD ROOM FOR THE two of them, he failed to mention that he just *barely* had room. What he had was a small but soft rug on the floor of a tiny compartment in his tent. A compartment so tiny that the rug pulled up at the edges of the tent, not quite small enough to lie flat against the floor.

Sepora lies on her side facing the canvas wall, her back turned to him. Even so, there is barely a breath of space between them on the pallet. He will have to stay up the entire night to ensure that he doesn't touch her.

And to ensure that she doesn't wake up in his arms in the morning.

Even now, the full curves of her figure call to him, so much so that he must keep his fists balled at his side in order not to let them wander. It is not difficult to recall how soft she is, how well her body fits against his. How is he supposed to sleep with her so very close?

He tries not to give thought to what it would be like to sleep next to her as her husband, to enfold her in his embrace, to fall asleep each and every night with the scent of her intoxicating him. What would it be like to wake up next to her? To watch her open those silver eyes for the first time to the sunlight of a new day? It's all too easy to imagine, and even more so to pretend it was still going to happen one day.

No, better to keep awake and think of kingdom matters than this kind of cruel fantasy, which only breeds disappointment and even anger.

Still, his eyes feel heavy, weighted down by exhaustion. Perhaps he should just sleep, and let things fall as they will. She is tense and awake anyway, he can tell. If she keeps awake, then she'll be the one to ensure they don't find themselves entangled in the morning.

"Are you asleep yet?" Sepora whispers so faintly he almost doesn't hear it.

"Why do you keep asking me that?" It is the third time in an hour she's inquired about it. Or at least, he thinks it's only been an hour. He has no idea of how late it is. All he knows is how fatigued he is, even with desire singing through him. "Are you worried I'll fall asleep and smother you?"

"Yes."

"Liar."

She turns over so swiftly that it startles him fully awake. Anger flashes on her face as she narrows her eyes at him. "You're the liar."

Something she truly believes. "How's that exactly?" he says, incredulous.

"You said you loved me. You said you wanted marriage. Yet, the first mistake I make, and you call off the entire thing."

This is unexpected. He swiftly props himself up on his elbow, glaring down at her. "Be serious. You, Princess, are the liar. You kept the other Forgers hidden from me, even when I asked if you had any other secrets."

Her lips form a straight line. She's going to refute it, he can tell, but she can save her breath.

He continues, "Not to mention that you weren't even being

guarded in Pelusia. You didn't have a care or regard for my feelings after you disappeared. The entire time I searched for you, worried about you, and you could have left at any time."

"Surely *you* jest. You think with the plans my mother had for me that I really could have left of my own accord? Things were smooth as long as I was willing. If that changed, I'd have been locked away tightly, you can be assured."

He blinks. He had not thought of it that way. His expression must belie his feelings, because she continues without a response from him.

"How can *I* trust *you*? You're so confusing all the time! You want so much to believe in my disloyalty that you refuse to seek me out for the truth. How dare you!" By this time she is all but in his face, her breath pushing against his lips.

And it is more than he can take.

She doesn't even fight the kiss; she simply melds to him there on the pallet, fusing her body against his. She does fight *with* the kiss, however, taking more than she gives, kissing him with a sort of anger he's never experienced before. Nonetheless, she's kissing him, and he'll not complain about her motivations at the moment.

Finally, finally, his hands traverse her body, memorizing and appreciating each curve, the feel of her heated skin beneath his touch. He moves to lie over her, leaning part of his weight on her and against her moan, he traces his lips from her mouth down her jaw and then her neck, the scent of her devastating his senses and his sense.

Her hands lift to entwine in his hair while his mouth makes its way down the center of her, and to her stomach. She arches against him then, and he realizes at once that his control is completely gone, the consequences of his actions a dim memory lurking in the shadows of his mind. Nothing else matters except Sepora, her breathless gasps, her racing heart, the beauty of her flushed cheeks glowing in the faint candlelight seeping into the room. Even so, he will take his time. He will cherish her the way he'd dreamed about so many times, slowly and thoroughly and meticulously. There will not be an inch of her that he hasn't touched. Not this night.

He lifts her hands from his hair to above her head, holding them in place with one hand while his other makes a trail down the length of her, grasping at the curve of her thigh. Again he captures her mouth with his, kissing her with renewed purpose. She seems to sense it immediately, and embrace it, moving her lips on his with a need to match his own.

His senses come crashing back to him in a rush when loud, angry voices erupt outside the tent. Sepora's eyes are now open and alert, and he releases her immediately. Patra's low rumble of warning sweeps into their small compartment, and Tarik pulls Sepora to her feet. He motions for her to stay back as he peeks out of the flap of their room, scanning the inner chamber of Cantor's tent. The outside entryway is pulled open, and Cantor stands there with crossed arms, nearly yelling at whoever has interrupted his evening. "My guests have already departed, and you've no right to enter my home," Cantor is saying, his voice resonating through the tent in warning.

"We demand to know who you keep here, old man," another voice says gruffly. He's obviously a Stray; there's a wildness to his voice, a feral tone that suggests he'll not be reasoned with. "It is rumored the high servant of the king has visited you this night."

Patra is poised behind Cantor, her hair standing up at the nape of her neck. She senses danger in the man speaking to Cantor, and she's ready to pounce. This is not good. "Patra, come," Tarik whispers.

Reluctantly, his cat does as she's told.

Sepora makes room for her as she saunters into the compartment and scratches behind her ear, for Patra nearly seems to pout at being called off.

Tarik turns to Sepora. "We need to leave. Cantor cannot hold them off for long. They'll have recognized Patra."

Sepora glances about the room and points at the bottom of the tent. "We'll have to crawl out. Hopefully, they don't have us surrounded."

"If they do, I'll loose Patra on them. Hurry, before they come inside to collect us." But he is already lifting the canvas and inspecting the outside area around him. Satisfied that there is no one, he slides out on his belly, and motions for Sepora to follow.

Patra's exit is less graceful, her body pulling up one of the stakes holding down the tent. But at least they are all out safely. "We'll have to make a run for it," Tarik says. "Are you up to it?"

Sepora nods. In the moonlight, he sees that her lips are still swollen from their kisses. It had been a momentary lapse of judgment on his part, to initiate such an intimacy between them. He resolves to apologize for it later, though. Now, they must get out of Anyar. The moon is so bright that they need not bring attention to themselves by carrying torches, or stealing dying spectorium from one of the hanging lamps outside some of the booths in the Bazaar.

Behind them, Cantor bellows, "You see? There is no one here."

"Hurry!" Tarik whispers, and they take off running into the night, Patra trotting closely behind them. Every now and then, she emits a low growl, but he is unable to see what she sees in the darkness. All he knows is that coming to Anyar was not a good idea and bringing Sepora was an even worse one.

Against his will, he admits his fear for her safety is still very real. His anger at her deception does not, and will never, negate his feelings for her. But feelings have no place in the way he rules. He realizes that now more than ever.

As the Baseborn Quarters come into view, Tarik stops, pulling Sepora with him. "We need to speak about what happened in the tent," he says softly.

Sepora glances down at the sand, biting her lip. "Go on."

"That must never happen again. We are not to be wed. And I would have taken things too far, if given the chance."

"Then why kiss me in the first place?" Her voice is shaky, and even in the moonlight he can see tears filling her eyes, threatening to spill over onto her cheeks. He berates himself for hurting her. She did nothing wrong at Cantor's. It was all his own doing.

"It was a mistake. A momentary lapse in judgment. I assure you, it won't happen again." The words come out differently than he intended, sounding harsh instead of apologetic. The only person he wishes to be harsh with is himself.

But within two blinks, Sepora's expression hardens. "Keep away from me, Highness. Touch me again, and I'll murder you in your sleep." She turns toward the Baseborn Quarters, walking at a pace he's too exhausted to keep up with.

It is better this way, he tells himself. *It is better that she hates me rather than having false hope of reuniting.*

But more and more, his excuses for keeping her at bay seem born out of sheer stubbornness rather than reason.

33

SEPORA

THE DAY TULLE RETURNS FROM WACHUK, I AM collecting water at the edge of the River Nefari, one hand on my dagger, the other holding the skin flask underneath the surface. Patra stands guard behind me, in case of a Parani attack. The sky ahead of me looks as though a storm is rolling through. But storms in Theoria do not exist.

And this storm is red in color, a stark contrast against the blue sky.

Can it be possible? But as the red horizon grows bigger in size, I know for certain that it is.

Tulle has brought back with her a fleet of Scaldlings.

They pass over me quickly, heading toward the Baseborn Quarters behind me. I've never seen a live Scaldling before—they are extinct in Serubel, destroyed when their trainers could no longer control them. They are much larger than even Defender Serpens, and red as blood. Their three sets of wings have sharp, sicklelike claws at the tips, which almost appear as hands with long nails. They are awe-inspiring, to be sure, but what's more, they are not as wild as my tutor, Aldon, would have me believe. Perhaps the Serubelan trainers could not subdue them, but the warrior women who ride these fearsome Serpens command their beasts with authority, guiding them through the air as though they were an extension of themselves. I count at least thirty of them, their bodies casting glorious shadows on the ground where I stand.

Thirty Scaldlings, with three riders on the back of each. Tulle is apparently a very good negotiator.

I sheathe my dagger and break into a run to get back to the quarters; I don't want to miss a thing. Especially Tarik's face when he beholds what a Scaldling actually looks like, and what an asset Tulle has brought him from Wachuk.

THE GREAT COUNCIL CONVENES JUST A SHORT HOUR later. Tulle and Queen Emula take the speaking circle, along with Tarik, to translate what the Wachuk warrior queen says.

Emula is fierce, every bit a warrior queen. She is unnervingly beautiful, her skin almost as black as onyx, and she has many scars on her arms and legs, which are rippled with muscles. Two spears are strapped to her back, a sword at her side, and two throwing daggers are laced at her calves. I wonder at how she got the scars, as Wachuk is a peaceable nation, and why she would have need for so many weapons—aside from the fact that she may have come here to help us overtake the palace.

I remember then that Aldon said the Wachuk women are great hunters, choosing the meat of carnivores because of their belief that what they consume becomes a part of them. I'm given to share their beliefs; Queen Emula looks like someone who could take on a Theorian cat and walk away with its hide, never mind the gashes and bites she would endure in the taking of it.

Beside Emula is another warrior woman, shorter than Emula and strikingly blond and pale like a Serubelan. I'm reminded about what my tutor Aldon taught me about Wachuk: The citizens are a melting pot of the fiercest females of all the kingdoms, women who found dislike in their lots in life and abandoned them altogether in favor of living peacefully among each other in the forest. Aldon's words were heavy with disapproval whenever he spoke of them, and now I know why; he was afraid of them. Afraid of anyone who would dare to seek out something bigger than perhaps Serubel or Theoria or Hemut. Afraid of any woman who dared to reject men for leaders.

Even Sethos, I think, is afraid of them. He once told me they were beastly creatures who treated their men like whelps, forcing them to raise the children and do the cooking while the women warriors hunted for food and sport. I'd called him on his hypocrisy, and he'd blundered something incoherent but most assuredly ignorant, for he'd refused to meet my eyes when he'd said it.

My entire life, it seems, the men in charge of me had taught me half-truths and faulty impressions. I cannot help but feel ashamed at my ignorance of Wachuk. And I'm determined to rectify that very soon. These women are to be admired for their courage. Not feared for their values.

Tulle is the first to speak, addressing Olna directly. "This is Queen Emula of Wachuk. She has heard our request for assistance, and has pledged thirty-five Scaldlings and three hundred warriors. The rest of them travel here by foot and will arrive in a matter of days."

Olna's mouth falls slightly ajar. "Did she say what she would like in return?"

At this, Tulle hesitates. "She wants nothing in return. She is convinced that I am the reincarnation of their Ember Goddess. She will do as I ask." At this, Tulle blushes. I wonder what it is like to be considered a goddess. Of course they would worship Tulle as their deity; they worship the element of fire, because of its purifying power, and Tulle creates that with her bare hands. We'd hoped she would make an impression on them, but this is more than we could have ever imagined.

"I've told her many times that she is mistaken, that I'm not to be worshipped. She insists that I would not know that I am the Ember Goddess, because I was born to the ice kingdom where they teach subservience to men. That my duty . . . my *purpose* there . . . is to melt Hemut for not respecting the power of a woman."

That's certainly an idea, I think bitterly. The males of Hemut are even more overbearing than the males of Serubel. In Hemut, a woman must not even touch a weapon. At least in Serubel, we are trained to fight and defend ourselves and if necessary, our land. Too, the idea is fetching because if Hemut refuses to make peace with Theoria, we could simply send Tulle, Emula, and her army of Scaldlings there as retribution. Why not head off an attack from that nation before it begins?

What has gotten into me? Now I'm thinking as Rashidi or Commander Morg. I must not lose my respect for human life. I must remember that eventually, whether there is war or negotiation, peace must be made again between all the kingdoms. Peace has a better chance of prevailing if *none* of the kingdoms suffer the bitterness of an overwhelming loss.

Tarik speaks to Emula with a series of clicks and chirps and grunts. Aldon once told me that it is a primitive language, the most inferior of all the five kingdoms. When I'd repeated this to Tarik, the Falcon King had laughed. He explained to me that to the Wachuk, the same sound could mean many different things depending on the emotion put into communicating it, that almost like a Lingot perceives lies, the Wachuk are able to see through words and home in on the feelings behind them—which takes far more skill than learning any of the other languages. In fact, there is a section of the scroll vault in the Lyceum completely devoted to the language and its history, and it takes even a skilled Lingot years to master it because of the human feeling that must be put into it. Making sounds is one thing, Tarik says, but conveying how one feels without the convenience of words is quite another. He impressed upon me that long ago the Wachuk were the most proficient at all the languages of the five kingdoms, but willingly abandoned words for a more pure way of communicating. Words, to them, can be fraught with deception. "Saying the Wachuk language is inferior because the sounds are simple," Tarik had said, "is like saying the pyramids are easy to build, because their shape is simple."

When Tarik puts it like that, Aldon seems less and less a tutor, and more and more a teacher of prejudice. And no matter where I end up after this is all said and done, I have no room for prejudice.

Emula returns a response, her face solemn. I can hear gratitude in her voice.

Tarik addresses Olna. "I've thanked Emula for her generosity and willingness to help. She requests that her Scaldlings are watered and her women are fed and given a place to rest. She awaits Tulle's next request."

Olna nods to a man in the back of the chamber. He disappears outside, probably to do Emula's bidding. She returns her attention to Tarik. "It will be done immediately, as we speak. We've been making tents in preparation for a favorable response from Wachuk and should be able to accommodate her warriors. I know they are used to the shade of their forests. Please tell her she is an esteemed guest in the Baseborn Quarters, and that if she requires anything at all, we will be happy to oblige."

Tarik relays the message to Emula, who nods. She speaks again, and Tarik translates for us all. "She also requests that fires be built for them. They do not abandon their rituals even while traveling. They've brought wood with them to burn. She invites us to join them, if we please."

"We do not worship elements here. Still, she is welcome to build her fires on the far south side of the quarters," Olna says. "Those of us who wish may join them. I will not speak on behalf of the people in that regard."

"My only concern is that the fires may be seen from Anyar," Tarik says. "The Strays will wonder what is amiss."

Olna laughs softly. "With respect, I think the Strays will get more than they bargained for if they wish to intrude on us at this point."

Tarik nods. "So be it."

"We will adjourn this meeting, then, to attend to our guests if there is nothing else—"

"There is something else," a voice calls from the back of the chamber.

I had not noticed that Rashidi had slipped in. From the look on his face, he does not bear good news from Hemut. Not that Rashidi smiles excessively all the time, but when he is especially annoyed, his mouth twitches reflexively when he wishes to appear neutral. Mouth atwitch, he strides with his long staff to the center of the speaking circle. "Please give my extreme gratitude and respect to Queen Emula," Rashidi tells Tarik. "It is an honor to have her here."

Tarik relays Rashidi's sentiments to the queen, who simply nods. I wonder what the old man really thinks of the queen. I wonder from where Sethos extracted his prejudices. Maybe it wasn't Rashidi. After all, Tarik carries no such disregard.

"What have you to report to us, friend?" Tarik says, relief at his adviser's return marked on his face.

"I have secured the support of Hemut," Rashidi announces, but there is no pride nor happiness in his tone.

Tarik must sense this as well, because he says, "What do they want?"

Rashidi looks pointedly at Tulle.

Oh no.

"King Ankor demands the return of his daughter immediately."

Tulle's sharp intake of breath draws Tarik's attention. "Under the circumstances of your departure, this was not unexpected, Princess. But if you are an outcast in your own kingdom, why would he want you back all the same?"

"Because I demonstrated my powers when I escaped. He had no idea of my ability to create fire. No doubt he sees me as an asset now."

Tarik frowns. "You do not have to go. We can manage without Hemut. We can even manage against it, if we must." But there is an uncertainty in Tarik's voice I do not care for. He doesn't believe we can manage. And if he doesn't believe it, I don't.

Rashidi nods. "If you do not return her, Hemut will attack. But I'm afraid that's not the extent of the king's requirements."

"What else?"

"Ankor requires that Prince Sethos weds Tulle, and that the pair reside in the Ice Palace with him."

Tarik's eyes widen. "Sethos will never agree to that."

No, he won't. He had told me of his experience traipsing about the ice kingdom in search of me. He'd said it was bitterly cold, devoid of sunshine, and a dismal, depressing place to be. Sethos will not consent to live there, I know it.

"I will speak to him," Tulle says. "Whether or not he weds me, I must return to Hemut—but not before my work here is done. I cannot have the blood of your kingdom on my hands. We will send word immediately that my father's terms will be met one way or the other. That should stave off an attack."

I'm beginning to like Tulle more and more. She is capable but gentle, determined but kind. And we share the same hope for peace.

I wonder what Sethos will do when he learns that she will return to her home with or without him. Probably a tantrum is in our near future. I only hope he takes Tulle's thoughts and feelings into consideration before acting out of temper.

"How soon can Ankor assemble his forces?" Tarik asks Rashidi. "If Sethos agrees to this . . . proposal?"

"As soon as we send him word of our compliance."

So then, we must wait for Sethos to return with Cy. I bite my lip. The room is silent. There is not one of us who thinks waiting is a good idea. Yet we need Hemut.

"The Strays must be stopped," Tarik counters. "We cannot wait for Sethos's return. I'll send word to Cantor to collect the Majai together. With our loyal Majai and Queen Emula's army, we should have no problem overtaking the Strays."

I step into the circle uninvited. "I wish to speak," I say, addressing Olna instead of Tarik. Olna still recognizes me as a princess of Serubel, even if Tarik does not want my opinion in his own kingdom's matters.

Olna nods to me.

"We must remember that the Strays are not evil, they are just ill," I say. "If we kill them, we will be killing citizens of Theoria. Capturing them and holding them until Cy returns would, in my opinion, be the wisest course."

"You and I share the same opinion," Tarik says. "Efforts will be made to subdue, not to kill. The Majai are trained in such ways. I'll make sure Queen Emula understands our purpose." He turns back to Olna. "Please send for your fastest messenger. It is time I took my kingdom back."

34

TARIK

IT TAKES THE BETTER PART OF A DAY TO SECURE and clear the palace once more.

More than seven hundred Strays and Serubelans were captured and imprisoned, transported, and guarded heavily at the Lyceum by loyal Majai and Wachuk warriors. The palace is in disarray, from crude and insulting paintings on the walls to spoiled food in each hallway, in addition to dried blood and the stench of death infused throughout. It will take a solid month to restore everything to its proper order, but Tarik is more than happy to take on the endeavor.

He finds his day chambers have been ransacked, scrolls torn to pieces and strewn about the floor, his desk overturned, and most of the sheers overlooking the balcony ripped down and trampled upon. His bedchamber fares no better. The mattress has been ripped to shreds, his sheets cut into strips and hung about the room, and his seating area burned on the stone it once stood upon. The ornate carvings of his bed, his father's bed, have been sliced through and ruined beyond repair. The latrine is full of excrement where the Strays had not bothered to use the running water meant for that purpose.

He wonders how Sepora's chambers fare and is certain they are no better. He'd sent word through Morg to allow her into the palace now that everything has settled down and it was cleared of all miscreants. She'd been angry that he ordered her to stay behind with Olna until the task had been completed, insisting her swordsmanship could help. But Tarik had seen the way she fought with Sethos in the courtyard below his balcony.

And she is certainly not ready to face a Stray Majai.

She'd already informed him that she would collect her things from her chambers and move herself to the Baseborn Quarters forthwith. He'd been at a loss for words at her decision, though he'd known it was only a matter of time until she decided what her own fate would be. He has tried to conjure up reasons for her to stay in the palace, particularly as his guest, but she would have none of it. She is no longer to wed him. She could not stay as an adviser to him, since he no longer trusts her judgment. Other than a guest of Theoria, as the misplaced princess of Serubel, he could not offer her an alternative. And she is set against "imposing on an offer made out of pity," she'd said.

How had she come to be so stubborn?

And of course, he cannot consider her stubbornness without first examining his own. Throughout the ordeal in the Baseborn Quarters, ever since her return to Theoria from Pelusia, she has acted time and time again on behalf of his citizens. When she openly pleaded that the Strays be treated and not killed, it had deeply moved him. His reasons for not taking her as his queen are becoming weaker and weaker. He senses that even Rashidi disapproves of his decision; the old man may not care for Sepora, but he carries a tone of admiration in his voice when he speaks of her nowadays. If Rashidi is convinced she would make a good queen, why should Tarik not be?

And—what if she will no longer have him anyway?

Perhaps that is what keeps his tongue silent. Perhaps that is why he does not reapproach her about the matter. He is afraid of rejection.

What could I say to make things right between us now? There is nothing, he thinks.

And pride of the pyramids, but where is she? She should have arrived by now. Surely she wouldn't move her things without the courtesy of an official farewell. Of course, she certainly is angry enough to—

The realization strikes him so hard it nearly steals his breath. Sepora is no doubt here.

And she no doubt went straight to the stables for Nuna.

35

SEPORA

I SINK TO MY KNEES BESIDE HER. SHE HAS BEEN GONE for some time now, as flies have gathered around her, maggots breed in her mouth, and the blood from where they skinned her of scales has dried and crisped in the Theorian heat. Spears poke out from everywhere. She suffered.

Not Nuna.

Not my Nuna.

There are a few dead men scattered about the stable where she's housed, men who were probably victims of her sharp teeth, if their gashes are any indication. I wish those men alive, so I could kill them all over again. After she'd shown her power, they obviously came at her in numbers. That is the only way to take a Defender down.

I bury my face in my hands and let out a scream. The tears come in an instant deluge that I can't stop even if I wanted to. But why should I not cry? Nuna deserves my tears, my anguish. She deserves it, because I abandoned her to this fate. Did she wonder why I did not come for her? Do Serpens think on that level? Was she hungry when she died? Thirsty?

It is good that I wonder those things, that I torture myself with them. That I suffer from not knowing, that I suffer at all, because she suffered. She died alone and without help.

There is so much loss within me. Father. Mother. My queenship. Tarik himself. And now Nuna. How much loss can people handle before they become Strays themselves? It is unbearable, this. It's unthinkable. I could handle all the rest. Tears at night, sorrow at my losses, but a show of strength during the day. It hasn't been easy, but it's gotten me by. Now I have no strength left to give.

Not Nuna.

"Sepora," Tarik says softly. I feel his hand on my shoulder. I'd told him to never touch me again. At the time, I had meant it. He's hurt me in so many ways. Humiliated me, betrayed me. But now, at this moment, I want to bury myself in his arms and let him comfort me. I want to use him, the way he used me that night in Cantor's tent. I want warmth and affection and something more than loss.

I look up at him, too weak in the knees to stand. "I should have come for her. But you were too blasted vigilant for me to leave Cantor's tent. This is your fault."

"Yes," he agrees, to my surprise, "it is my fault. Not yours."

I know what he is doing. He's trying to relieve me of the burden of guilt. And as much as I want to give it to him, as much as I truly want to blame him, I cannot. Nuna was my responsibility. I should have found a way. Tarik is not all-knowing. He is just a boy king. I could have come.

I should have come.

"There is a burial ground in the back of the palace for generations upon generations of royal cats," he says, crouching down on his haunches next to me. "We will see that she receives a proper Theorian burial and honors, if you wish it."

"She's not a Theorian cat," I say, even as I decide in my head that I'll allow it. Nuna deserves what she can get. What I can get for her.

"No. She's more fearsome that any Theorian cat. And she served a Serubelan princess. She deserves a proper farewell."

My bottom lip quivers as more tears slide down my face. "I should have come for her."

He doesn't answer, just scoops me up in his arms and carries me to the door of the stable. His strength is unimaginable. He carries me as the wind carries dust, or as the Serubelan breeze carries leaves from a vine. I don't have the energy, the will to fight against him. I don't have the desire. I lean my cheek upon his bare chest and cry into it. He brings me this way back to the palace, me sobbing like a small child, and him cooing words of comfort for my ears only. Many people come to aid him. Rashidi, Morg, servants.

But he nods them all away, carrying me through the palace as I cling to him and weep. I recognize where he is taking me and as we enter his bedchamber I suck in a breath at the state of it. Everything is strewn about as if a riot had happened here. Servants hurry about the room, cleaning up what they can. Tarik's enormous bed has been ruined, torn at the mattress with vulgar scenes carved into the once beautiful wood. The usual smell of lavender is replaced by a lingering stench of feces mixed with the familiar scent of a cleaning solution as servants work in the lavatory.

"Leave us, please," Tarik says loudly, and one by one the men and women stop what they are doing and leave the chamber. Tarik is still holding me when the last one shuts the door behind him.

"The Strays are nothing but beasts," I say.

"They are ill," he reminds me as he gently lays me upon the bed. He slides next to me, and pulls me to him, tucking my face back against his chest. "I want you to cry, Sepora. Cry until you've nothing left in you. Cry for all you've lost."

"I don't want to."

"For once in your life, don't fight me. You need to mourn your losses. Please, Sepora."

The gesture is so tender that the last bit of bitterness I have toward him is stamped out. I fold myself into his arms and give in to the grief. I cry mostly for Nuna, but I cry for other things, too. I cry for the loss of my kingdom, for the loss of my future with Tarik, for the loss of my trust for my mother. I even cry for the loss of my father, though not for his death, but for the way he chose to live his life. For causing all of this to happen in the first place.

I weep and sob and scream into the shelter of Tarik, and he holds me tightly, saying nothing at all. I'm aware of the last few moments before I fall asleep. Tarik must think I've already succumbed, because he kisses the top of my head and relaxes against me.

I slip into oblivion, completely spent.

WHEN I AWAKEN, I'M SURPRISED TO FIND THAT THE sun has not yet risen. There is a tray of breakfast food and drink beside me on the bed, with a note from Tarik:

Gather your strength and seek me out when you're ready.

I take the chalice of water and drink it dry, grabbing the chalice of juice as well and downing it just the same. I could use more, as the dehydration from hours of crying has set in, but I'm not ready to call for a servant. I'm not ready to face Tarik yet. Or anyone, for that matter. Almost everyone in the palace saw me broken and defeated yesterday. Those who didn't witness it for themselves will have heard about it by now. About the Serubelan princess who could not keep her composure the way royalty should.

I take a piece of bread from the tray and make my way to Tarik's grand balcony, intending to watch the sun rise. But as I pull aside a sheer shredded into thin strips, I nearly drop my bread. The balcony is sopping wet.

Because it is raining in Theoria.

PART FOUR

36

TARIK

WHEN SETHOS AND CY RETURN FROM PELUSIA, it is still raining. They enter Tarik's day chambers soaked through, and with another person in tow, a stranger to Tarik—and clearly Pelusian. She is much older than Rashidi; wrinkles crease her skin, which hangs from her bones like fleshly cloth. Her head of hair is solidly white, and she is skinny enough for Tarik to assume she has not eaten properly in a very long time.

Why is it that when I send Sethos for something, he always returns with an extra person?

Sethos greets his brother with, "The courtyard is flooded to my ankles. What's the meaning of this?" He shakes his head to relieve himself of the excess water the way Patra does when she's finished with a bath. "Rain is insufferable."

Tarik could not agree more. The first day, it was a novelty, something not seen in Theoria for centuries. Young and old alike went outside to experience the storm, reveling in the downpour and the absence of the sun, peering up at the lightning in wonder and awe.

Now that a week has passed, it's nothing more than a nuisance. His kingdom is not outfitted for days upon days of rain. The streets of the Bazaar are flooded, the courtyard is inaccessible, and the River Nefari continues to rise. As of this morning, it was reported to him that it is halfway up the hills of the bank. And, he has learned, Patra is afraid of the thunder.

"We are taking measures to drain the courtyard," Tarik says, "but my first priority is the Majai training yard. Cy, welcome back. Whom do I have the pleasure of welcoming into my chambers today?"

Cy grimaces. "I don't know if you'll have much pleasure in meeting her, but this is Esmelda. She is the best Healer in all of King Graylin's kingdom."

Tarik raises a brow. Sethos has really outdone himself this time. First a princess, now a Master Healer of an enemy kingdom. Perhaps he's more than just a mouth to feed after all. "Why would I not want to make her acquaintance? We need all the help we can attain."

"She created the Quiet Plague to begin with," Sethos spits, pulling up a chair for himself. He laces his hands behind his head. "So do keep your pleasure at a minimum."

Tarik levels his gaze at Esmelda. For what it's worth, she seems remorseful.

"You *created* the Quiet Plague?" he says, incredulous.

She nods. "It was a request of my king's, Highness."

"Whatever for?"

"I do not question my king, Highness." She folds her hands in front of her with finality. "But I suspected it was for the demise of Theoria."

At this, Cy clears his throat and pulls out the chair next to Sethos, gesturing for Esmelda to sit. Sethos rolls his eyes. Esmelda shakes like a chariot with one wheel as she lowers herself into the seat. "Thank you, young Cy."

"You see, Esmelda was tasked with creating a disease only Theorians could catch," Cy explains. "One day, King Graylin and

Queen Hanlyn came to her and asked her if such a thing were possible, bringing with them Theorians whom they'd captured in the Dismals. She performed her tests on them and found a method to isolate only Theorians for the plague."

Tarik feels his gut twisting. Hanlyn and Graylin have been planning this for longer than he expected. "That's why my father was the first to die," he says, his voice tight. "As king, he was the obvious choice. How did they infiltrate the palace?" Many emotions threaten to surface, but Tarik stamps them down as best he can. This woman is essentially his father's murderer. He cannot come unraveled now. He simply cannot, not when Sepora herself is so delicately mourning the loss of Nuna. She needs him. He has failed her too many times to fail her now.

Too, he must be strong as a king and as a son.

Esmelda shakes her head. "I do not know the details, Your Majesty. And I'm sorry to have been involved in your father's death."

The truth.

But it is not good enough. Too many of his people have suffered and even perished because of this wisp of a woman. "Why did you bring her here?" he barks at Sethos, letting a bit of his ire slip. He must do better. "Why would we want such a woman among us?"

"She has the cure," Sethos drawls, unconcerned with his brother's anger. "As we were in a bit of a hurry, Cy couldn't learn the steps quickly enough. So we brought her with us as a consolation prize. Put her to work, put her to death. I couldn't care less."

"She's really quite brilliant," Cy says before catching himself. "I mean, for being a murderer and all."

Esmelda doesn't deny the accusations. She also does not seem concerned for her own well-being—when Sethos mentioned putting her to death, her expression remained solemn. She has probably seen much in her many years of service to Graylin. Death, to her, is probably a part of life. Too, the woman is ancient. Death would probably be a relief to her.

So then, putting her to work it is.

"We've been treating the prisoners with spectorium," he tells Cy. He leaves out the part where they are doing so by force. Cy has always been an advocate of voluntary treatment. Still, it is time the young Healer becomes savvy in the ways of how to rule a kingdom. If Tarik must learn, so must Cy. "It has done much to calm them down. There are some who are still afflicted with madness. The spectorium seems to have no effect on them."

Esmelda nods. "That would be because spectorium was never intended as the cure. Though it's interesting that it helps with treatment."

"Bore someone else with your interest," Sethos says. "Tell the king what he needs to know."

Esmelda cuts him a vicious look but addresses Tarik with respect. "The cure is derived from the root of the Acutus plant. The root is ground up and boiled, and with a few more ingredients, administered by mouth. The afflicted will recover within two days."

A plant. The Quiet Plague can be conquered by a mere plant. If Tarik were not covered in gold paint, he would run a hand down his face. That is one thing he misses about living in the Baseborn Quarters, the glorious relief from his royal body paint. He looks at Cy. "I've never heard of the Acutus plant."

"It doesn't grow in Theoria, Highness," Cy says. "But we've brought a sackful of seeds back with us from Pelusia. We'll set about planting them right away. Though I'm not sure how they'll fare in this weather."

"You'll have to grow them inside," Esmelda interjects. "They need very little sunlight, fortunately for you. But they thrive on the salt water from the oceans. You'll have to add salt to any water you irrigate them with."

"And fortunately for *you*," Sethos says, "I have a fondness for Cy and his fascination with you. Otherwise, you'd be dead."

Cy waves his hand. "Yes, yes. She deserves to be put to death for her crimes. But I must recommend we bring her health into good standing before she dies of starvation."

"Your king did not take care of you?" Tarik says.

Esmelda nods. "At first, he did. But when Theoria began to treat the patients with spectorium, and the plague did not have its desired effect . . ." She shrugs. If she pities herself, she does not show it. In fact, she shows no emotion at all.

If she is not concerned with her predicament, why should I be? "How long will the Acutus take to grow, to be useful to us?"

"It's a fast-growing plant, Highness. Two weeks under the proper care, and we'll have enough root to make the first batch."

Tarik gives Cy a stern look. "Have the fountains in the palace drained and plant the seeds there. In this weather, I doubt you'll find soil that is suitable for planting so you'll need to dry the mud first. You are personally responsible for the care of the seeds. See that it happens as she says."

"And the Lady Esmelda?"

"Keep her under lock and key and guards. And pride of the pyramids, get her some food."

Cy nods. "As you wish it." He helps Esmelda to her feet, steadying her as they make their way to the door. When they are gone, Sethos gives Tarik a look of disgust. "You could have waited until I returned before taking back the palace. I've been itching for a good fight."

"Then you should have started a few in Pelusia. Particularly with King Graylin, I think."

Sethos yawns. "Where is Tulle? I could use some comforting."

"You've always hated her, ever since we were children, Sethos. What changed? Why must I even ask?"

"I've always loved her. Hate and love are closely related, you know. I just didn't realize it until I saw her again."

Tarik mulls over the words and finds truth in them. He supposes passion can be mistaken for many things. "Tulle and Sepora are visiting the Baseborn Quarters. I sense a secret between them, but Sepora continues to evade my questioning."

Sethos grins. "You've met your match with that one. And you're a fool to have called it off. I could still punch you for that."

Tarik sits and leans back in his chair. He'll not discuss his personal affairs with the likes of Sethos. His mouth is more active than his prowess for women. "Speaking of engagements, I have some news for you. King Ankor has consented to allow you to marry his daughter."

"You jest."

"I swear it."

"Do not toy with me, brother."

"If you don't believe me, ask Tulle for yourself. Rashidi's visit was a success."

"What could have changed his mind? Last time I saw him, he was leading his entire army in pursuit of us."

Tarik tries to suppress his grin and fails miserably. This is going to be great fun. "As it turns out, *you'll* be leading his army from now on. Because you and Tulle are to reside in the Ice Palace."

AFTER FOUR WEEKS OF NOTHING BUT RAIN, THE city of Anyar was flooded. The River Nefari overflowed and Parani swam the Bazaar, attacking the citizens and merchants who chose not to seek out higher ground by the palace. Many chose to stay behind and guard their possessions and lost their life to the great flood in one fell swoop. Those who didn't drown in the wake of the flood were taken by the Parani, suffering an even worse death than being snuffed out by water. The Wachuk warriors did their best to use the Scaldlings to extract as many Parani from the waters as they could, but the death toll continued to rise.

After eight weeks of rain, even the first floor of the palace is underwater. A makeshift kitchen has been set up in the upper west wings, and servants are forced to double up in the sleeping chambers aboveground. From his balcony, Tarik can only see the tops of roofs at the Bazaar, and the small single lights of boats drifting along the water covering what was once desert. He is weary of the sound of rain and thunder. If he never heard it again, it would be too soon.

Tarik turns to Sepora, who sits in a chair in his seating area. She sketches a pyramid on parchment with a piece of kohl, absently rubbing a bare foot up and down Patra's belly. The cat lies in front of Sepora's chair, purring in appreciation, flicking her tail now and again contentedly.

He's more grateful now than ever that in the end, Sepora decided to stay as a guest in the palace instead of returning to the Baseborn Quarters—which are now flooded and unlivable. He's met with the Great Council and his best engineers. It was decided that they'd build up shelters in front of the palace, laboring in the rain to complete their homes on stilts. In fact, most of the citizens have chosen this option, and Wachuk has supplied an abundance of wood for the job.

Chariots have been replaced by small boats and skiffs. Citizens who had solid structures to begin with have moved to their rooftops, using tents as shelter from the rain. Trading has all but halted. The Middling crops are ruined. The people have resorted to eating the Parani and other fish that venture into the city.

It would seem the treaty with the Parani will never recover from this.

Tarik shakes his head. "We eradicated the Quiet Plague only to be taken down by a weather anomaly?"

Sepora looks up from her drawing. She has been obsessed with pyramids of late, drawing them and asking questions about their construction. Such detailed questions that he'd had to refer her to his architect. Still, he's grateful that she's able to focus on something other than her losses. Yes, he had wanted her to mourn her losses, but he'd wanted her to recover from them, and not only because he's been waiting for the right moment to ask her again to wed him. He wants her mind at ease. He wants her to feel better. And for all his Lingot abilities, he still senses a great sadness in her.

"It can't last forever," she says, "and you're doing all that you can."

He sits across from her and nods at Patra. "She's restless. I've been running her up and down the stairs between the second and third floor, but she longs to get out of the palace."

"We all do. Sethos is going to drive me mad with his whining."

"Sethos has no reason to whine. He has a wife to see to his every comfort," Tarik says dryly. He'd taken the news of King Ankor's requirements quite well, actually. It had been no fun at all, when he'd readily agreed to live at the Ice Palace if it meant wedding Tulle and keeping the peace. Perhaps he'd meant to make up for starting a potential war in the first place. But Tarik suspects his new and improved mood has everything to do with Tulle. They'd requested to marry immediately—which had been a good idea, since Sethos could barely keep his hands off her—and they'd moved into Sethos's old child-hood chambers within the palace. It is a cozy set of rooms for the two of them, Tarik is sure. He is sure, and he is jealous of what his brother has.

He tries not to stare at Sepora while she draws, but he can't help but wonder what it would be like to wed her. To climb into bed with her every night, to wake up to her in the morning, to confide in her all his secrets and hopes and wishes.

But can he confide in her, truly? He isn't sure, even now. For still, she hides something from him. When he asks her about her visits with the citizens of the Baseborn Quarters, she glosses over the truth, opting instead for evasive answers. What she might be up to, he couldn't say. He even asked her directly once, and she changed the subject altogether. It can be unnerving, to always be engaged in a battle of wits with her.

Unnerving, and a pleasure at the same time.

A knock at the door draws him from his thoughts. Commander Morg lets himself in. He bows before them. Tarik can already tell from his face that he will not like whatever Morg has to say.

"Highness, I have urgent news for you."

"Yes, I gathered that, Morg. Speak your peace."

"Ships have been spotted in the Dismals, Your Majesty. Many ships, of great size. They move toward Anyar."

"*Ships?*" Sepora repeats, sitting straight in her chair. "Ships meant for the ocean?"

Morg nods. "Indeed, Princess. There are dozens of them."

She gives Tarik a grim look. "Pelusia," she says, but he is already thinking it. He'd been waiting for Hanlyn to make her move and preparing accordingly. Of course, he'd thought by now that he'd be warring with her on dry land. But the woman has brought ships with her instead. How could she have prepared for such weather?

Tarik has no ships of his own. He has no shipbuilders. Of course, he has faith in his engineers, but they've no experience in the matter. And now, they have no time.

"What are your thoughts, Commander Morg?"

"It would be foolish to meet them in the Dismals with smaller vessels, Highness. I say we wait it out and fight them here."

"That's a greater chance for damage to our buildings and structures," Rashidi calls from the door. He makes his way to them, his staff clinking against the floor as he walks. "We cannot protect our citizens if they are in the fray."

"I was hoping we could evacuate most of the citizens to the Lyceum," Morg says. "And inside the palace."

The Lyceum is the only building in all of Anyar that remains unflooded, simply because it was built upon a high foundation meant to symbolize higher learning. Its steps are mostly underwater, but the living quarters remain intact and dry. A kingdom-wide invitation had been sent for families to fill it as needed, but many chose to remain at their homes and build from the ground upward. Tarik understood the choice of his people; it is the Theorian way to persevere. But this time, he needs them to obey. Tarik nods. "Send the women and children to the Lyceum, and keep Majai there to watch over them. Bring the men to the palace—and start arming them."

Tarik paces the room, his mind reeling. "Set up a Slinger on every rooftop." The Slingers can be used to tear down sails, rendering the ships dead in the water. Morg has fine-tuned the aim of these mechanisms so that they can separate a man's head from his body with a simple arrow. "Send for Queen Emula and tell her to prepare her warriors and Scaldlings. And fetch Sethos. I need him to cooperate." Because he's going to ask for Tulle's assistance. She is a weapon all on her own. And Sethos will not like putting her into the battle. "How long do you think we have before their arrival?"

Morg scowls. "They move impossibly fast. Their sails are open, even though there is no wind to push them."

Curious. But Tarik has no time to ponder over it. "Prepare our citizens for war, Morg. Send a messenger for Olna and ask for every Forger she has." They'd been milking venom from the Scaldlings for weeks. With that and the fresh spectorium, their supply of cratorium will be virtually endless.

Sepora settles her gaze on him. "How can I help?"

"By staying put and out of harm's way."

And he'll not argue on the subject.

37

SEPORA

"BLAST TARIK AND HIS COMMANDS," I MUTTER, as another cannonball strikes the outside of the palace walls, shaking the room where I, along with the older and infirm men of Theoria, wait for our fate. I hear the shriek of a Scaldling nearby and wonder if it's been injured. And if a Scaldling is injured, how many *people* have suffered and died already?

"I need to go out there." I pace back and forth, hugging myself in indecision.

"You would add another worry to the king's list?" Rashidi calls from the stairs where he sits.

I growl under my breath. "Tulle is out there," I argue.

"Sethos is watching over her, and Tulle is more than capable of defending herself."

"Are you implying that I'm not?"

Rashidi shrugs. I thought by now I would come to like the old adviser. I'd been mistaken. "Whether you can or can't is not my concern. You've been ordered by the Falcon King to stay inside."

Ordered. Tarik wants to keep me safe, and I want the same for him. Who is he to tell me what to do? I'm a guest in his palace, not his servant. I'm a person in this war. A person who cannot stand idly by and watch the outcome unfold and do nothing to sway it one way or the other.

And so, I take the stairs two at a time, passing Rashidi in a rush even as he reaches out to grasp my ankle. There is a window on the landing before more steps lead to the third floor, and it's just big enough for me to crawl through. The rain and wind hit me as I step out onto the ledge of the window.

Dead bodies—mostly Theorians—float in the water beneath me. Scaldlings pepper the sky and spit flames at the huge vessels, but everything is too drenched to catch fire. Majai jump from rooftops onto the ships while Serubelan and Pelusian men from the ships jump onto rooftops. We are outnumbered by half. The clamor of swords meeting, the screams of death, the shouting of orders to two separate armies.

In the distance, I see Tulle on a ship throwing her flames, Sethos fending off the men who would strike her down. She's not able to catch anything afire, either, but she singes the men coming toward them, her blazes reaching out the length of a Serpen. It's amazing to watch.

Amazing, and horrifying.

Above me, I catch the attention of a pair of Wachuk women circling the sky on the back of a Scaldling. I motion as best I can that I need a ride. They swoop down to my level, the one with the bow and arrow reaching her hand out to me.

I will have to make a jump for it.

I hear Rashidi behind me, calling my name. A glance back reveals he's finally made it to the top of the steps.

It's now or never.

I jump just as Rashidi grabs my ankle. I topple forward, unable to catch my balance. The Wachuk warrior latches on to my hand as I dangle in the air and as Rashidi dangles from me. *What have I done?*

"Hang on, Rashidi!" I scream. But Rashidi's old hands have not been strong for some time, and the weather has made the joints in them painful. His grip slides from my ankle to my toes, and terror bulges in his eyes. "Do not let go!" I command, even as he looks down. When he raises his gaze back to mine, I see a decision has been made. "No!"

"Take care of him," he says. "He loves you yet." He lets go then, falling into the water below.

And he never comes back to the surface.

38

TARIK

THERE IS SOMETHING STRANGE ABOUT THE FOREIGNERS on these ships, Tarik decides.

There are not many of them, perhaps two per ship. They are not Pelusian or Serubelan. Their skin is darker, but their hair is white in stark contrast. They wear intricately styled beards and silken lavender robes, which, when soaked through with rain, cling to muscular bodies. Bodies that would be more than able to fight, yet they are guarded, protected at all times by at least three men—and all they do is stand there and raise their hands to the sky.

The sky? Are they priests summoning whatever gods they worship to help them through this battle? Pelusia and Serubel are not the kind of kingdoms to give in to such nonsense worship of gods. Too, Queen Hanlyn is much too practical and resourceful to send priests—especially priests that need so many of her capable men to protect.

No, these foreigners have a purpose, and Tarik aims to find out what that is.

He fights his way up, climbing upon rooftops to get a better view. There is a ship nearby, close enough for him to study for a bit without too much of a threat against his person. Still, his bow and arrow hit their mark on several men, leaving them alive but incapacitated, before he reaches a good vantage point.

He watches one of the foreigners for a few minutes, releasing arrows when necessary to fend off charging attackers. Each time the man thrusts his palms in the air, lightning strikes around them. A bolt seizes a Scaldling midair, and it falls immediately into the water below, carrying its Wachuk riders with it.

That's not possible.

Could these foreigners be controlling the weather? He searches out Tulle and Sethos, whom he finds a few rooftops away. Tulle aims her flames toward the three men protecting another foreigner, but the foreigner thrusts his hands against the flames, sending them back in her direction. She falls to the ground, barely escaping her own fire, while Sethos fights a Pelusian combatant several arm lengths behind her.

Once the foreigner has deflected Tulle, he turns his attention to the other side of the ship, propelling his hands toward a Majai trying to board. The Majai is caught midair as if hit by an invisible wall and thrown backward into the water below.

Lightning, and now wind. It explains how the ships moved so quickly upon Anyar, their sails opened wide even though there was not enough wind in the city to blow about the flaps of a tent. If these men are weather summoners, then one of them must be controlling the rain. And that one must be stopped.

Queen Hanlyn is behind the flooding. Of course she is. She must have sent one of her foreign allies here, disguised as a Theorian to open up the skies and bring down the rains. She has proven to be a more cunning adversary than Eron could have ever hoped to be.

Tarik must get to Commander Morg, to tell him to concentrate on the summoners. But Commander Morg is nowhere in sight. A Scaldling swoops overhead then, the draft from its flapping wings whipping the rain before him.

And to his horror, Sepora is on it, preparing to dismount onto this rooftop.

She is too high above, yet she leaps from the back of the beast, landing beside him and rolling several feet before coming to a halt at the edge of the building. Already she is being reckless.

"You're supposed to be hiding," he says, grasping her arm. An arrow narrowly misses them both, infuriating him even more. "Go back, Sepora."

"I will not," she says, and blast it all, it's the truth. He can send her away from him now, but she'll not obey his command to retreat to the palace. She'll simply join the fray and get herself killed.

"Go back, or I swear to you I'll have you thrown from the Half Bridge after this is all over with!"

"I can help. My spectorium—"

"I cannot concentrate knowing you are in danger. Sepora, how can you not know this? I need you safe. It is not a question of whether you can help." Another arrow zings by his head. Sepora would have taken that shot if she had chosen to stand two feet to the right. He cannot stomach this now.

"You can endanger yourself and I cannot? Tulle can use her powers, but you would ask me not to use mine?"

He closes his eyes against her logic. Logic has no place where his heart is concerned and this girl who stands before him has become his heart.

She places a hand on his forearm. "Let me help. I'll stay close to you. I'll fight only when attacked. But do not shut me away. Not now. Not like this. Not when I can be useful."

"Very well. Be at the ready at all times." It's the most difficult thing he's ever said in his life. He wonders how much more he can take.

"I have to find Commander Morg," he yells over the commotion around them. "Your mother has sent foreigners with the ability to control the weather. We must target them first if we are to infiltrate the ships and make any headway." He points to one of the silken-robed men, showing her how he summons lightning from the air.

Sepora gasps as another Scaldling is struck and plummets into the water. "We are losing," she says. It isn't a question. But Tarik does not hesitate with his answer.

"Yes, we are." Sepora must understand the odds, the risk she's taking in deciding to stay outside the palace.

"What about Tulle?"

"The wind summoner deflects her."

"We must move her to the lightning summoner, then. Distract him from the other side so she can have the opening she needs. The more Scaldlings we lose, the worse our chances of survival."

Survival. Tarik's stomach clenches. Many of his men have already fallen, and Sepora is of a mind to die herself if need be. Why could she not stay in the palace as he requested? Why must she always do the exact opposite of what he wants? What if he loses her this day?

The thought is unbearable and beyond distracting. But there is no time to fret over things he cannot change. The only thing he can do is protect her as much as possible. He slings his bow over his shoulder and cups her face in his hands, willing her to focus on his eyes. "I need you to find Morg," he tells her. "Do not fight unless you have to defend yourself. Tell Morg of the summoners. Tell him to target them at all costs, if he has not already. Then we will be on level fighting grounds, I think."

She nods. "I will. Where did you last see him?"

"I haven't seen him since the battle began."

She turns to leave but whirls on her heel to face him again. She swiftly plants a kiss to his lips and steps back. "Stay safe, Highness."

"A hypocritical request, don't you think?" he calls after her, but she is already gone.

Not wasting any time, Tarik makes his way toward Sethos and Tulle. He tells Sethos of the summoners, and asks Tulle to focus on scorching as many fighters as she can and to steer clear of the wind summoners who can send her flames back to her in an instant.

"Send word to your Majai to aim the Slingers at the summoners. Surely they cannot deflect dozens of arrows at a time," he tells Sethos. "And if they can, those closest to them will suffer the consequences." If the wind summoner protects himself, he'll be diverting the arrows in the direction of his own protectors. At least, that is what Tarik is hoping for.

He turns to leave, to find the best vantage point for his bow and arrow, but Sethos grabs his arm. "Tarik, look," he says, pointing toward the ocean that used to be the Dismals. The horizon is full of ships, at least thirty more.

This is not good. Theoria cannot stand a second wave of attack.

"No," Sethos says, as if reading his thoughts. "Those ships are from Hemut. I would recognize them anywhere. I searched through their ports while I was looking for Sepora."

"You're sure?" Tarik says, hope swelling inside him.

"Positive. If you look closely, you can see the images of the whales on their sails. They are definitely from Hemut."

"Yes," Tulle shouts over the thunder. "My father has sent his help!"

As if that weren't good enough news already, the downpour from the sky suddenly stops as quickly as it had started all those weeks ago. Sepora must have found Morg. And Morg must have found a way to incapacitate the rain summoner.

With Hemut attacking from behind, and with the Majai taking

out the summoners, surely they will defeat Hanlyn's forces. Perhaps that was the one thing Hanlyn did not account for: Theoria's ability to form allies.

But the battle is not over yet. Tarik takes aim at a man on the closest ship to him. He targets the man's leg; rendering him useless is better than rendering him dead. In the end, he will want to seek peace with Serubel and Pelusia, and perhaps even this new foreign kingdom. In the end, peace is always the answer.

Before he dispatches the arrow, he receives a tap on the shoulder. He turns to find Rashidi standing there. *Does no one follow my commands anymore?* He'd ordered Rashidi to watch out for Sepora—obviously she'd outsmarted him. Has he now come to collect her? Does he really think the task will be so easy?

"Sepora is with Commander Morg," Tarik tells his friend. "You may go back to the palace." This is no place for an old man such as Rashidi. He is not swift on his feet and does not have the skill of warfare. His gift is his tongue, and that will do little this day.

"I think not," Rashidi says, but his voice sounds different. With a swift motion, he lunges at Tarik, faster than Rashidi has ever moved. Tarik never saw the dagger in his hand. He only felt the pain of it thrusting into his gut, Rashidi twisting it for good measure.

Tarik slumps to his knees, pulling the dagger from his belly, his hand covered in blood. He peers up at his oldest friend. "But why?"

The old adviser takes the sleeve of his wet robe and wipes it down his face. Queen Hanlyn's features appear. She laughs softly. "Because even if your kingdom survives this day, you will not. And I will come for your people again and again, until there is nothing left of Theoria."

Tarik leans forward, placing his weight on his hands. The wound is deep, and he feels the warmth of the blood oozing from the gash. She is right. He will not survive.

She removes another dagger from her belt and grabs a handful of his hair, pulling his head up, no doubt so that she can deliver a swipe to his throat. Just as the blade touches the skin of his neck, the point of a sword slams through her chest. She screams in agony as Sethos kicks her from behind, sending her plummeting to the ground next to Tarik. He wastes no time in finishing her off, raking his sword across her throat.

Sethos sinks beside his brother and examines his wound. "We need to get you to Cy. Now."

It is the last thing Tarik remembers.

39

SEPORA

WAKE UP.
It is all I can think, sitting here in the chair I've dragged over to the bed from Tarik's seating area. The war has ended with a victory for Theoria. But is it really a victory if it loses its Falcon King?

Wake up, Tarik.

But the Falcon King doesn't stir, even at the loudest of noises. For days, the servants have come in and out with trays of food for me, have cleaned the chamber, have implored me to get some rest of my own. For days, Cy has changed Tarik's dressing around his wound, cleaning it thoroughly and administering some salve, giving his body nourishment through injections of something that smells awful.

And for days, I have conducted the business of Theoria from Tarik's bedside.

Officially, the duty belongs to Sethos, next in line for the throne. But the kingdom still doesn't know of Tarik's renouncement of our engagement, and Sethos is not the ruling type, not to mention he has been busy keeping his new father-in-law occupied, so he has unceremoniously left me in charge. He tries to help at times, advising me of kingdom intricacies that I'm unfamiliar with, but otherwise, he steps aside and enforces my decisions.

It is a time for rebuilding in Theoria. It is a time of change. And the kingdom needs its king.

I peer down at the scrolls in my lap, at the correspondence from Commander Morg, at the instructions for Tarik's care from Cy, at an invitation from Olna to meet with the Great Council. I've also dragged a marble table to the bedside, and it is now burdened with scrolls of my own penmanship. They are messages of peace to Pelusia tempered with the threat of attack, news to Serubel of my mother's death and orders to await my command, and requests for a meeting with King Hujio of Clima, the kingdom of the foreign weather summoners. The latter is the one I am most concerned about. I know Tarik would once again seek peace with King Graylin if at all possible, because sending his army so far north would not be ideal. But I also know that if Graylin doesn't accept the terms of the treaty, I will order the Majai to move accordingly—and with no regret. In fact, it would be best and most efficient if the Majai deliver the terms of the treaty themselves, I think.

But whether I should pursue peace with the weather summoners, I'm not sure. Tarik would no doubt want to meet with their King Hujio, so that his discerning ears could sort out the extent of his involvement in the battle. I've had Lingots interrogate what was left of the summoners themselves, and the verdict has come back that they acted of their own volition, having been made grand promises by my mother and King Graylin.

Still, if an entire kingdom of weather summoners exists north of the ocean, both Theoria and Serubel would do well to secure it as an ally. And so I've invited King Hujio to the desert kingdom to meet with me, hoping against the odds that Tarik will wake up.

Cy says the Falcon King has little chance of survival, that I should prepare myself. Even now, his breathing is shallow and not nearly as frequent as it should be. He has simply lost too much blood. Even the Healer Esmelda has examined him and come to the same conclusion.

Tarik is not likely to live.

And that is why I stay at his side. I will not abandon him in his last hours. I will not leave him to die as I did Nuna. I'll not let him die alone.

The door to the chambers opens and Sethos enters, his expression grim. He is not taking his brother's condition well. His way of dealing with it has been to avoid the subject altogether. He wasn't there when his father, King Knosi, died. He'd just missed his passing when he'd arrived from the Lyceum. But Sethos is having a difficult time staying away from Tarik's bedchamber. He doesn't talk of Tarik, or the state of his health, but he visits every few hours to tell me news, though none of it is really news. He tends to repeat himself, talking absently as he stares at his brother's lifeless body on the bed.

"You look malnourished," Sethos tells me as he sits on the bed next to Tarik. "You're not eating enough."

"I'm not hungry."

"My brother wouldn't like that."

"I will fight with him about it when he awakens."

Sethos's lips curl up into a grin. "See that you do."

"How are things with King Ankor? Give him my apologies for my absence at dinner."

Sethos shrugs. "If he's offended, he hasn't said as much. All he wants to speak of is my commanding his army, teaching them the way of the Majai. The Lady Gita is set to arrive soon. Tulle says she will be angry that we've already wed."

"You could always stage a public wedding ceremony to appease the people."

He grimaces. "Why would you say such a thing?"

I cannot help but giggle. A public ceremony would involve body paint, headdresses, and hours of parading about like the royalty he would rather not be. "Tulle does not want a lavish ceremony?"

"Of course not. She's entirely too practical for that."

"Every princess secretly wants a lavish ceremony, Sethos."

"Do you?" Only, the question does not come from Sethos, but a raspy voice on the bed behind him.

Tarik's eyes are open, though his lids are heavy. He looks at me and nods his head. Hope floods my insides like the Nefari had flooded Theoria. It is not healthy to feel hope, I know. But mourning the loss of someone who is staring me in the eyes is not something I will do. Not yet.

"Well, how could you expect me to sleep when the two of you are making so much noise?" Tarik says.

Sethos scoots closer to him on the bed, his face flush with excitement. A litany of emotions attack me at once, and I almost cry out from the intensity of it. His eyes are open. His eyes are open and he's speaking!

"You've slept through the rest of the battle, idiot," Sethos says. "And if you're going to complain, it should be about how ridiculous your hair looks at this moment."

Tarik feigns a scalding glare. "Why were you born with a mouth?"

I stand, taking a few apprehensive steps toward the bed, afraid that if I get too close, I'll smother him—I stay my instincts to throw myself at him and weep. Tarik frowns up at me. I am trembling on the inside; I'm careful to keep my hands folded in front of me lest he sees me shiver with every emotion slamming against me at the moment.

"Sethos is right. You look thin," Tarik admonishes.

"How are you feeling?"

"A bit like death."

"You look it," Sethos says cheerily. "I'm going to fetch Cy."

"Fetch some water while you're at it," Tarik says, licking his lips. "My lips are more parched than the Dismals. Well, before the rain came."

"Things are already drying up," I tell him, taking Sethos's spot on the bed after he leaves. "The people are returning to their homes and many are rebuilding."

Tarik reaches a hand for me, and I take it. "I'm sorry," he says. "For your mother."

It's not something I've had time to think about, what with managing the kingdom affairs and restoring order to Theoria. And truth told, it's something I will have to grieve in my own time. My mother betrayed me, yes. But I didn't want her dead. Sethos had acted out of love for his brother. I can't fault him for that. But somehow I'd envisioned a reconciling with my mother. A chance to get answers. That will never happen now. "Thank you" is all I can say.

"Tell me all that has happened," he says. "What have I missed?"

I take a deep breath.

And I start with Rashidi's death.

40

TARIK

TARIK IS SITTING IN THE GARDEN WITH PATRA, sharpening a new set of arrows, when Sepora seeks him out. It is a rare occasion that she wears her hair down anymore, and he appreciates the beauty of it cascading about her shoulders.

But of course, he appreciates the beauty of her in general. She has gained her weight back, and now stands before him, full-figured and solemn. "You asked for me?" she says.

"You didn't have to come so soon." He pats the seat on the stone bench next to him, urging her to sit. Yet, he realizes now that he summoned her too soon. He doesn't quite know how to begin. An apology would be a mere start, he thinks. But how to ask her to wed him again after calling off their engagement so callously? How can he make up for his actions with simple words?

It had been easy to negotiate with her father for her, easy to navigate the arrangement as a kingdom matter. But this is a matter of the heart. This has nothing to do with the kingdom and everything to do with the fact that he loves her and wants her to be his wife. This is between two people, not two kingdoms. And the thought of exposing himself to that kind of vulnerability has him terrified.

But not so terrified that he won't actually do it. Because the sooner she is his, the better. He simply must get on with the asking of it.

In the days that he's been healing, she has taken on much responsibility. She has proven that she cares for the people and that she is capable of leading them. His mind no longer wars with his heart. She is fit to be queen.

And he's ready to act as king again. Yes, he has already reclaimed some of his obligations while he heals, but it is time he returns to his proper position. Perhaps that is where he should begin. "I cannot begin to tell you how appreciative I am of all you've done for Theoria. But each day I get stronger and stronger. In fact, I grow bored of laying about. It is time for me to resume my duties."

She nods, a hint of sadness in her eyes. "I agree."

"King Hujio arrives in a few weeks. I'd like for you to meet him as well."

"I'm afraid that's not possible, Highness," she says.

"I don't follow."

She sucks in a breath. "You know I've been spending a great deal of time in the Baseborn Quarters. I've been meeting with the Great Council. We have decided that it's time to go home."

"Home?"

"Yes, to Serubel. With Mother and Father gone, I'm heir to the throne. I cannot leave Serubel without a ruler. I'm taking the Great Council with me as my advisers, with your permission, of course."

It is the last thing he was expecting to hear. She's shown much concern for the Serubelans that have stayed behind in Theoria after the war. She's set up tents for them and seen to their needs, helping them to return home little by little. He'd thought it natural, for her to see them home. They were her people once.

As it turns out, they still are.

And why shouldn't they be? She is right; she has a responsibility toward her home kingdom now that it is left without a ruler. She is the heir, the rightful queen of Serubel now. With the Great Council at her disposal, she will most certainly shine.

"I will invite King Hujio to Serubel on his way back to Clima. I think it's fitting that we make our own treaty with him, separate from Theoria."

Separate from Theoria. All Tarik can do is nod. All his heart can do is stammer. "When do you leave?"

Her lips form a straight line. "In the morning." She pauses. "Unless you need me for anything else?"

I need you for my wife, he wants to say. But it would be unfair to ask that of her now. And it would be foolish; Sepora would turn him down, as she should. She must think of her kingdom now. "I think I can manage," he forces out.

When she stands, he does, too. "Be well, Falcon King." She leans in and pulls his head down to hers, planting the barest of kisses on his forehead. "And stay out of trouble."

He tries to make his smile look genuine as he watches her go.

PART FIVE

41

TARIK

KING HUJIO OF CLIMA IS NOTHING LIKE TARIK expected him to be. In fact, the older man reminds Tarik of his own father, King Knosi. He's built like a warrior, with a shaved head, and a thick gray beard that Tarik is sure used to be solidly black. He's a reasonable man and wise.

Even Sethos likes him. He may well be the only person Sethos is fond of, except for Tulle.

Tarik cannot help but think Sepora would like him, too.

He cannot help but think of Sepora all the time, in fact.

But things are as they should be, he knows. At least, that is what he tells himself to fight against the emptiness inside him. All this time he had deemed her unworthy as a queen, and yet, in the end, she had made all the sacrifices a queen should make to serve her people. She even made sacrifices to serve his people while they still thought she would be their queen. How foolish he'd been. And now he must pay the price for it.

"You seem distant today, friend," King Hujio says, taking a generous sip of wine from his dinner chalice. They have had a long day talking of peace and trading, but dinner with the king is always a pleasure. He has a great many stories to tell, his favorites being of his time secretly spent as a pirate in the great ocean above Pelusia, stealing ships and men from his own father's fleets. He also speaks of his dead queen, a female pirate with the gift of the Cumuli—a person who can control the wind. As it turns out, the king himself is not a weather summoner—though they are not rare in Clima, he reports. His own daughter is one, in fact. However, their activities are outlawed, because wielding their powers can make things quite chaotic.

But about this, the king shrugs. "I would allow them their freedom, but you see what they did to Theoria. Can you imagine if they all banded together?" He chuckles. "But I keep them happy with riches and titles. They have no reason to rebel."

Tarik is not so sure of that. Not if Queen Hanlyn had something of more value to offer those who attacked Theoria. He wonders what she offered them at all, what promises she made, and if she would have kept those promises. She was never dishonest in her dealings with him. She was always genuine. She was just very good at hiding and evading.

Much like her daughter.

Hujio sets down his chalice and scrutinizes Tarik in a way that makes him feel uncomfortable. It is not so much that he's staring, but that he examines Tarik with a purpose. An idea has struck the king, he can tell. He can also imagine what it is, since Hujio has been hinting at it for days now. It seems the Climan king is ready to ask directly.

"We've spoken of peace and trading," Hujio begins, "and that is all well and good. But if you really wanted to unite our kingdoms, the northern realm with the southern realm, we need more than just a connection through trade."

"How do you mean?" But Tarik knows what he means. And he knows the king is right. He knows that if Rashidi were here, he would have already suggested it himself.

"I mean to say that you should wed my daughter. Unite us in that way, cross our bloodlines, and you will always have us at your disposal."

At Tarik's hesitation, the king continues, "Oh, don't look so put out. My daughter is a rare beauty, sought after by many in the northern realm and not just because of the wealth she brings to the union. She has been groomed from birth to be a good queen. She would not disappoint Theoria."

"I'm sure she wouldn't."

"So then, when shall I send for her?"

Tarik picks up his own chalice and draws deeply from it. He does not know how to answer. No, that is not true. He does know what he *should* say—he simply doesn't know what he *will* say. Perhaps he needs more wine. Wine will ease his inhibitions. "I agree that wedding your daughter would be a good union," Tarik begins. Yes, that is a good start, he thinks. But again, he stops.

King Hujio leans back in his seat, tapping his fingers upon the table in an impatient rhythm. "So then, I should send for her."

Tarik sighs. "Before you send for her, there is something you must know."

"Have out with it, then. I'm beginning to feel insulted." Though delivered with a small smile, it is the truth. And why wouldn't he? Tarik is, in essence, rejecting an alliance here, if he's not more careful.

"I mean you no disrespect, nor do I mean to diminish your daughter's good name. It's just that I . . . I'm not sure if I would make a good husband. You see, I—"

"You're in love with the Serubelan queen," King Hujio finishes, inspecting his fingernails. He takes a table knife and digs something from beneath one of them, not even bothering to look at Tarik. "Everyone knows that."

Tarik blinks. "Well, I wouldn't say everyone."

The king bellows his laughter. "Your servants drink with my servants, who drink inside the palace and out. It is the talk of the kingdom. Plus, Queen Hanlyn was to marry her off to Prince Bahrain. That kingdom was already prepared for your attack, if it came. Hanlyn was not indirect in implying your affection for the Princess Magar, and the blow it would be to your honor."

"And you thought the whole thing was fair? That I should stand by and allow my future queen to be married to someone else?"

Hujio purses his lips. "I did not know you, friend. And it was not my kingdom negotiating these things, nor did they affect my kingdom whatsoever. They were rumors. Rumors that were, apparently, true."

Tarik makes a note to ask Ptolem of it. He is supposed to be reporting everything he hears about the throne to his king. Somehow, he'd left out that tiny detail about the servants gossiping. Tarik nearly flushes. What must his people think of him? Do they think him weak since Sepora was, in the end, the one to leave and return to Serubel, the one to publicly break off the engagement to assume her own throne? Do they view him as Sethos always has—a lovesick fop who was unable to persuade her to stay?

And if they see him as all these things, should he not prove to the people that he is still their king and will make sound decisions by at least taking Hujio's daughter as wife and forming this alliance?

"This is quite the conundrum," Hujio says, amusement dancing in his eyes. "Are you saying you would not produce an heir with my daughter?"

Tarik nearly spits out his wine, but his guest only laughs again. "Do not mistake my merriment, young friend," he says, scratching at his beard thoughtfully. "This is a serious matter we must discuss. Does your Serubelan queen return your sentiments?"

This is not a conversation Tarik should be having with a prospective father-in-law, he knows. But he cannot resist. Besides, he gets the feeling Hujio will not be quieted until he has answers. The man is as stubborn as Sethos—another trait that reminds him of his father. And with Rashidi gone, he could use fatherly advice right now.

"I do not know," Tarik says finally.

"There is only one way to find out," the king announces. "And I, my friend, am going to help you."

Pride of the pyramids, what have I gotten myself into?

42

SEPORA

OLNA IS GIVING ME A QUIZZICAL LOOK, WHICH means she's just asked me a question—and I was not paying attention at all. I glance around the long wooden table at all my advisers, former members of the Great Council who'd accompanied me back home with most of the freed slaves. They all look at me expectantly, some with impatience, some with polite indifference, and some with certain knowing smirks.

I sigh, flushing just a bit, and not just because of my embarrassment. I tug at the collar of my gown, stifled almost beyond breath. I am no longer used to Serubelan attire. Where I used to feel insecure in the scanty Theorian styles, I now feel smothered in my Serubelan clothes. Being home has taken quite some getting used to. "I apologize, Olna. Could you repeat that?"

I see a flash of frustration cross Olna's face, but she answers with graciousness, "We were discussing whom to select as ambassadors to other kingdoms, Highness. Now that we've settled, we must begin to strengthen our relationships with all the five."

Yes, of course. Ambassadors. I had heard the beginning of the conversation. Something about appointing a representative for each kingdom from among my advisers. That's when I'd started to lament the fact that while my ambassadors would be traveling, I would be staying here in the castle, going mad waiting for even the smallest morsel of news from other kingdoms.

From Theoria.

At least King Hujio from Clima will be arriving soon, if his sojourn in Theoria goes well. He'll bring with him the tidings of an entirely new kingdom to Serubel. I'm quite sure I'll pay attention to King Hujio. Perhaps his visit will excite me enough to want to partake in the activities of the council. Or perhaps I'll accompany him back to Clima myself, instead of sending an ambassador. I must remember to fish for an invitation. . . .

A few moments pass before I realize Olna has asked me another question. This time, she is the one who sighs. "Queen Sepora, we do not wish to bore you with such mundane matters. We can always vote on the matter and bring the issue to you for a final decision later."

What she means is, I am dismissed. I should object to that, I know, being dismissed from my own council meeting, but I jump at the chance to escape the confines of this assembly hall. I feel guilty for the relief that overcomes me when I stand and push my high-backed chair from the table. "Yes, I think that's a wonderful idea." I fail wretchedly at hiding my enthusiasm to leave.

Olna folds her hands on the table in front of her. "I'll seek you out later, Highness, to report on our arrangements."

I nod respectfully but am out of the door before the council can stand at my leaving.

OLNA FINDS ME ON THE MAIN TERRACE OF THE castle a few hours later, sitting on the stone bench and watching the waterfall on the mountain across from me. I remember a time when I wanted to pitch myself from it, to escape the power of my father, but couldn't bring myself to do it. To this day, I still don't know if I made the right decision. I've caused so much trouble since then, and lost so much, that it's difficult to look at things objectively anymore.

Olna takes a seat beside me and nudges me with her elbow. "You are not yourself of late, Highness. Not since we left Theoria."

"Perhaps this is my new self."

"I certainly hope not."

I do, too. It would be a shame to live out my days moping around the castle. Surely I'll snap out of it. Surely it was not always like this at home, tremendously boring and such. Of course, I was always kept busy Forging for Father. Now that I'm no longer under that obligation, it seems I don't know what to do with myself. Of course, I still Forge, but I do so when I want or when I need energy. Many Forgers from the Baseborn Quarters made their journey with us in our return to Serubel. They take care of Forging for trade with the kingdoms. These days, I find myself nearly useless.

"I'm sorry about the council meeting earlier. I just felt restless."

She nods, gently patting my leg. "Some kingdom concerns are more interesting than others."

She reaches into the pocket of her gown and pulls out an unopened scroll. I recognize the seal immediately as one from Tarik's architect. "This came for you just now," she says.

I have been waiting for this correspondence, yet I dread opening it. It meant so much to me before. But now it only brings me pain. I unravel it, already knowing what it will say, and already knowing what it will mean for me. It reads simply:

Our task is completed, Highness.

My chest aches at the words. "I must return to Theoria soon," I tell Olna. It's a duty I must fulfill, a mistake I must aright. Yet, when can I? Tarik entertains King Hujio now, and after that, I will be entertaining him. Perhaps I should go now, and meet with them both.

"Yes," she says. "We agree."

I blink at her. "We?" The council could not know why I mean to return to Theoria. How could the council agree to something of which they have no idea?

"After you left today, it was discussed in the meeting how the council could assist with your apparent . . . melancholy. We took a vote on it, and it was unanimous that you must be the ambassador to Theoria. You have many connections there, connections and relationships that Serubel could use."

"But I can't be an ambassador," I say, a bit frustrated at the very suggestion. "I am the queen. It is simply unheard of." The work of an ambassador is considered unfit for royalty. What would the other kingdoms think? Surely they would see it as a weakness, that I do not have sufficient advisers for the task when it couldn't be further from the truth. I have more advisers than Sethos has pride.

"Many things that were once unheard of have taken place in recent months, wouldn't you agree, Highness? There is an air of change in the five kingdoms. Things are not as traditional as they once were."

Of course she has a point. The war has changed the five kingdoms forever. They've united in a way never before seen. Even Pelusia has been quick to make amends. Graylin himself welcomed the Majai army to his gates and negotiated peaceful terms henceforth. These alliances are not made up from fragile words penned on a treaty scroll. They are forged of blood and loss and sacrifice. And if Tarik, with his Lingot abilities, sensed insincerity in Graylin's apologies, he would have razed that kingdom to the ground, I know. After the war fought in Anyar itself, the Falcon King will never risk his people's safety again.

Still, ambassadors have delivered all of these messages. Not kings and queens themselves.

"There are some changes, yes. But the way the kingdoms handle their dealings with each other?" I shake my head doubtfully. "A queen's place is to be served, not to do the serving." I remember Rashidi saying the same thing to Tarik back in the Baseborn Quarters. Olna had agreed with it at the time. Now she purses her lips at me in dissent.

"That is true, for the most part," she says. "But a queen also has the responsibility to serve her people. Your father did not take that responsibility to heart. And so I urge you to consider this, Highness: How much are *you* serving Serubel as its queen?"

"I don't follow." I'm not sure if I should feel insulted. After all, it sounds as though Olna is implying I don't perform the duties expected of me, that she's in some way comparing the way I rule to the way my father did. If she's still sore about this afternoon's council meeting, she could come out and speak directly. It's the first one I've been excused from, so I cannot believe that my ability to rule depends upon my absence today.

"Would you not better serve Serubel as an ambassador?"

"I cannot *be* the ambassador, Olna. I'm the queen."

She smiles. It is an odd reaction to my frustration. "Actually, you can. We've been discussing Serubelan law with your tutor, Aldon. He recalls in the histories where a king was deemed unfit to rule, and the throne was turned over to his advisers until his son was old enough to preside over the kingdom." Olna sees that I'm horrified and quickly raises her hand. "We are not implying that you are unfit. We admire your ability to rule, Highness. If not for you, Theoria would have crumbled to pieces after the war. But there is a law in Serubelan history that allows a ruler to relinquish the crown."

"I have no heir."

"The law does not specify that you must pass it on to an heir.

Aldon is quite sure you could pass it on to a group of advisers—as was done before."

"The Great Council," I breathe.

Olna nods. "Of course, if that is not your wish, we will never speak of it again, Highness. But if it is, we are prepared to take on the responsibility. The decision is yours, by law." Her face softens. "You see, you will soon be expected to wed, Highness, if you choose to remain on the throne. But, of course, your husband would be expected to reside in Serubel, as it is your place to rule. As ambassador, you could wed whom you wished."

I do not miss her meaning. "The Falcon King does not want me, anyway," I tell her softly. "He made that clear when he renounced our engagement. And he would not leave the throne of Theoria for the throne of Serubel."

"Sometimes we cannot see a way out of conundrums. And sometimes the way presents itself."

She pulls another scroll from her pocket, this one opened. "This arrived today as well. We were going to discuss it at the assembly today, but you seemed too distracted. I thought perhaps you should read it in private."

She leaves me then, her stiff gown rustling in the breeze.

I unroll the parchment—and promptly drop it to the ground.

Tarik is to marry the princess of Clima, and I am cordially invited to the ceremony in three weeks' time.

Over my bloated, rotting corpse.

43

TARIK

WHEN PTOLEM ANNOUNCES THAT THE AMBAS-sador from Serubel has arrived, it is late in the evening and Tarik is weary of visitors. He has half a mind to put off the meeting until the morning, when his mind will be refreshed from sleep. But he already has meetings scheduled again with King Hujio; he is seeing Sethos and Tulle off to Hemut as well. Too, delaying a meeting until tomorrow afternoon with an ambassador who has traveled so far and is likely as weary as he is would be considered rude.

Tarik waves Ptolem off, gesturing for him to allow his visitor in.

He decides he'll greet him or her, and beg off from there, out of concern for his guest's long travel, of course. That is, after he ascertains that their queen is well—and gleans as much information about her as he can without looking like the whelp that he is.

The door opens, and Tarik stands to welcome his visitor.

When Sepora enters, he feels his mouth fall open.

"Greetings, Highness," she says, her long Serubelan gown flowing in a train behind her. "How do you fare?"

She's as lovely as he remembers, her cheeks tinged pink, her white hair braided down her back, and her curves barely visible underneath that wretched garment—which was obviously meant to suppress attraction of any sort.

Unlucky for him, it only makes him long to see the voluptuous figure he adores.

"I . . . I was under the impression I was to be meeting with an ambassador," he says.

She nods. "I am the ambassador for Theoria, Highness. May I sit?"

The truth. The *ambassador* for Theoria? He waits for someone else to come through the door. A member of the Great Council perhaps. Noting that Sepora raises a brow at him, he says, "Of course. But—"

"I want to offer my congratulations on your forthcoming wedding," she says. "I'm happy you have found the proper queen."

A lie. And she well knows that he knows it, too. But he'll not get his hopes up. Not just yet. And he must get to the bottom of all this ambassador nonsense.

"Thank you," he says, taking his seat across from her. "To what do I owe the pleasure of your visit, Queen Sepora?"

She smiles. "It seems I've arrived before my own correspondence. You see, I'm no longer queen of Serubel. I've appointed by law for the kingdom to be ruled by the Great Council."

Pride of the pyramids, but she's telling the truth. What sort of upheaval has happened in Serubel? And where is the blasted correspondence telling him of it? "I did not know that was possible."

"Neither did I. But the histories prove it to be so. Of course, I still wanted to be of use, so I will now serve as ambassador for Theoria. You and I disagree often, but I'm sure where our kingdoms are concerned, we can come to some sort of resolution."

"I see," he says, but he truly doesn't. "How often will you be visiting?" He can't help but ask. In the past, Serubelan ambassadors visited infrequently, but that was under different circumstances. Now that there is true peace between the kingdoms, an ambassador would likely visit three or four times a year. That's up to four times per year he'll have to be tortured with her presence for the rest of his life. He scowls at the thought.

"Visiting? Oh no, you misunderstand me. I'm to live in Theoria. My visits will be to Serubel."

"You're going to *live* here?"

"I find the dry Theorian air suits me."

It's a tangle of truth and lie, and he decides it's unimportant to sort out which is which. In any case, it is not the entire reason she has chosen to reside in his kingdom and she reveals nothing more than that. Speaking riddles to him is a talent of hers, it always has been. And it is more than he can bear at the moment. He removes his head-dress and runs a hand through his hair. "You'll have to excuse the informality," he says, "but you've taken me by surprise."

"I imagine I did," she says. Her face softens. "Speaking of surprises, I actually have one for you. But . . . we must travel by Serpen to get to it. Are you up for it tonight?"

No should be his answer and he well knows it. He remembers what it is like to travel by Serpen with Sepora. As she guides the beast, he clutches her waist for dear life—and his body reacts to the feel of her against him. Since he is now engaged, it is not a good idea at all. "Allow me some time to remove my body paint and I'll join you in the stables."

I'M A DOLT, HE DECIDES AS HE SCOOTS EVER CLOSER to her on the Serpen's back. *An absolute dolt.* If things do not go as planned, what he is doing is detrimental to his engagement.

Sepora smells of chamomile and lavender, infused with a scent he thinks must originate in Serubel. Together, they overwhelm his senses, and he finds holding conversation with her distracting. She seems to sense this, for she stops attempting to speak to him after half an hour has passed.

They glide through the air silently, hovering lower to the ground than she normally does as if searching for something spread among the desert sand. Occasionally they pass boulders that seem to have cropped up from nowhere at all, and curiously, seem to point in the direction in which they fly.

It is liberating to fly rather than travel by foot or wheel. The ride is smooth and since the Serpen can go much faster than a man and his horse, the wind keeps them comfortably cool in the night air. The stars twinkle above them, a gentle light when the moon hides behind clouds at times. It is intimate, he knows. Much more intimate than he has a right to expect from her.

After another half hour has passed, he presses his cheek to her ear, knowing full well that the act is inappropriate. She leans into him; he's not sure if it's reflex or willful seduction, but secretly hopes it's the latter.

"How much farther do we have?" he says. They've traveled farther south than he's ever been, even past the burnt city of Kyra. Yet, even as he questions her, he sees a tiny white speck of light in the distance.

"We're almost there," she whispers, shifting on the Serpen in an obvious bid to speed up.

As they get closer, as the light materializes into a pyramid, Tarik sucks in a breath. "What is this?"

"It's your wedding present," she says, not bothering to keep the bitterness out of her tone. "Sethos told me about your father's pyramid. I've had a new one constructed for him. He rests there already."

"How . . . how did you keep this from me?" he asks as they land smoothly in front of the great structure. He slides from the Serpen and takes a few cautious steps toward the monument in front of him. It is unlike any pyramid he's ever seen. It is much larger than his father's old one, and in the front there stands a statue. A figure of King Knosi himself, and a very true likeness indeed. Tarik laces his hands behind his head and stares in disbelief. Emotion wrestles about his gut. Sadness, awe, gratitude—they all vie for his attention.

"I told you, secrets can be kept if you don't ask direct questions. And I had much help from friends."

He turns on her. "This is what you were doing in the Baseborn Quarters. This is why you had such an obsession with pyramids. All this time, you were having this built? This is the result of the lies and evasiveness you demonstrated after we took back the palace."

"Yes," she says softly, gesturing for him to walk with her to the entrance. "You mistrusted me already. What else did I have to lose?"

"You had this made before you knew I was to wed the princess of Clima," he says, peering down at her in the glowing white light. "You could not possibly have intended for it to be a wedding present."

"I had hoped it would be a gift for *our* wedding." She takes a step back, as if he'd struck her. "I had hoped we would reconcile things. But I see now that there was nothing to reconcile." She smiles weakly. "You have your duties. An alliance with Clima will be good."

"Sepora—"

"Forgive me," she says, nearly choking on her words. "I do not mean to belittle your upcoming marriage. It's just that . . . this is not how I intended for the evening to go. Perhaps we should return to the palace."

"Sepora, please."

She takes yet another step back. He cannot bear it any longer. "Sepora, I won't marry the princess of Clima. Not if you tell me here and now that you're mine."

"Wh-what?"

"I'll call off the engagement."

She shakes her head. "You can't do that! You'll start another war! You've seen what they can do, the weather summoners. We'll fight for decades! You'll—"

"No," he says, closing the distance between them and taking her hand in his. "You don't understand. King Hujio made a deal with me. He proposed that I send you an invitation to my wedding to his daughter. If you came for me, he would not force me to honor the engagement. If not, I'm to wed her. The decision is yours, Sepora. It always has been."

"Do not toy with me," she says, her voice shaking.

"Do not toy with *me*, Sepora. Are you mine or not? You're not the queen of Serubel anymore. You can do as you please, marry as you please. Did you think that fact was lost on me when you first told me you were no longer queen? I assure you, it wasn't. Now I ask you. Will you be my ambassador, Sepora? Or will you be my wife?"

A tear slips down her cheek, and he wipes it away with the crook of his finger. She laughs softly. "I was prepared to fight for you. Yet I did not even have to seduce you."

"Seduce me?"

"I came here with a purpose. I would seduce you away from the princess. I would make you want me again."

"I never stopped wanting you."

"You were very convincing that you did."

"A Lingot can lie."

"What of the other kingdoms? They are preparing for your royal wedding in a mere two weeks."

He grins. "You're the only one who received an invitation, love." But he feels his face fall. "Yet you still have not given me an answer. Why do you evade me even now?" Pride of the pyramids, but at a moment like this, she still plays a game of wits with him. He's flustered and delighted all at once.

She laughs, a sound he's missed so very much. "I must practice, my king. I'm to spend the rest of my life with you. It will not do to let my guard down."

I'm to spend the rest of my life with you.

The truth. The glorious, magnificent truth.

EPILOGUE

SEPORA

THERE IS A KNOCK AT THE DOOR TO OUR BED-chamber, and I nearly dive beneath the linens of Tarik's massive bed. Of *our* massive bed. Tarik grins down at me, planting a kiss on my nose before securing the sheets up to my neck to cover my naked-ness. "I am expecting a visitor, love."

"At this late hour?" I say, but what I really mean is, *On our wedding night?*

Tarik smiles down at me as—to my disappointment—he wraps his shendyt around his waist and heads for the door. "I know it seems odd, but I think you'll be pleased."

Pleased. I can't think of anything at this moment that would please me more than for him to send whoever it is at the door away, and rejoin me in the bed. Tonight we have loved each other in ways I could never have imagined, in ways that make me blush even as he opens the door and allows entrance for my servant, Cara, carrying a small wooden box. I blush all the more that Cara is our visitor, because she has known me from the beginning of my time here in Theoria—and she knows well what we have been doing on our wedding night.

Tarik does not miss the warmth to my cheeks, and he grins. Blast him. I'll punish him for this. How, I'm not sure, because he loves for me to speak to him in riddles, to test his Lingot abilities. Perhaps I'll not speak to him for the rest of the evening. He will not enjoy that at all.

Still, he does not allow Cara to linger, taking the box from her gently and giving her shoulder a soft squeeze. "Thank you, Cara. Please leave us, as my bride just might burst into flames at any moment at your presence."

To my horror, Cara giggles. Then she turns on her sandaled heel and exits, shutting the door softly behind her. I glare at Tarik as he makes his way back to the bed. "You'll pay for that," I tell him sweetly.

He laughs. "I'm looking forward to it."

With great care, he places the beautifully carved case next to me on the bed and slides under the sheets on the other side of it. It stays between us for some time, as we both look at it. Tarik wants me to inquire after it, I know, but I won't. Not when he needs to be punished.

Something rustles within the box, and I tighten my hold on the covers. Perhaps the matter should be discussed after all. "Wh-what is that?" I finally ask, giving in to curiosity and a bit of terror. Something live is in that chest, and at any moment I expect it to spring out and . . . I'm not sure what will come after that.

Tarik reaches across and captures a tendril of my hair, twirling it between his fingers without looking at me. "Your wedding present for me was . . . incredible. I could never top it, and I'm sorry if this gift to you pales in comparison. But . . . I'd like for you to open the box, Sepora. I think that you will come to love what is inside."

"This . . . is a gift?"

"Your wedding present. I'm sorry that it's late. It took me a long time to . . . find it."

The box rustles again, and I can't help but feel alarmed. Tarik is thoughtful and kind, I remind myself. He would not play a cruel prank on me the night of our wedding. Yet, I ask, "Does it bite?"

"Most assuredly."

Well then. Perhaps I've misjudged my husband altogether.

He sighs. "Sepora, open the blasted box before I die of anticipation."

I let out an exasperated breath. A restless thing in a box that most assuredly bites. My Falcon King is not a good present giver, I decide. Even Sethos managed to be romantic with Tulle, gifting her a throne made of gold for their wedding instead of one made of ice.

Still, I can tell Tarik is eager for me to see his gift. And so I reach for the latch and gently unhook it. The lid is heavier than I imagined, and it's then that I realize the sides of the crate have small holes in them. This present was meant to be alive when I opened it. I should probably get on with it, then.

I remove the lid and peer inside, clutching the sheet at my throat for safety at first—and then in astonishment. On the silken pillow within the box is a baby Serpen. A Defender Serpen. A Defender Serpen that looks very achingly familiar.

A sob escapes me. "Tarik. I . . . What have you done?"

Needing no further instruction, he grasps the tiny creature with both hands and holds it up for me to see. "She is not Nuna," he says quietly. "Nuna could never be replaced. But this youngling is a relative of her. Nuna had siblings. Those siblings had offspring. And this, my love, is Nuna's great-niece."

Tears slide down my face as he hands the infant Serpen to me, its long tail entwining about my wrists, clinging to me for dear life. "She looks just like Nuna," I say, helpless against the small creature's little whines. "She even has her coloring."

Tarik nods. "While you sought to rebuild my father's pyramid, I sought to soothe your losses. It would seem that even while we were at odds, we were not enemies." But I have no words for him. I have no words for the man who was once my nemesis, for the man who is now and forever my ally.

ACKNOWLEDGMENTS

Reading the acknowledgments of a book should take as long as sitting through the credits of an epic movie. There are so many people to thank, and so many pages to write of gratitude, that another book should be published for that alone. When you tweet me or email me and say you read my book in a day, know that I love you for it. But also know that there was so much hard work and sweat and coffee and laxatives that went into making it what it was, and so, so many people, that it is amazing you could read that book in a twenty-four-hour period when almost a year of community sacrifice went into the production of it. I'm just the up-front face of it all. The real party is in the back, I promise.

That said, it all starts with having an agent who believes in your work. Lucy, you took something I thought was good and you pushed me to make it better, and I'll be eternally grateful to you for that. You made something from nothing of me. Thank you. To my editors, Liz and Anna, what can I say to you that will make what you do easier? That will make what you do any more valuable? What you do is priceless and I can't express it in any other terms. Tell me what I can say, and I'll say it. For now, my deepest gratitude will have to do. To the publicity team at Macmillan, is there any way you can all just move to Florida and live with me and work from my house together? I'd make it worth your time. But don't tell your other authors. It will be our little secret.

Also, Kelsey: Stop answering your emails on the weekend! :)

A big thanks to April Ward for the amazing cover designs of both *Nemesis* and *Ally* (insert goose bumps here).

I wouldn't be where I am now if it weren't for my critique partners, Heather R. and Kaylyn W. You two hand me my butt in the form of red ink, and I love it, and I can't wait to start our Red Ink Tank podcast this year. If it weren't for your snarky yet on-point critiques, I'd be a babbling mess on the page. And we all freaking know it.

Before I actually turn into that babbling mess now, I need to thank my fans/readers/book bloggers, and anyone and everyone who has picked up one of my books and kind-of sort-of liked it at least a little bit. You're the reason I get to write these acknowledgments. You're the reason I get to write at all. And I know it very, very well. THANK YOU.

I want to give a huge, bigger-than-my-own-butt thank-you to my friend Sanjana. Our daily chats, our venting, our encouraging, our fighting, our forgiving, our laughing, and our sarcasm have given my life such dimension that I consider you one of the best friends I've ever had. I don't know what I would do without you. I can't believe we accidentally met all those years ago on our writing journeys and that we're still sticking with it, through all the ups and downs. Until the next time we meet, which I hope is very soon.

For my Navy Fed peeps: You complete me. You jerks. :)

And finally, for my family, I have no words. I love you. For what we were, and for what we are now, and for whatever may come.

THANK YOU FOR READING THIS FEIWEL AND FRIENDS BOOK.

THE FRIENDS WHO MADE

POSSIBLE ARE:

JEAN FEIWEL
publisher

LIZ SZABLA
associate publisher

RICH DEAS
senior creative director

ALEXEI ESIKOFF
senior managing editor

KIM WAYMER
senior production manager

HOLLY WEST
editor

ANNA ROBERTO
editor

CHRISTINE BARCELLONA
editor

KAT BRZOZOWSKI
editor

ANNA POON
assistant editor

EMILY SETTLE
administrative assistant

STARR BAER
production editor

FOLLOW US ON FACEBOOK OR VISIT US ONLINE AT MACKIDS.COM.

OUR BOOKS ARE FRIENDS FOR LIFE.